"Cate. Cate Dalton, St. Anthony's Resort," she said, not missing a beat.

The lie came out of her mouth smooth as silk.

Cate. The woman hadn't even changed her first name. Now it all seemed so obvious, but before, when he'd been rummaging through hundreds of records, he never would've guessed she'd done something so careless. Everything else, every bit of her trail, had been so carefully scrubbed. She'd left hardly any clues. But she'd kept her first name.

He wanted to know why.

A tiny little scar barely the length of a nickel ran across her chin. It hadn't been in the photographs he'd pored over, and he wondered what it was from.

"We spoke on the phone," she said. "This is your first time to the Caribbean?"

"That's right."

He could lie, too. No need to tell her he'd been hopping from island to island for the last four months, on one goose chase after another, starting to wonder if he needed to rethink his new career as a private eye.

Dear Reader,

I'm excited to share with you my new book, *Shelter in the Tropics*, a story about two people running from their pasts and desperately hoping for a fresh start. It takes place on a Caribbean island I created, St. Anthony's, after the patron saint of lost things.

I loved the idea of a place where people who might be lost in different ways come to find themselves—and each other. This is the first story I wrote on this island, and I hope it won't be the last!

Cate has fled an abusive relationship with her child, hoping to hide from her very powerful and very rich ex-husband, who will stop at nothing to get her and his son back. Tack Reeves, riddled by guilt from his service in Afghanistan and haunted by a dishonorable discharge, is a private eye hired by Cate's ex.

Except Tack discovers very quickly that his own redemption might come by protecting Cate from the man who wants to destroy her.

Together, Cate and Tack must learn to face the demons of their pasts and move on. Together, they'll find the strength to do it on this very special island.

I think life can be complicated and we all deserve second chances. Sometimes, the hardest thing to do is to forgive ourselves for mistakes we've made, but with love and patience, I believe we can do it. I hope you enjoy this book and St. Anthony's Island.

Here's to the restorative power of Caribbean sunshine, love and forgiveness!

All my best,

Cara

CARA LOCKWOOD

Shelter in the Tropics

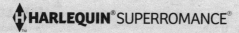

Recycling programs
for this product may
not exist in your area.

ISBN-13: 978-0-373-64031-7

Shelter in the Tropics

Copyright © 2017 by Cara Lockwood

Printed in U.S.A.

Cara Lockwood is the *USA TODAY* bestselling author of more than fourteen books, including *I Do (But I Don't)*, which was made into a Lifetime Original Movie. She's written the Bard Academy series for young adults and has had her work translated into several languages around the world. Born and raised in Dallas, Cara now lives near Chicago with her two wonderful daughters. Find out more about her at caralockwood.com, friend her on Facebook, www.Facebook.com/authorcaralockwood, or follow her on Twitter, @caralockwood.

Books by Cara Lockwood

HARLEQUIN SUPERROMANCE

The Big Break
Her Hawaiian Homecoming

**COSMOPOLITAN RED-HOT READS
FROM HARLEQUIN**

Boys and Toys
Texting Under the Influence

Dedicated to my daughters, who challenge me to be my best self.

CHAPTER ONE

St. Anthony's Island, the Caribbean Sea

WELCOME TO THE Island of Lost Causes.

Tack Reeves couldn't help but shake his head at the sign that greeted him at St. Anthony's baggage claim. Looking around at the crowd of tourists in T-shirts and flip-flops, nothing seemed very lost about this tiny Caribbean airport. He grabbed his old faded olive green seabag from the ground near his feet and moved with the tourists, though his jeans and plain black T-shirt looked out of place in the sea of neon around him. People herded together like this reminded him of the markets in Kabul, Afghanistan, where it was impossible to tell the citizens in the crowd from the insurgents. He felt that old familiar steel ball of unease at the center of his stomach.

One redhead wearing too-high platform sandals bumped into him, making him flinch. She looked up, smiling sheepishly as she apologized for the accidental contact. The old Tack, the one before his sixth deployment, would've found time to talk to the twentysomething in the barely there sundress. Maybe even had the clothes off that fit little body before she'd managed to get her first tan lines. But those carefree days were long gone.

Besides, he had a job to do.

It was probably another dead end, like the dozens he'd run down in the last year. His target, Cate Allen, was like a ghost. Her billionaire husband had hired him to find her and his son, but after nearly a year of working the case, he was starting to think seriously the woman might be dead.

At the very least, she really, *really*, didn't want to be found. He was following the latest lead to this small island, hoping *this* time he'd finally get a break. But it was a long shot. Cate Allen was a missing wife to a famously reclusive billionaire. He'd quietly offered ten million dollars for her return, but nobody knew about this except a chosen few. How he'd kept it out of the news was anyone's guess, but Tack figured money had something to do with it. He steered clear of the other tank-top-clad college coeds on their way to spring break. At the end of the gleaming steel baggage carousels stood a group of drivers, holding up signs. One of them bore his name: Reeves.

He looked up at the woman holding it and for a second nearly froze in his tracks.

Could it be…?

On the surface, this woman looked nothing like Cate Allen, the dazzling, overly made-up brunette socialite, always in designer stilettos, Chanel suits and bright red lipstick. This woman screamed quintessential beach bum with the long blond hair in a loose braid down her back, the aviator sunglasses perched casually in the neckline of her scooped tee and the flip-flops on her feet exposing toes that lacked nail polish. But Tack had memorized the photos he'd trolled through online. He knew every laugh line, every little quirk of her face. His gut told him, *This was her.*

Nobody else had a dimple like that on her right cheek, that flirty "dare you to ask me to dance" upward quirk of her pouty lips. And no matter what she did, the woman couldn't hide the fact that she was gorgeous. No matter how much she dressed down.

She hadn't seen him yet, and for that Tack was grateful. He needed a minute to compose himself. He'd been hunting this woman for *almost a year*, and she'd stymied him at every turn. He couldn't let himself be carried away. This could still be another dead end, the welling of hope in his chest just another precursor to disappointment.

And *everything* was riding on this case.

Her eyes met his then, and his knees locked up. They were greener than her photographs—a clear blue-green, like the Caribbean Sea. Damn, but she was so much more beautiful than her pictures. And they were near a perfect ten. He was just a few feet from her. She smiled at him, hesitant.

"Mr. Reeves?" she asked, and then her eyes widened a bit as he took another step closer. "You're...tall," she managed.

"Six-four," Tack said. "Got my dad's height and my mother's forearms, just don't tell her that," he joked as he always did when people asked him why he was built like a tank. His mother was a big-boned woman who, years ago, didn't mind getting after her boys with a wooden spoon when they got out of hand. The tough love apparently worked as she was now the proud mother of two marines and an army ranger.

Cate smiled, and the brightness of it took him by surprise. She certainly didn't look like a woman with a backyard full of buried secrets. But then, the best liars always believed their own tales.

"You're…?" He deliberately paused, studying her face.

"Cate. Cate Dalton, St. Anthony's Resort," she said, not missing a beat, the lie coming out of her mouth as smooth as silk.

Cate. The woman hadn't even changed her first name. Now it all seemed so obvious, but before, when he'd been rummaging through hundreds of records, he never would've guessed she would've done something so careless. Everything else, every bit of her trail, had been so carefully scrubbed. She'd left hardly any clues. But she kept her first name.

He wanted to know why.

A little scar barely the length of a nickel ran across her chin. It hadn't been in the photographs he'd pored through, and he wondered what it was from. "We spoke on the phone. This is your first time to the Caribbean?"

"That's right." He could lie, too. No need to tell her he'd been hopping from island to island for the last four months, on one goose chase after another, starting to think he needed to rethink his new career as a private eye. "Need a little R and R."

"You'll find it here. Where are you from?" she asked, beaming at him as she put on her sunglasses.

"Seattle." The lie came smoothly. No need to

tell her he lived in Chicago now, the same city her ex-husband, the real estate mogul, called home these days. Tack's younger brother lived in Seattle. He visited often enough, and he'd be able to bluff his way through any further questions.

She nodded and beckoned for him to follow as she moved to the exit. She headed out the first sliding door to the bright tropical sunshine. Tack couldn't help but watch her hips sway like a palm tree on a breezy beach. The sunlight shone on her tanned thighs, the bleached denim cutoffs hitting right at his favorite spot.

"Great view, isn't it?" she asked him, nodding at the big blue sky above them and, in the distance, the sparkling aquamarine sea.

Tack, who couldn't take her eyes off Cate's just-short-enough shorts, nodded once. His view was spectacular.

Distant alarm bells in his brain told him his thoughts were wandering into dangerous territory. He needed to keep this all business. He had a job to do. A job that had more riding on it than just money.

They made their way to the small airport parking lot and an old, slightly battered minibus with St. Anthony's Resort in faded blue paint on the side. She wasn't exactly living the luxury resort life he'd thought she would be after taking off with so much cash. Clever, he thought. Wouldn't be good to be flashing money around that she'd taken. Maybe she was smarter than he thought.

He stuffed his seabag into the luggage caddie behind the bus driver's seat and settled into a worn blue bench where he could watch her drive. She climbed up into the big bus seat and looked like a child trying to reach the pedals.

"Okay, just want to apologize in advance," she said. "I don't normally do shuttle duty. My driver, Henry, is out today."

Henry the driver? Maybe the socialite hasn't wandered so far from the money, after all.

"He had to take his wife to the doctor, and I'm all left feet when it comes to driving the beast."

"The beast?"

Cate patted the old, cracked dash affectionately. "This old girl doesn't know how to quit, but she does know how to give one heck of a bumpy ride. You might want to fasten your seat belt." With that, she threw the bus into gear and they launched out on the road, with Tack nearly flattened against the bus window as they jostled down the bumpy asphalt.

"Are you all right there, Mr. Reeves? Hope you don't get carsick."

"Nope. And call me Tack." He stared at her decidedly *not* manicured nails and felt a flicker of doubt. He was 90 percent sure this was Cate Allen. But that left 10 percent uncertainty, and he didn't like it.

He met her gaze in the oversize rearview mirror above her head.

"Sure…Tack. Unusual name."

"Nickname, for tactical, I guess. You could say I'm a planner." Nobody went over a mission like he did. He thought of every possible scenario far in advance. His unit thought he was crazy, but when the shit hit the fan, he was ready. He was never without a backup plan. "My parents named me Thomas, but nobody calls me that."

"Tack." His name sounded good coming from her pink lips. "I like it."

He ought to be friendly, try to fish out some information, but he didn't feel like letting down his guard. This woman, if she really was Cate Allen, was cunning and dangerous, he reminded himself, no matter how pretty her smile happened to be.

She shifted gears on the bus, and the beast protested with a black puff of smoke out the back. Tack wasn't 100 percent sure they'd make it to the resort in this old clunker.

"You in the marines?" she asked nonchalantly, as if somehow his service were emblazoned on his forehead like a tattoo.

"Why do you say that?" He knew he sounded overly defensive. He needed to calm down. There was no way she'd be able to trace him to his employer, no way she'd find out what he was really doing on St. Anthony's.

Cate glanced at him in the rearview, surprised. "Your luggage," she said. "The seabag? My dad was a navy man. Let's just say I saw a few of those in my time."

Tack glanced at the olive-colored knapsack, wondering if he should lie, but decided not to, remembering the cardinal rule of deep cover: the truth was easier to remember. "Yeah, I used to be in the marines."

"Where'd you serve?"

"Six tours of duty in Afghanistan." *And a dishonorable discharge.* Tack wasn't proud of that. Who would be? But if it came down to it, he'd do the same damn thing all over again. He'd take that court-martial, again and again. Sometimes, principle outranked rules.

"Well, thank you for your service," Cate said.

He knew she probably meant well, but he wished she hadn't said that. He'd served his country, and he'd gone through hell, so what? Lots of guys did. Lots of good men died. Some men served America who weren't even in the armed forces. He thought of his brave translator, a local Afghan named Adeeb, who'd saved him more than once. Now, he was the one in trouble.

But this job could change all that. Allen had promised to help. That's all that mattered. Tack had a job to do, and when he did it, everything would be made right.

Tack grew silent, watching as she steered the old clunker down the road. Still, why did she have to be so…nice?

She jostled them down a narrow, barely two-lane road with no lane markers and no shoulders. The tiny road wound up the coast, the view of the water brilliant below them. Cars drove on the left side here, probably because the island used to be British, before it was French and then Dutch. Battered trucks and rental hatchbacks passed them in the opposite direction. Just a line of wildflowers separated them from a plunge down a fairly steep cliff to the water below.

A loud bang shook Tack to his core, and for a second, he was right back in the godforsaken desert. Then he heard the rim of the front left tire hit the road with a deafening screech as they careened sharply to the left.

Cate went silent as her hands gripped the

oversize steering wheel. The old minibus lurched dangerously close to the cliff face. Another foot and they'd be taking the shortcut to the beach, grille first. She struggled to keep the three good tires on the asphalt. Tack leaped to his feet. He leaned over the back of Cate's seat and clutched the wheel. Her hands looked tiny compared to his as he gripped the plastic hard and tugged them away from the cliff. They managed to come to a precarious stop in the middle of the road.

"Oh, my God," Cate breathed, her chest heaving. "We could've…"

"We didn't," Tack said, reaching over and throwing the vehicle into Park. "You okay?" He knew shock when he saw it, and Cate looked like she might faint. He moved over beside her in the open area between her and the accordion door of the minibus. "Hey, look at me."

She stared numbly at him, eyes wide and pupils dilated. For a split second, she wasn't a mark, and he wasn't a detective. This was just a scared woman about to hyperventilate sitting in front of him.

"We're okay," he said.

Behind them, someone slammed on their brakes, honked and veered around them.

"I know." She abruptly pulled her hands

away and was herself once more, regaining her senses, almost as if she'd woken up from a daydream, or day nightmare. She flipped on her hazard lights and stood. "I've got a spare tire in the back. Hopefully, a jack that works."

The record time she'd taken to recover from the near accident impressed him. This was a woman who didn't crack under pressure.

Of course, women who try to kill their husbands usually don't.

Tack glanced out the window and the other cars speeding around them. They wouldn't be safe for long here, and they needed to get the minibus moving before someone slammed into them on this narrow road. Cate was already at the back panel, wrenching up the trapdoor and lugging out a near bald Michelin.

"Whoa, there," Tack began. "I can help…"

"What? This old thing?" She grinned at him, a gorgeous, effortlessly flirty smile, and he felt his crotch grow tight. "I've got it."

And it looked like she was going to take that tire and the partly rusted jack with the paint flecking off and fix this thing before Tack could even get a word in about it. When she leaned in to get the tire iron, Tack easily slipped it from her hands. No need to arm the woman. From what he'd heard, she was dangerous enough all on her own.

"Please, ma'am. I insist."

CATE EYED THE muscled marine kneeling by the front tire of her ancient minibus and felt a ripple of unease. He attacked the rusted lug nuts, and she tried not to be distracted by the fact that the muscles in his forearms rippled when he loosened the nuts with hardly any effort. He glanced up and met her gaze, showing even white teeth, his brown eyes warm.

Bet he gets any girl he wants, she thought, feeling her own abdomen grow warm as she watched him wrench the old tire free, his biceps engaging as he lifted it up. *Sexy ex-marine probably never gets told no.* She felt a pull suddenly, a flush of desire run through her. How long had it been since she'd even had sex?

Normally, she was able to push those feelings aside, but watching the marine work made her mind go to places she thought she'd long since forgotten.

Relationships were too risky. *One-night stands are fine. Anything more and you're just asking for trouble, Cate.*

But Cate wasn't a one-night-stand kind of girl. Of course, after Rick Allen, she wasn't sure forever love even existed. *And, now, I can't try for it, either. It's too much of a risk.*

She knew she'd be giving up things when she took her boy and ran. She'd gladly sacrifice forever love if it meant her boy would be safe. If it meant Rick Allen could never hurt him—or her—again. Being alone was better than being hurt. Better than being...*controlled, imprisoned in her own house.*

You're mine, he'd said the night she left. *You belong to me. You'll never get away.*

That had been more than three years ago. *I did get away, Rick. I did. And I'm never going back.*

She focused on Tack's lean back, the muscles of his broad shoulders taut against the thin fabric of his shirt as he slipped the spare tire on the minibus. The loud whoosh of cars passing at speeds faster than they should whirred in her ears, yet she paid them no heed. Her whole focus was on Tack.

Something about this man made her feel distinctly off balance, and it wasn't the fact that he had the body of a Greek god, either. He was tan, far too tan to be a mainlander who'd only just come to St. Anthony's for a little getaway. As he turned his attention back to the tire, she saw the strip of red on his neck—a

fresh sunburn. *That's not the kind of tan anybody gets in Seattle in February,* she reasoned.

Could he be working for Rick?

As soon as the panic rose in in her throat,
she swallowed it. *Don't be paranoid. Guilty
people do that. Guilty people get jumpy, and
jumpy people get caught. And you're just being
paranoid.*

*Of course he's not working for Rick. Rick
doesn't know where you are. You're fine.*

For a bright second, she was back in her
husband's house, standing at the top of the
stairs, clutching her baby boy. She'd never forget the sight of Rick's body, lying motionless
at the bottom of the marble landing, the fear
and horror in her throat suffocating her. He'd
been so terribly still, lying in that unnatural
way, his leg bent at the wrong angle.

She felt her heart speed up, the blood thrum-
ming through her veins, the panic of that night
fresh in her mind. She had to will herself to
calm down. She wasn't there. She'd never be
there again. *Not if I can help it.*

He glanced up at her, squinting against the
sun, and flashed another smile. She forced herself to relax.

"So you live in Seattle. I love that city," she
said, trying not to sound like she was probing
his backstory, which she was. "I went there

once, after college. My roommate's house overlooked the Sound. Was gorgeous. Where do you live?"

"A neighborhood called Wallingford," he said, without so much as a hitch. "I've got a condo that looks out over Woodland Park. Ever been there?"

"No, I don't think so. It was a long time since I went." She bit her lip. So he passed the first test. *He's just a tourist, like any other tourist. Don't go looking for trouble where there's none.* He tightened the lug nuts on the new tire, a small bead of sweat visible on his smooth forehead. He lowered the bus on the jack and popped up, swiping his hands free of dirt.

"That ought to get us there," he said, and straightened. He was so damn tall. And those muscles. He took a step closer to her and without thinking, Cate backed up. He was too big, too…muscled… Too damn attractive. She felt his gravitational pull and the only way to break the spell was to somehow get out of his orbit. She took another step backward and a flash of alarm lit his face as he looked over her shoulder.

Before Cate knew it, he'd grabbed her by the shoulders and pressed her against the side of the minibus. Before she could even squeak, an oversize white delivery truck rumbled past. Too big for any one lane, its white cab would've knocked Cate flat if it weren't for Tack.

She could feel him breathing as hard as she was, his fit, muscled stomach against her, her face nearly eye to eye with his chest. She could smell him—sweat and salt and the hint of some fresh scent, like laundry drying on the line. Cate ought to have been thinking about how she'd almost been killed by a truck, but instead, all she could think about was Tack's hard body against hers, how every nerve ending in her body seemed to come alive. It felt like her body had been sleeping, and now, suddenly, every cell was awake, and they all wanted one thing. All she wanted to do was to press herself closer to him, to wrap her arms around his back and feel his sturdiness. She could feel his chest rise and fall and wondered if he felt it, too, this electric rush, this sudden, powerful *want*.

As she glanced up at his face, she saw his brown eyes studying hers, his eyebrows crinkled with worry.

"Are you okay?" he asked, keeping his body against hers, his bulk still protecting her from the rush of traffic behind him.

Considering all she wanted to do right at

that moment was stand on her tiptoes and see if she could taste his lips, she already knew the answer to that question. *I might never be okay again.*

CHAPTER TWO

TACK WAS ALL too aware of Cate's body against his, warm and pliant. The way she was looking at him right now made him want to kiss the life out of her, to make her moan with want. *Nothing like a life-or-death situation to speed up the libido*, he thought, but then wondered if saving her from a speeding truck had anything to do with the fact that he didn't want to take his hands off her.

Her green eyes studied him, her pink lips parted as he waited for an answer.

"I...I'm fine," she managed to say, but never broke eye contact. He'd always been able to read women, a talent he'd learned early when overnight in high school he'd grown a foot and put on thirty pounds of muscle. They'd gone from ignoring him to waiting at his locker, giggling and blushing all the while.

He could swear the way she craned her neck, the way she leaned into him, she *wanted* him. The thought sent a thrill down his spine. *She wanted him*. He had her pinned against the minibus, but she made no move to flee. Her eyes told him she wanted to stay right where she was.

The deep-seated satisfaction this little revelation brought him surprised even him. He wanted her to want him. He'd felt the desire to put his hands on her since he saw her waiting for him at the baggage claim.

He felt drawn closer to her and before he knew it, he was just inches away from her lips. All he'd have to do was drop down a little more…and he'd be kissing her. He wondered what she tasted like. He wanted to find out.

But he couldn't. Not now.

With great reluctance, he pulled himself away. He saw a flicker of disappointment in her eyes. *She wanted that kiss as much as I did.* There was no doubt in Tack's mind.

And then, another, not-so-nice thought popped into his mind. *I could use that.*

He wasn't proud of himself for it. Didn't like how the thought felt oily in his mind, but it was the truth. He had to use every advantage he had. He knew that better than anyone.

Tack watched Cate as she scurried to pick up the wrench and carried it back to the van. He reached out and grabbed the flat, easily lifting it and putting it underneath the carriage where the spare had been. They both climbed back into the minibus.

"Uh…we're not too far from the resort," she said, not looking him in the eye, a blush creeping up the side of her cheek as she settled into the driver's seat once more.

Cate's mobile phone came to life then, blaring an easy Caribbean tune, and Tack saw her grab the phone from her pocket. "Mark?" she breathed into the phone. "Yes, I'm on the way. Just had a flat, but…" She paused, listening. "No, a guest helped me change it." For the briefest of seconds, Cate met Tack's gaze and a deep blush swept her neck as she swiftly looked away. She might as well have been telling him how she felt about their almost-kiss. He wondered how a woman who wore her emotions so clearly on her face could plot to kill her husband, steal from him and flee the country with his only son. She looked to him like an open book.

Which was probably what made her so very dangerous.

Cate glanced away and pressed the phone to her ear. "We're fine…Really…We'll be there in two minutes…I will. I promise…Okay. Bye."

She tucked the phone in her pocket and smiled sheepishly at Tack. "That's my current business partner. He…" She paused. "He was just checking up on me. Wondering what was taking so long."

"Protective?" *More like possessive*, Tack thought and then wondered why he felt a pang of jealousy.

"He just worries about me." She smiled at Tack in the rearview mirror, but her answer didn't make him feel any better. A man who called when a woman was ten minutes late from the airport had to be more than a business partner.

"Sounds like he cares about you. Boyfriend?" he asked, and wondered why the word felt so bitter on his tongue.

A laugh burst from Cate, and she shook her head. "Oh, no. Mark's happily married. His wife, Carol, helps me run the resort, and they've got a fifteen-year-old daughter, Grace, who is an amazing high diver. Might even try to get a scholarship in the States." Cate guided the minibus around the cliff bank and then took a right turn into what seemed like jungle.

The tightness in Tack's chest eased.

"So, he's not the boyfriend. Dating someone else? Or are you married?" Technically, he already knew she was divorced. Rick Allen had filed for divorce in her absence and had the courts push it through about a year ago.

Cate didn't even flinch. "God, no," she said,

and laughed, flicking her long blond hair over one shoulder. The laugh sounded so genuine. "Too busy being a single mom," she said lightly. No trace of irony in that at all.

"Oh, how old is your child?"

"He's four," she said, and he could hear the pride in her voice. "He's an amazing swimmer. And so very sweet."

"It's probably none of my business, but... what happened to his dad?" Tack watched Cate carefully, studying her reflection in the rearview mirror and trying to pick up on any signs of discomfort, of deceit. Her narrow shoulders stiffened ever so slightly, he noted, but she kept her expression neutral.

"He died," Cate said, voice flat. Her foot nudged the accelerator a little bit more. Seemed like she might want to get to the resort a bit faster.

"I'm sorry. I shouldn't have asked."

"No. It's okay." Cate shrugged and then turned, throwing an almost too-bright smile over one tanned shoulder. "Looks like we're here."

Tack glanced out the window and realized they'd taken a turn and were now out of the thick brush and into a cleared parking lot, with a three-story, white brick hotel sitting about a hundred yards from the pristine beach. The blue-green water of the Caribbean sparkled in the sunlight, and a sole, mature palm tree offered shade for a few empty white lounge chairs. Beyond that lay a boat moored at a long wooden dock. Tack could just make out the name painted on the stern: *Lost and Found*.

Indeed, Cate Allen, he thought as he looked at the lithe blonde who shut off the minibus's engine. *You were lost, but now you're found.* He was more convinced than ever he'd found his target.

"Gorgeous view," Tack said as he grabbed his seabag and slung it over one shoulder.

"We provided the clean sheets and breakfast buffet, but I can't take credit for the view," she said. "Mr. Reeves, if you'll follow me? I'll get you checked in."

The formality wasn't lost on Tack. He'd been kicked back from first-name basis to formal stranger. As the two walked into the hotel's lobby, Tack felt a cool blast of air-conditioning, and the air smelled like coconut oil. White marble tile lined the floor, and dark wicker furniture made up the spacious check-in area. Tasteful, he thought. A man with gray, nearly white hair, wearing khaki Bermuda shorts, sprang up from the love seat.

"You okay, Cate?" he asked in gruff voice, concern etched in his face.

"Mark, I'm fine. Uh…Mr. Reeves helped with the flat." Cate turned and nodded. "Mr. Reeves…this is Mark Gurda. He co-owns the resort with me."

"Nice to meet you," Tack said, and extended a hand, noticing that Mark eyed him with suspicion, taking in his build and his seabag.

"Marines, huh?" Mark said, but it didn't sound like he approved.

"Yep." Tack nodded. "Retired, though. If you can ever be retired from the marines." He'd leave out the part about the dishonorable discharge. No need to split hairs.

Mark gave a curt nod but quickly shifted his attention back to Cate. "I…need to talk to you. Do you have a minute?"

Cate hesitated. The man wasn't just a business partner, that much was clear. And Tack knew more than anyone that being married didn't mean he wasn't sleeping with Cate. He'd been hired to catch more than one cheating spouse. As Tack glanced down at Cate's long, tanned legs, he thought, *Who wouldn't throw away marriage vows for that?*

"Mr. Reeves, if you'll head to the front desk…" Mark nodded curtly away from them, leaving no mistake about his meaning. *Get lost.* Tack eyed the older man. He hadn't heard of Gurda before now. She must've met him after she'd run away, and somehow convinced him to invest in the resort. But, given all she was said to have stolen, why would she need a coinvestor? Tack would find out.

"May I help you, sir?" called a pretty forty-ish woman with short, bobbed hair and a quick smile. She stood behind the front desk. Reluctantly, Tack left Mark, who was speaking in low tones to Cate about something he wanted to overhear. "Don't mind my husband," she added. "He's gruff on the outside, but a teddy bear on the inside. I'm Carol Gurda. Welcome to St. Anthony's Resort." She tapped on the computer behind the desk, and when she looked up again, Tack was leaning on the counter near her. "Oh…my…you're tall." She craned her neck to look up at him. "Bet you get that a lot."

Tack shrugged. "A little bit." He grinned. While Carol looked up his reservation, Tack couldn't help but glance over his shoulder at Mark and Cate. They'd walked off a few more paces and stood by the window, talking in low tones about something a little too serious for Tack's liking. Lover's tiff?

"Cate's great, isn't she? Just a doll," Carol gushed, watching Tack watching Cate.

"She's captured my attention, that's for sure," Tack said, which wasn't a lie.

Carol eyed him with interest. "You're staying for a week?" she asked him.

"So far," he said smoothly. "But I've got a flexible schedule, so could I extend the trip if I wanted to?"

Carol brightened further. "Absolutely, you can."

"I might want to get to know one particular local better." He grinned at Carol and she returned the smile.

"Cate? You know, Cate's just the best. I keep hoping she'll *find* someone, though my husband tells me to quit meddling. That it's none of my business, but *look* at her. Why is she single?"

"Indeed. She's one of the most beautiful women I've ever seen," Tack said. This was also not a lie.

Carol beamed as she grabbed the newly minted key card from the register. "Beautiful inside and out. She really is a sweetheart. Honestly."

Here's someone else who thinks she's nice. Tack had interviewed every person he could find who knew Cate, down to her high school algebra teacher. They all said the same thing— about how sweet she was. Still, people could be fooled. Besides, what sweet person would take a son away from his father? It didn't make sense.

"Are you single?" Carol asked, glancing at Tack's empty ring finger.

"You running a matchmaking service?" Tack joked, and Carol grinned.

"Maybe." Carol sighed. "I just want Cate to be happy. She's been very—" she hesitated "—unlucky."

"Her husband dying."

Carol hesitated a beat too long.

"Right." Carol nodded. She kept her eyes fixed on the computer screen in front of her.

"Sometimes feeling normal again takes a while," he added. "My dad died when I was twelve, and it took me years to get over it."

Instant pity registered on Carol's face, and her mothering instincts seemed to take over. "Oh, you poor thing."

"Bad things happen sometimes." He shrugged. "If I did want to get to know her better…" Tack let the insinuation linger. "What would *you* suggest?"

Carol's eyes brightened. "Well, dinner for guests starts at seven, but Cate…she always eats in the dining room around six." Carol lowered her voice and leaned over the counter. "But you didn't hear that from me."

"Hear what? You told me what time dinner

was, but darned if I just couldn't remember." They both shared a little laugh. "I'll just be early to be on the safe side," Tack said, exchanging a conspiratorial grin with Carol.

"I like you already," Carol said, and handed him his room key.

CHAPTER THREE

HE'S GONE. MAYBE I can avoid him for the coming week he's here, Cate thought as she watched Tack's tall, lean form leave the lobby and felt a little breath of relief escape her. Something about him… And it wasn't just his intelligent eyes and capable hands, either. Something about him just screamed trouble. Just because she went all gooey in his arms didn't mean she ought to ignore her instincts. *They've got me this far. I'll need to keep my guard up.* Cate almost laughed to herself. When did she ever let her guard *down*? She'd chosen a life where she now had to look over her shoulder every day. But it was better than the life she had with Rick. There was no doubt in her mind about that.

"Did you hear me?" Mark asked her as he drew her attention back to him. "We're in the red, Cate. Big time. I'm not sure how we're going to keep the lights on next month if we don't get more guests here."

Cate sighed. This was becoming nearly a daily conversation with Mark. "I know."

"We need to do more marketing," Mark insisted, tapping his open palm. "More Yelp. More social media."

"No." It came out harsher sounding than she intended. "And you know why."

And he did. Mark had been there almost from the beginning of her escape. He was the one who got her a fake passport, who snuck her out of the country.

Cate had met Mark by chance at one of the big charity galas Rick so liked to attend. Her ex always wanted everyone to think he was so generous, so magnanimous. Cate remembered watching Rick from the corner of the elegantly appointed hotel ballroom, sipping a glass of expensive champagne, thinking about how she felt like she was suffocating.

"You're mine," he'd said in the limo ride over. He'd clutched at her arm in the back seat, his hand a metal cuff, his fingers digging into her flesh like teeth. "You and my son. Don't you ever forget it."

How could she ever? He treated his wife and son like possessions, toys that belonged to him, to do with as he pleased. To the outside world, he was the reclusive billionaire, the mysterious genius who'd turned over one amazing land deal after another but never granted an interview. But no one knew the dark, brooding, insecure man like Cate did. No one knew how much he secretly drank, how hard he worked to make the small, elite circle who did know him think he was charming, how desperate he was to keep things in his control. The lengths he'd go to make sure they stayed that way.

When she'd first met him, she thought he'd just loved her more than anyone else had loved her. He was dogged in his pursuit, determined to have her, and she'd been flattered. That was the truth of it. At first, she thought his intense interest was a compliment, a testament to his love. She never dreamed it would become so twisted.

Then, inexplicably, there at the ball, watching him surrounded by a small circle of admirers and sycophants, watching him pretend to be the man he wasn't, she felt sick to her stomach. She'd glanced at herself in a mirrored column and saw to her dismay a bruise blooming on her upper arm. She realized she'd sweated off some of her concealer, and it was the middle of the summer so she wore no wrap for her sleeveless gown. How could she be so stupid? She felt exposed and desperate to cover it up.

"Are you all right?" Carol had asked, a

woman she didn't even know, with her husband by her side, a sympathetic look on his face.

It was that small act of kindness that underlined just how long it had been since someone was kind and considerate, that broke her. She started to lose it. Her hands shook. Tears sprung to her eyes, and tears would only wash away the caked concealer she'd used to cover the fading bruise on her cheek. Cate remembered Carol had somehow steered her to the bathroom. How she'd remarked on the bruise on her arm. "I don't think you're all right at all," she'd said. "How can I help?"

She'd graciously accepted Carol's tissues but told her she'd be fine.

"Here," Carol had said, handing her a business card with their Caribbean address. The two had been in town only for the charity event, one they attended every year. "My husband used to be a lawyer. We can help you. When…it's the right time."

It was only a few months later, when everything went so terribly wrong, so out of control, that she reached out to them for help. She'd be eternally grateful they answered the call. She felt someone up there was looking out for her that night. A chance encounter with kind strangers would save her life. Yet even now, three years later, she was still scared, still worried that it wasn't over.

"I know this doesn't make sense," she said. "I know we should do more advertising... but..."

"You're scared." Mark always seemed to know what she was thinking. "There's no link to your old life. I made sure of that," Mark said. She knew he was right. Before he retired early and moved his family to the Caribbean, Mark had spent his career helping clients set up shell companies so they could hide things they didn't want found. But Rick Allen was never one to take no for an answer. He always used to say you don't build a billion-dollar empire by giving up. How many different ways had he told her the Allen family didn't have quit in their blood?

After what she'd done to him... After how she'd left him...

She shuddered. No, he'd never give up. Not now.

"We don't have to use pictures of you. We could find a way to advertise this without... putting you out there. We have to do something."

"I know. I know we do." Cate felt the sudden weight on her shoulders. If they didn't make this resort work, then what? Cate had pawned the jewelry she felt couldn't be traced back to her. But she still had the quarter-million-dollar engagement ring. Though, if she sold that, she knew it would come back to her. He'd had it custom made, and probably had every major jeweler looking for it. She had more real estate, too, adjacent to the resort, but she'd been hoping to keep that. Expand the hotel in better times.

"Besides, maybe he's stopped looking for you." Mark met Cate's gaze, but even he didn't believe those words.

"You know he won't."

Mark sighed. "I know." He glanced toward the hallway, where Tack had walked, and shook his head. "Maybe we should hire that new guest for extra muscle. He's built like a wall and what is he? Like six-four? He feels like a cop."

"He's a former marine."

"Yeah, I saw the seabag," Mark said, and grinned. "If he were your bodyguard, you know who wouldn't even dream of coming near you."

"I'm not so desperate that I'm going to go recruiting our guests, Mark." Though, she had to admit, the thought of Tack by her side made her shiver just a little. She glanced at her watch and realized it was time to pick up her son from preschool. "I need to get Avery. We'll talk about this later?"

"We'll have to," Mark grumbled.

THE SMALL PRESCHOOL sat in a cluster of palm trees next door to the island's only aquarium, a tiny but clean building mostly frequented by tourists with kids. A pretty glass mural of a sea turtle swimming in gleaming green water kicked back the light. In the parking lot, iguanas sunned themselves on the stucco path, not even bothering to move as Cate walked by, her big straw bag slung over one shoulder. The sound of little kids laughing found her, and she walked back around to the fenced-in play yard. She saw Avery climbing up the ladder of a slide, his curly blond hair flying into his eyes as he sped down the plastic chute.

"Mommy!" he cried as he saw her and bounded to the gate. Her heart felt like it might explode. She felt this way every time she looked at her son, unable to believe that such a sweet boy had come from her...and Rick. The minute he was born, Cate remembered vowing that she'd protect him from every harm the world had to offer. Even if that harm might come from his own father.

The preschool teacher nodded at Cate, recognizing her and opening the gate from the inside. Avery bounded into his mother's arms and squeezed her neck tightly.

"Avery!" she cried as she scooped him up, giving him a kiss on the cheek. "How are you today, bud?"

"I made a crown!" he told her, showing her the construction-paper craft he'd decorated with markers and glitter. "It means I'm king!" His green eyes sparkled in delight.

"You sure are," she said, and hugged him a little tighter, whipping his too long honey-colored hair from his face. "And the king needs a haircut."

"Aw. Weally?" His adorable lisp temporarily disarmed her. As did the truly disappointed look in his green eyes. They were *her* green eyes. Every time she looked at Avery she saw herself. She was grateful for that. Though, of course, there were reminders of Rick. In the way Avery smiled sometimes, the expressions on his face. But Avery was all rainbows and sunshine, a bright ball of love and nothing like Rick in all the ways that mattered.

"Yes, *really*, sire. You need a cut." She mussed his soft hair and he laughed. Cate carried him over to her little hatchback.

"Look, Mommy. Blue! My favorite color," Avery said, grabbing the crown and showing her his scribbles. He might just be four, but he was an expert at diversional tactics.

"Blue is pretty, honey." She was strapping him into his car seat when he held up the crown.

"Do you think Daddy likes blue?"

The question stopped her in her tracks. Avery had gone nearly a year without even mentioning his dad. Now, suddenly, here he was asking questions.

"I don't know, sweetie." She tried to keep her voice steady. Rick didn't have a favorite color. Not that she knew of. *If he did, he'd probably get a copyright and then declare that color off-limits to everyone else*, she thought.

"Do you think there's a lot of blue in heaven? Where Daddy lives?"

"I don't know." Cate felt rattled by the questions. More so than usual. She also felt an unexpected pang of guilt. Yes, she'd told her boy his father was dead. That was a lie, but what else could she do? Tell her perfect little boy the truth?

Your father is a monster.

No. She never wanted him to know that. Because Avery wasn't anything like his father, and she planned to keep it that way.

"I bet you're hungry," she said instead. "Ready for dinner?"

Avery nodded. "Snack!" he demanded, opening up his hands.

Cate knew the fifteen-minute drive back to the resort would be a lot easier with a few crackers than without. Besides, the boy burned through calories. He needed to eat every ten minutes, so there was almost zero chance of spoiling his dinner.

"Want some graham crackers?"

"Yes!" he cried with enthusiasm. She grabbed the Ziploc snack bag filled with animal-shaped grahams and handed it to him. Feeling relieved, she made her way to the driver's seat and looked forward to a nice, quiet dinner, before the rest of the guests. Not that there were that many, she thought. The resort was less than half full. It was one of the reasons Mark wanted to do more advertising. And she should, she guessed. She should get over this irrational idea that ads would somehow catch Rick's attention.

She wouldn't be in any of the ads, and she could use a picture of the resort on social media. She needed to let go of the fear that drove her. She knew it didn't make sense. But fear never did.

She pulled up to the resort, noticing the mostly empty parking lot. Her stomach sank. What would she do if the resort went under?

When she sold her jewelry—the only thing she took from Rick Allen—she'd put much of it into the hotel. Mark had suggested it. He could be the public face of the resort, and she could be a silent investor, hidden away from the public and from anyone who could recognize her.

Then it had been booming, and she thought it was a sound investment. Of course, that was before the island opened itself up to the big cruise ships. Now, fewer people came to St. Anthony's to stay. Most opted for a floating hotel, and that meant letting staff go and her taking on a larger role in the resort. She saw two big liners off in the distance. She wondered how many of her guests they'd stolen in the last year.

How many different ways had Rick told her she wasn't capable of doing anything on her own? There were the hundreds of small household decisions he'd called into question: *How could you let the gardener plant those ugly shrubs? Am I wrong, or were you supposed to be supervising him?* And then there was the time she wanted to try writing a novel, but he'd ridiculed her mercilessly and in front of others: *Cate wants to write. God, can you imagine? A romance! Lord help us.* He'd even had an opinion about what she wore: *You don't even know what looks good on you, Cate. How did you last this long with me?* When she got upset, he'd tell her she was overreacting. That it was her fault. After all, there was never anything wrong with Rick Allen. The problem had to be with her.

She'd been with him five years, married for three, but in some ways it felt like a life sentence. His nagging voice in her head never quite seemed to go away. He was always telling her something was *wrong* with her—she wasn't smart enough, wasn't interesting enough, wasn't pretty enough. She got now that it was his way of controlling her, just another aspect of the abuse. But while the bruises healed, the insults and criticisms just festered, wounds that never seemed to scab over.

Maybe I'm not smart enough to run this resort. Maybe Rick was right.

The second the evil thoughts weaseled their way into her head, she pushed them out once more. She was done letting Rick push her around, whether that was physically or in her own head. *You'd never survive out there without me*, he'd told her once. *Well, that's just not true*, she thought, *I'm surviving just fine.*

She killed the ignition and glanced at the resort.

For now, at least.

Cate bustled Avery out of the car, carrying his fire truck backpack, and steered him straight into the lobby and to the dining room, where the dinner buffet was just being set up. She looked at all the food—the simple fish fillets and bright veggies prepared with such loving care by the cooks in the kitchen—and felt a bit of sadness. It was lovely, but couldn't touch the amazing buffets of the good old days with fresh crab legs and delicate sushi rolls. The scaled-back buffet was a shadow of its former self. She steered Avery to his favorite spot, near the window looking out to the blue-green water, and turned to head back to the food.

She piled on chicken strips and apple slices, and then hesitated at the broccoli, wondering if it would be too much of a fight to get him to eat some. She felt a sudden presence by her elbow.

"Hi, Cate," came the deep, unmistakably sexy voice. She knew before looking who stood there.

Cate nearly dropped the plate as she whirled away from the buffet. So much for avoiding the man.

"Tack," she cried, surprised, her heart rate doubling as she took in his tall frame. The man moved like a big cat. She hadn't even heard him approach. He'd changed and now wore a linen button-down, short-sleeved, pale blue shirt and khaki cargo shorts. His face broke into an easy smile, and she felt her stomach clench as she looked at his clean-shaven tanned face. She'd just seen him earlier that afternoon, but it seemed in that time he'd managed to get sexier, if such a thing was possible.

"Uh…the dining room is closed," she managed to say, though the gruff way it came out made her want to kick herself. Why was she being so rude?

Tack grinned, and nodded at the buffet and the plate in her hands. "It looks pretty open to me." He seemed completely unruffled by her, and even worse, he wasn't leaving. "Mind if I…join you?"

"Uh…I'm eating with my son…" She nodded toward the table where Avery was happily pretending his snack cup was a car, and making it zoom across the table.

"I love kids," Tack said smoothly. "I don't want to brag, but I've been told I'm the world's greatest uncle. I might just have a mug that says the same thing."

He flashed another bright white smile, and all of the excuses as to why she wouldn't want a handsome stranger to join her rushed from her mind.

She giggled a little, feeling like she was thirteen again and standing by the lockers in front of the cutest boy in school. *Get it together, Cate. He's not interested in you, anyway. You're not nearly pretty enough for him. Not without all the expensive jewelry and clothes that Rick said made you an "eight" when you were naturally just a "six."*

Tack reached behind her to get a plate, and his strong arm brushed her elbow. She was hyperaware of every movement he made. She realized, suddenly, she was still holding her son's half-filled plate, watching Tack reach for scalloped potatoes. She decided to leave the broccoli and opted for raw carrots instead, then headed back with a cup of juice to the table, where she plunked the plate in front of her little boy. He went for the chicken fingers first, naturally, and happily chomped his food while she turned back to the buffet. Deliberately, she started on the opposite side as far from Tack as she could get, though it wasn't long before he was again by her side.

"What do you recommend?" he asked her, dark eyes studying her. Her mouth went a little dry beneath the intensity of his gaze.

"Everything is good," she said. "But you should try the conch chowder. It's the island specialty." She nodded toward the soup bowl on the other side of the glass-partitioned buffet. She thought it would be better if she could move him from her side, but when he walked around, she realized now, he was right in front of her, glass buffet or not, and he was watching her even as he ladled soup into a small bowl. If he was going to study her like that, she might not be able to eat. Her once growling stomach now exploded into a riot of nerves. Why did the man make her so nervous?

She managed to keep her eyes on the broiled fish she scooped onto her plate, then she moved on to the steamed veggies. He watched her every move. She made the mistake of glancing up at him once, and they made eye contact. She held his gaze for a beat too long, unable to break free. It had been so long since a man had been this focused on her.

Not since Rick, she thought.

She glanced down at her own frumpy cut-offs, her faded T-shirt and flip-flops. She wasn't even wearing any makeup, and she'd swept up her hair into a messy, careless knot at her nape. She had no idea why Tack studied her like he was trying to figure out a puzzle. It made her uneasy.

She hurriedly finished filling her plate and then scurried it back to her son's table. *The faster I eat, the faster I can get away from that man.*

Cate sat and Tack followed, slipping into the chair opposite her. His shoulders were enormous, she decided, like a well-muscled wall, sitting in front of her. It was going to take effort to eat with this hulking man sitting at the table.

Avery just grinned at the stranger. "Hi! I'm Avery," he said, beaming. The boy wasn't the least bit shy. Raised in a resort, he was more than used to strangers. Mark had joked that they ought to put the boy out in the lobby as a concierge.

"Hi, Avery. I'm Tack."

"Nice to meet you," the precocious four-year-old said. He grinned. "You've got lots of muscles. Are you Captain America?"

"Avery," Cate said reprovingly, feeling the blush of embarrassment creep up her neck. The air-conditioning suddenly seemed a little too weak in the room. Leave it to a preschooler to say exactly what's on his mind.

"He's in a superhero phase," she said, apologetically.

"I'm not Captain America," Tack said, trying to sound serious. "But I *used* to be a marine, actually. First Lieutenant Thomas Reeves, at your service. I *might* know a thing or two about saving the day."

"I knew it! You are a superhero! Can you fly?"

"Oh, now you've started it," Cate said, and Tack chuckled a little.

Over Tack's shoulder, Cate saw Carol peek out from the door to the kitchen. The woman was spying! When she was caught, she gave Cate a huge thumbs-up, and that's when Cate knew somehow that this was all Carol's doing. It would be just like her to try to set her up on some kind of date. Carol was under the misguided impression that Cate was lonely, that she needed a man's company. Cate had sworn off men. She didn't trust herself to pick a good one, and she'd never, ever be beholden to one again.

Tack took a sip of soup and nodded his appreciation at the taste of the conch chowder.

"My daddy can fly," Avery said suddenly. "He's an angel in heaven."

Cate nearly spit out her food. Tack coughed, as if the soup had gone down the wrong way. He coughed louder, face turning red as he gave his chest a hard pat.

"Is that right?" he managed to say, recovering.

Now Cate *really* wanted to be anywhere

but here. Carol was still spying, and she sent her what she hoped was a look of stern disapproval.

"I don't have a dad. Do you want to be my dad?" Avery asked.

"Avery! That's not…" Cate wanted the ground to open her up and swallow her whole.

Tack laughed a little. "Don't worry. It's okay. Well, how about we see first if we can get through dinner, all right, champ?"

Cate had never felt more embarrassed in her whole life. The table sunk into silence then, the only sound the clink of Tack's spoon on his soup bowl. Tack seemed to be preoccupied, no doubt thinking she was the most desperate woman on earth. She'd not put Avery up to that, though, she swore.

That's when Cate saw Carol bustle out of the kitchen, seeming determined.

Oh, no. This was not going to be good.

"Everything all right here?" Carol said brightly. "Can I get you anything else?"

"No, we're *fine*." Cate wanted Carol to go away. Besides, this was a buffet, not tableside service.

"So, Mr. Reeves, I know it's your first trip to St. Anthony's. Do you snorkel?" She barreled on, not picking up on the cue from Tack's now-somber face that he probably wasn't interested in any tour. He looked like a man who wanted to escape. Not that Cate blamed him. Kids at all were a nonstarter for most men, but kids talking about dead fathers and wanting new dads were probably more serious deal breakers.

"Snorkel?" Tack looked momentarily taken aback.

Cate knew exactly what Carol was doing. She was talking about the boat tour around the island that Cate led every morning around ten.

"I'm sure Mr. Reeves has other things to do with his first morning on vacation," Cate said.

Tack studied her. "Well, I…"

"Cate gives the *best* tours, and she knows the best snorkeling spots. She leads a group every morning…"

Cate mentally shook her head. *No, Carol. No!* She tried very hard to telepathically tell her friend to stop what she was doing. The last thing she needed was Tack on board her boat at nine in the morning.

"I love to snorkel. Sounds like fun." Tack stared at Cate as he said that. Avery happily chomped his chicken tender and Carol just beamed, like she'd won a prize at the state fair. Oh, she'd won a prize, but it wasn't anything she'd like, Cate thought. *She's going to get an earful when I get her alone.*

"The boat is already full," she lied. Only four other guests had booked a trip for the morning. And two of them were simply strong *maybes.* The boat could hold ten easily.

"One already canceled just this afternoon," Carol said. "You've got room for one more." The woman wasn't going to let this go. The steely look in her eyes told her she was not going to be deterred from this matchmaking mission. Tack quirked an eyebrow, almost as if daring her to deny him now.

"All right," Cate said, giving in. There was no use fighting them both.

CHAPTER FOUR

TACK LAY ON the soft bed in his room and stared at the second hand of the clock sitting on his nightstand as it ticked forward. The sunlight streamed in; he'd seen the slow progression of light since dawn. He'd been up since three in the morning, his usual wake-up call. He hadn't sleep through a night since he'd left Afghanistan. And every time he woke up, he thought of Adeeb, fighting side by side with them in some of the worst firefights.

He sent up a little prayer that he was okay. That he'd eluded the Taliban another day.

Tack had met Adeeb when he was twenty-five and worked with him for three years straight on sensitive ops to find Taliban strongholds in Helmand Province, one of the most dangerous areas of Afghanistan. Adeeb, a lanky and thoughtful man, never once got rattled, not even under heavy gunfire.

Tack had been suspicious of the idea of a local translator at first. After all, what reason did he have to help the Americans? But

Adeeb hated the Taliban and everything they stood for. "They are terrible people. They're not about Islam, they're about power."

Adeeb had watched his sister be terrorized by the Taliban, and his family threatened when they tried to send her to school. He had every reason to hate them.

Still, Tack wasn't sure. How could he trust a translator he just met? Sure, he'd volunteered and been vetted by the military, but still. Tack didn't like wild cards, especially when the lives of his men were on the line.

On their first mission together, Tack and his team were looking for a Taliban leader who'd been causing a lot of trouble. Adeeb interviewed a local family, and after several minutes of discussion as Tack stood by, not understanding a word they said, Adeeb turned to Tack and said, "They told me he's not here. But they're lying, and here's why. They have a son, and he was kidnapped by the Taliban last year. They're scared."

Adeeb had been right about everything from that day forward. He knew the bad guys from the good guys, he was smart, he was a fantastic read of people and he'd saved more marines than Tack could count, all by giving them life-saving intel. He was worth his weight in gold.

But it didn't take long after that before the

threats from the Taliban came in. Phone calls, notes left at his house. They saw him as a traitor and planned to cut off his head. They said they wouldn't stop there. They'd kill his entire family, all of his relatives. But nothing ever rattled the man, not the threats, not gunfire. He held firm in his beliefs. He told Tack that he believed the Taliban was ruining his country, and that he'd risk his life if need be to stop them. Let them do what they wanted, but he wasn't going to let them ruin his country without a fight.

Tack respected the position. It was exactly what he would do if a group of extremists took over his own country.

The marines promised Adeeb and his family a visa to come to America, but they'd reneged on their promise. Scratch that. The marines hadn't reneged on their promise, Tack's sniveling coward of a commanding officer, Derek Hollie, had.

He checked his phone and found a message from Adeeb. Relief flooded Tack's body. He only heard from the former translator a couple of times a week, when the man went close enough to town to get a signal.

We are fine. Wanted to let you know. Medeeha says thanks for the candy.

Medeeha was Adeeb's little girl, who'd just

turned three. Tack had sent a care package, as he did every month, filled with dry goods and treats. None of it would do any good if the Taliban found them. Tack quickly messaged back.

Keep safe, man. I haven't forgotten my promise.

Tack had promised to bring Adeeb to the United States, and he wasn't giving up on that. He'd left Helmand Province years ago feeling like he'd left one man behind, something he'd vowed never to do.

Adeeb had saved Tack more than once. Had saved all the men in his company more than once. And he helped the Americans at great personal peril after the Taliban labeled him a traitor. Tack knew better than anyone that the Taliban didn't make idle threats.

Tack had lobbied his senators, wrote letters, did all he could think of to do to get a visa for his friend. Then he had found out that Rick Allen, major donor to political causes, might be able to get him the visa Adeeb so badly needed. That's why Tack couldn't fail. Not to mention, the ten-million-dollar reward money could help Adeeb and so many more resettle in the United States.

Tack breathed a sigh of relief that Adeeb and his family fought to live another day, and focused on the case at hand. Already, he'd taken too long in looking for the missing woman. Every day that went by was a day that Adeeb didn't have.

He glanced at his watch. Time had slipped by, and he realized he ought to get a move on if he wanted to get to the dock for the promised tour. *Better watch your back, Tack. She gets one whiff of who you work for, and she might throw you overboard.*

He grinned at the thought. *Let her try.* He'd faced more cunning enemies before. But maybe not prettier ones, he thought, remembering her clear green eyes. He had to admit that.

He stepped into some swim trunks and an old tee, and then grabbed a baseball cap and shoved it on his head. He reached for his mesh bag where he kept his own flippers, mask and snorkel—he'd been scuba certified since even before he enlisted in the marines—and headed out of his room, maneuvering down the stairs and out to the lobby. The ocean was just past the resort pool and down the short stairs to the smooth, nearly white sand. He saw the twenty-foot boat with the blue canopy floating at the end of a long, wooden dock and headed that way. He expected to see a crowd of tourists but found the dock empty, except for Cate.

She wore a pair of worn cutoffs and a tank,

the bright teal bikini strap tied at the back of her neck poking through. Her back was to him, and she was bent over an old red plastic cooler, working to lug it to the boat. For a few seconds, he watched her struggle with the heavy old red plastic box, admiring her muscled, tanned legs. The sound of the ocean and the rush of waves hitting the beach made it easy to sneak up on her. He put down his mesh snorkel bag.

"Can I help?" he asked, and watched her jump nearly a mile.

"God, you scared me," she said, pushing her oversize sunglasses up on her nose and flattening the other hand against her chest. "Where did you come from?"

"Iowa," he joked. "At least, that's where I was born and raised, before I moved to Seattle." She sent him a wry smile as she went back to her work with the cooler.

"Here, let me." He easily lifted the cooler, packed with ice and drinks, and she stepped back, a little surprised.

"Uh...thanks," she said, and he noticed she kept her attention focused on him. Good, that's where it needed to be. "Just put it there." She pointed to the stern, where a carved out little indention fit the cooler perfectly. He set it in. She hopped in after him and fastened straps around the cooler to make sure it didn't fall overboard.

"I've got snorkel gear if you need it..." she began, turning to one of the seats of the boat. She flipped up the cushioned top to reveal mounds of flippers, snorkels and diving masks.

"I came prepared," he said, nodding back to the dock. He hopped off the boat and grabbed his gear.

"Oh, I see." She glanced anxiously about, looking unnerved and clearly distracted, or she would've noticed he already had gear. She glanced at the sports watch on her wrist and then back at the hotel, as she kept one foot on the dock and one resting on the stern of the boat.

"Where is everyone?" Tack asked, glancing around the empty boat.

"We were supposed to have at least one more couple join us today," she explained. "The others have already dropped out, which is unusual, but...it happens. Did you see anyone else in the lobby on your way out?"

He shook his head. "No one in the lobby."

"We can give them a few more minutes," she said, biting her lip. Then her phone dinged with an incoming message and she pulled it out of the back pocket of her shorts. "Dammit," she murmured, and then she glanced up apologetically. "Sorry. I…uh…" She peered at the screen of her phone. "Just one minute."

She tapped her screen and then put the phone against her ear as she made a phone call. "Carol! It's Cate. Are you sure they canceled?" She stood and anxiously paced the boat, putting a hand on her head and looking unnerved. "You're *sure* that *they* canceled?"

The intonation wasn't lost on Tack.

"Carol…if…" She stopped, listening. "Yes, but…maybe we should just reschedule the trip?" Tack, on high alert, listened in. She let out a long, defeated-sounding sigh. "All right then. Fine." She hung up and angrily tucked the phone back in her pocket. Then she grinned at him sheepishly. "Looks like it's just us."

"Don't sound so disappointed." Tack grinned, and Cate barked an uneasy laugh. He slung his mesh diver's bag onto the floor of the boat and as he did so, brushed her arm ever so slightly. She jumped back and almost toppled onto the bench. He reached out a hand to steady her, and he could just make out her wide-eyed surprise behind her tinted lenses. Oh, yes, this would be an interesting morning, of that he had no doubt.

"Uh…thanks." She withdrew her arm and rubbed it, now looking anywhere but at him.

"Can you get that rope, please?" She tried to be all business, but he could tell she was rattled. He hopped off the boat and easily untied the line holding them to the dock. He stepped back on board and gave the boat a shove with his foot as Cate kicked on the motor and took the boat out to sea. She handled the controls with confidence. The waves slapped against the bow as the ship moved across the green water, sparkling in the sun.

"Where did you learn how to pilot a boat?" he called over the roar of the engine. Of course, he already knew the answer. He'd done his homework on Cate long before now. He already knew she'd grown up in a small town in Louisiana, near Cado Lake, known for cypress trees and a few alligators. While trying to track her down, he'd damn near interviewed every one of her relatives and nearly anybody else who'd ever known her.

Her dad scraped by repairing boats, and probably took her out on the lake more than once. Her mother worked various waitressing jobs. She came from no money. Hers was a typical Cinderella story, if Cinderella tried to murder Prince Charming.

Cate kept her attention on the water. "My dad," she said. "Dad loved to fish. He taught me how to do both."

Tack already knew that. He'd interviewed the man, a tattooed sixty-four-year-old who drank beer for breakfast, cursed worse than a sailor and still ran a tiny little bait shop off the small, dirt turnoff for the lake. It had been a shock to his system trying to imagine the spoiled, greedy socialite living in the bayou. Her father, and everybody else he interviewed from her childhood, praised her as having a heart the size of Texas. Tack never could make sense of how she'd gone bad, except that money did funny things to people. Even nice people.

Rick Allen had told him that she plotted to kill him because a prenup meant she'd get nothing if they divorced. His death was the only way she'd get out of the marriage with a single cent.

Cate's father had told him in no uncertain terms that he had no idea where she'd gone. Hadn't heard from her since she'd disappeared and hoped she was doing well, wherever she was.

Tack had assumed, given how drunk the man was by the end of the interview, that her daddy issues ran deep. Probably what made her so focused on squeezing her husband dry.

"Your dad taught you?" Tack still couldn't see how the old man managed it. Unless he wasn't drinking so much then. "That must've been nice."

"Well, sure, but Dad always got so drunk he'd pass out, and I'd have to steer the boat back to the dock. What I really learned was how to handle a boat," she said, without a trace of self-pity, which Tack found remarkable. Tack grew up on a farm in Iowa where self-pity was about the worst sin you could manage. Despite his better judgment, he found himself admiring Cate's no-nonsense approach to her clearly less-than-stellar childhood.

"You don't sound mad about it."

Cate shrugged. "Just the way things were. Like my gran said, 'You can cry about it, or you can get over it.' And I never much liked crying." Right then, Tack heard just the faintest trace of Louisiana in her accent, which in other times she so carefully tamped down. Before now, he never could imagine Cate fitting in down in the bayou, no matter the old picture her father had shown him of her in cutoff jeans and bare feet.

Of course, this Cate before him, the one who kicked off her flip-flips now and stood barefoot in her boat, maybe *this* Cate could've come from the bayou. He could imagine her, maybe, walking barefoot down by the muddy lakeshore.

This Cate reminded him of the girls back home in Iowa. Unassuming, no makeup, living on the family farm. It was the kind of girl he'd had a weak spot for since eighth grade.

He saw her shift her weight, the deliciously firm muscles in her calves rippling ever so slightly. He imagined what they'd feel like wrapped tightly around his waist, and felt himself becoming aroused. This woman was a walking visa to the United States for a brave man and his family, and he couldn't forget it.

He rummaged around in his bag and dug out the waterproof camera and began clicking pictures of the resort. His mission today was to get as many of Cate as he could. He'd need some to send to his employer, to see if he thought the resemblance was as strong as he did. Granted, Mr. Allen had asked for a DNA sample, which Tack had yet to get, but in the meantime, pictures would be a start. He turned the camera toward Cate, and instantly she held up her hand in front of her face.

"Not me! You don't want me in there ruining your shots." She laughed, but there was a hard edge to her voice, a warning.

"But you're the prettiest thing out here," he said, and for a second she hesitated.

"I hate having my picture taken," she said. And he knew it wasn't a lie. You couldn't hide too well if people started posting your picture on Facebook. Not when there's a ten-million-dollar bounty on your safe return to the States.

Tack tried to click a few more, but she'd turned, showing him her back.

Cate kicked up the motor, making any more conversation futile as the wind whipped across the bow of the boat and the maw of the engine buzzed loudly in his ears. Soon enough, Cate turned the boat into a small cove and slowed.

"Welcome to Blue Bay," she said, cutting the engine as the boat pulled into the small inlet, where she let it drift about twenty feet from shore. She released the anchor to steady the vessel. The bay was aptly named—the clear water looked more blue than green here, and when he glanced over the side of the boat, he could see brightly colored fish darting just below the surface along a large expanse of blue coral reefs.

Cate threw down the ladder from the back of the boat.

"Help yourself," she said, gesturing to the water. "We can stay here as long as you'd like."

Tack whipped off his T-shirt and noticed that Cate gawked at his bare chest before she quickly turned away. He worked hard keeping himself in shape, and he smiled to himself as he noticed her flushed face.

"You're not coming in?" he asked.

"Oh…" She looked genuinely taken off guard. "Well, I…"

"I thought I paid for a guided tour." He sat on the bench at the back of the boat, slipping on his flippers.

Cate studied him a moment as if trying to figure out a problem. "Sure. I'll join you." She kept her voice neutral as she unbuttoned her cutoffs and slipped out of them. She pulled her tank over her head and now it was Tack's turn to stare. The woman was a tanned, toned masterpiece in perfect symmetry. He couldn't help but stare at her belly button and the firm stomach that slipped down into her bright blue string bikini bottom. She sat and busied herself putting on her own gear. She attached a small knife belt to her thigh, and grabbed a small mesh bag.

"Fish food," she explained as she held it up. "You ready?" He swallowed, his mouth suddenly very dry as he tried his best not to look at how well she filled out her bikini top.

"As ready as I'll ever be," he said as he maneuvered to the end of the boat, bypassed the ladder and leaped into the warm Caribbean Sea.

The rush of warm water enveloped him, and when Cate jumped in a few feet nearby, he swam to her, playfully splashing her with water.

"Hey!" she called, retaliating by slapping the water up to his face. He coughed and swiped at his eyes, and as she advanced, he caught her off guard by diving beneath the waves and grabbing hold of her waist.

He realized how fit she was, how taut her skin felt beneath his hands. When they came up for air, their bodies pressed together, water ran down their faces. All he really wanted to do was kiss her.

CHAPTER FIVE

CATE FELT TACK'S strong arms around her. For a second, she froze, wondering what would happen if Tack pressed his lips to hers. Would she let him kiss her? Would she slap him? Did she want him to kiss her? Then she got the impression they were both starting to sink. With neither of them able to touch bottom, kicking alone—even with fins—would not keep their heads above water for long.

"You'd better let go of me or we're going to drown," she cautioned him.

"It would be worth it," he said, the flirting tone unmistakable.

Cate grinned, but then splashed him once more. He let go and she swam away, laughing. She realized she was actually having fun.

Swimming next to Tack, she wondered if a little fling would be good for her, after all. He was a tourist, so it's not like there could be anything serious. A week at most? What was the harm in that?

Plus, there was something about the man

that made her feel both at ease and anxious at the same time. He was built like a Renaissance statue, complete with chiseled abs. His muscles simply couldn't be real. That's what Cate told herself over and over again as they swam together in the fish-filled cove. She tried not to stare, but everywhere she looked, she saw his muscles working. His broad shoulder muscles tensed as he swam along the surface, and she wondered how easily he might be able to lift her up. *Or carry me to his bed.*

The thought popped up in her mind completely unwelcomed, and she squashed it down instantly. *I can't have a fling. I've got Avery to think about. And Tack's a perfect stranger. Can't be trusted.*

For all she knew, he could be on Rick's payroll.

The thought was paranoid and probably not true. She wondered when she'd stop thinking every stranger worked for Rick Allen. Maybe never.

Besides, if he were working for her husband, he'd have called in the cavalry by now, and Rick would be banging down her door. Right? He wouldn't take a morning off to go snorkeling.

He dived down to the silty bottom and brought up a small shiny piece of metal. Trash from a fishing boat, most likely. He broke the surface of the water and Cate followed. He spat out his snorkel as he held out the hook and line.

"This doesn't belong there," he said, and grinned.

"You've probably done enough cleaning," Cate said, nodding with approval to Tack's small mesh bag, which he'd filled with trash. "Ready for a break?"

Tack nodded, and the two of them swam back to the boat. The wind kicked up, and as the boat rocked back and forth, it was a little bit harder to get the ladder, especially with the swells about three feet instead of one.

Tack nodded to the rocking boat.

"Ladies first," he said. Cate felt like arguing. After all, he was her guest, but somehow, she knew she wouldn't win. She swam for the ladder, which was bucking up and down, and she managed to get hold of it. The wind blew harder and the boat dipped dangerously to the right, and she slipped, bumping her head hard against the second rung. Stars blurred her vision and for a paralyzing second, she thought she'd black out...go under...drown.

Suddenly, though, Tack was there, keeping her from falling off the ladder, pressing his body against hers, his strong arms cinched around her, holding her in place. Cate felt the hardness of his muscles, the safety of his thick arms. They felt so…right. She leaned into him, her vision returning. She glanced up at him and saw the salt water dripping from his chin, his eyes trained on hers, worried.

"You okay?"

"Uh…yeah," she managed to say as she worked on climbing awkwardly up the ladder— fins still on, wondering why she turned into the world's biggest klutz anytime Tack was near her. Normally, she wasn't so clumsy or careless. But how come every time Tack was around she found herself in peril? First the near car accident and now this. Honestly, he was going to think she was the clumsiest woman on earth. Tack eased himself on board, kicking off his fins on deck.

"You should sit down," he said, taking her by the shoulder and maneuvering her to the nearest cushioned bench. She sat, still feeling a little bit dazed. Tack knelt in front of her, and she was more than aware the man was half naked, wearing only swim trunks. She glanced down at his navel, and immediately realized her mistake. The expanse of bare, tanned skin, with that tantalizing V running down like a welcoming arrow to his lap, made her want to reach out and touch it, feel just how taut the muscles were beneath the skin. "Let me take a look."

"I'm fine." Cate covered her forehead with her palm, the sting of the hit only just beginning to fade. She pulled her attention reluctantly from his chest and met his gaze. He ran a hand over his dark hair, wet from snorkeling.

"This is getting embarrassing. You rescuing me all the time." Cate tried to sound playful but instead just sounded grumpy. "I really am not usually this accident prone."

"Really?" Tack made a disgruntled sound in his throat to show her how little he believed that. "Let me look." He gently peeled her hand away, assessing her forehead for damage. "You're going to have a serious knot there, by the looks of things. But…" He trailed off, meeting her eyes once more. How did he get so close to her? There was an intensity there in his gaze, so powerful that she felt the need to break the stare, but then realized her mistake. Now she was focused on his lips, slightly parted, almost as if asking her to kiss him as he knelt in front of her.

And then, her brain simply shut off. She forgot to be anxious or worried, or overthink anything. She forgot why it was she avoided men, why she worked so hard all the time to keep herself carefully removed from anyone who might find out her dark secret. In that moment, instinct took over. She inched a little closer, their lips nearly touching.

She paused suddenly, right before they touched, suddenly frozen by second thoughts. *What am I doing? Am I really going to kiss this man?* But before she could back away, retreat, his lips covered hers, and she felt the rest of the world melt away. She could taste the salty sea and felt the gentle exploration of his mouth on hers. It had been a long time since she'd kissed anyone, and yet her mouth remembered exactly what to do.

He began gently, a tentative touch, his expert lips on hers in a perfect dance. She'd forgotten how intimate a kiss was, how amazing it could be, closing her eyes and letting the warm, delicious sensation overtake her. She pressed her lips against his, wrapping her hands around the back of his strong neck. Want ran through her body, hot and searing, as the kiss turned deeper. Her lips parted as she felt the delicious warm wetness of his tongue. She felt like a switch had been thrown, and her body came alive, wanting more, ever more.

He pulled her down to him, and she went, their chests pressing against one another as they knelt together on the boat. Wet from the water, his muscled chest slid against hers. She felt desire rise in her, a strong need she hadn't felt in months. All she wanted to do was devour him, inch by inch.

Suddenly, a loud blast of a horn sounded, wrecking the moment. Cate pulled back, a little dazed, her eyes blinking back the bright sun. The horn sounded again, and she saw it came from a huge, white boat, blaring music and crowded with tourists, that had inched up to them, parking nearly right next to her smaller boat. She could hear the eighties hairband music blasting across the water.

Tack glared at the intrusion. Cate groaned.

"Great," she murmured.

"You know that boat?"

"Unfortunately, I do." Reluctantly, Cate pulled herself to her feet. Tack did the same. "Terry Blake owns that boat."

His tour excursion service had beaten out hers—and many others—to deal exclusively with two of the major cruise lines. He was also probably the most obnoxious and full of himself man on the island. Terry, with his sleek bald head, ample gut and furry gray chest, didn't care about anything but having a good time—and making sure all of his guests were usually hammered. He'd nearly clipped her boat more than once in these narrow coves. He was reckless and dangerous.

Then, she realized, he planned to block her in—putting his boat in between her and the sea, leaving her stuck between the shallow reef and the beach.

"He's going to block us in." She shouted Terry's name, but there was no way the captain could hear her over the blare of the music. He saw her and waved, not bothering to try to listen as he let out three more obnoxiously loud blasts of the horn right in their ears.

Cate laid on her own horn multiple times, but the boat kept coming. It almost looked as if he'd collide with her, but at the last minute it cruised to a stop. With about six inches between the two boats now, Terry dropped anchor and about thirty loud, and most certainly already drunk, tourists half fell, half jumped off the boat.

"Terry! You need to move!" Cate shouted when the boat lurched to a stop.

He put his hand to his ear and gestured to the blaring music. He was shirtless, his big furry chest visible, as was the bright gold chain around his neck. Terry was a walking stereotype. "Can't hear you, sweetheart," he called.

Tack's face flushed red with anger as he glared at the offending boat.

"I'll handle this." Tack climbed to the other boat with an easy long stride. Cate scrambled after him, not sure if she wanted Tack to clock Terry or if she should try to keep the peace.

Once on board, the smell of cheap mixed drinks hit her like a wave. The floor was also sticky with spilled mai tais.

"Cate!" Terry called, ignoring Tack. "Looks like you're finally *getting some*—" he paused in a vulgar way to let his meaning be perfectly clear "—R and R."

Cate decided to ignore that. "You've blocked us in, Terry. You have to move."

"What? No introduction?" Terry looked offended. He also looked drunk. And it was just eleven in the morning. Did the man get up early to drink?

Tack frowned. "Tack," he said, reaching out his hand. "And you are?"

"Terry." He reached out a beefy hand and shook Tack's, all the while assessing the man's stature. "You're tall."

"I get that a lot."

"Terry. *Move* your boat." Cate felt the anger rising in her throat.

"What's the rush? Why not stay awhile and have a drink." Terry offered her a plastic pitcher filled with a dubious red liquid.

"No, thanks. I don't drink while I'm working." Cate took in Terry's puffy, red face and bloodshot eyes. Definitely drunk.

"Didn't look like you were working. I saw how you two were sucking face." Terry leered at Cate, making her want to punch him in the face. He gave her a slow once-over, too, making Cate wish she'd thrown on a T-shirt to cover her bikini before she'd climbed on board his ship.

"I'm working. This is a guest at the resort."

"Oh, I see. Is *that* how you're luring guests to that ramshackle hut of yours? A little bit of sweet side action?"

Cate balled her fists at her sides, wanting to actually attack the man, but it was Tack who reached out and put his hand on Terry's furry shoulder.

"That's not very nice. I suggest you apologize," he growled, his meaning and the threat clear. He squeezed the shoulder harder than he should have, and Terry blanched.

"Hey! I was just joking. Come on. It's a *joke*. Yeah, I'm sorry. I'm sorry! Sheesh." Terry put up his hands and backed away from Tack, who let him go.

Cate had never seen Terry so quick to comply, but then again he'd probably never faced 195 pounds of muscled ex-marine, either.

Tack grinned, all easiness once more. "Now, if you wouldn't mind, move your boat, please."

Terry nodded reluctantly. "Fine. Sure." He

shook his head. "Is this any way to treat a friend who offered you help?"

"What help?" Cate spat.

"Oh…Mark didn't tell you?"

Now Cate felt her guard rise. "Tell me what?"

"I offered to buy you out. Seems maybe you're in the red? A little bit of love under old Terry, and that resort will be hopping with tourists."

Cate felt suddenly light-headed. Terry had approached Mark about *buying* the resort? Why hadn't Mark mentioned it? She felt suddenly hot and cold all at once. Was Mark trying to work a deal behind her back? Cate mentally shook herself. He wouldn't do that. Not to her.

Yet he'd invested as much of his life's savings into the place as she had. Would he want to cut and run?

She could feel Tack's eyes on her, assessing. She wished he hadn't heard the last part of this conversation.

"Seems like you two should talk," Terry said. "Because what I really want is something Mark can't sell me. I think you and I both know about the little beachside property Mark has nothing to do with."

Cate froze. Nobody was supposed to know about that little parcel of land. Well, Mark did, but it had been her side investment. She'd paid cash, proceeds from the jewelry she'd sold.

She felt a twinge of guilt and then instantly pressed it down. That money was hers. Fair and square. She didn't steal it.

"I'm not selling," Cate said, resolute.

"Suit yourself." Terry just grinned at her, showing a row of yellow teeth. God, she hated that man. She could feel Tack studying her, and Cate tried to keep her face neutral.

Stiffly, Cate returned to her boat, and Tack followed.

"What was that about?" Tack asked as Cate took the helm of her boat once more, watching Terry pull up the anchor so he could move.

"Nothing," Cate said, hoping that she was right.

THE MOOD ON board the boat for the rest of the morning felt muted as Cate struggled to put on a brave face. Tack could see her try to shrug off Mr. Gold Chain's remarks. She tried hard, but he could read every emotion on her face. He wondered how such a good liar had such a bad poker face.

Clearly, she was having money troubles, sealed by the fact that Terry offered to buy the place. Tack knew she had a lack of visitors. Anyone paying attention could see the hotel was less than half full, and yet he thought that was by design. According to Rick Allen, Cate stole enough cash and bearer bonds to be set up indefinitely. Millions, if his total was accurate. Had she gone through all that in just three years?

Maybe she used it all to buy the land that Terry mentioned.

That's the only hiding place that made sense.

She certainly didn't spend money on herself. Tack looked once more at her frayed jean shorts and worn flip-flops. Even the tour boat they were on had clearly seen better days. Some of the paint was peeling off the side, a few of the cushions had rips. Something about this wasn't adding up. Did she hide away the money? Was it somewhere she could get it if she needed to flee? Maybe she was just trying not to draw attention to herself. So far, she'd been meticulous in covering her tracks, and spending a lot of cash could certainly raise a red flag.

Another mystery. Just like the kiss they'd shared earlier. He wasn't sure how that had happened. He had not been planning it, but the woman was just so damn kissable. She'd been so close to him and so impossible to resist. Yet, he knew it was a mistake. He couldn't bed a woman who'd tried to kill her husband.

He shouldn't feel anything but disgust, and yet…that was not the feeling she stirred in him. He'd been really worried when she'd hit her head on the ladder, and then…when Mr. Gold Chain was being so obnoxious, he had felt protective of her. It was probably just his upbringing by a mother who insisted that it was his job to look after ladies—to open doors, to protect them when he could. And Cate sure did need protection.

Yet the way she kissed him, it just screamed want. And need. He'd had every intention of kissing her, but once he did, he'd lost a little of himself, lost the tight rein of control he always kept on himself. He hadn't intended to want her as much as she wanted him. It was supposed to be a game, a ruse, to ensure she let down her guard with him. It was all part of the investigation, until his body decided it wasn't.

He kept a rigid control of himself for a reason. When he let emotions get the best of him, bad things happened. Like when he'd hit his commanding officer. That had led to a court-martial. But the weasel had deserved it.

Adeeb's brother had died because Derek Hollie refused to let Tack save him. Then Derek conveniently scrapped all of Adeeb's paperwork for the visa promised to him by

Uncle Sam. By the time Tack realized the mistake, the visas had run out, the program had been nixed. There were none left for Adeeb.

Cate Allen was supposed to be the answer to his problems, but right now, she was making things far more complicated than he liked. He thought he was certain he'd been the one playing her, yet now he wasn't so sure. He couldn't let himself start thinking she was just your average girl. Nothing about her was average. Or safe.

"This is our last stop before I get you back to the resort for lunch," Cate said, pulling the boat into another small inlet. Tack didn't want the morning to end. He told himself it was because he wasn't done trying to pry information from her, but the truth was, he liked her company.

Tack glanced at the small town not far from their diving spot. He saw open-air cantinas and cafés, as well as a string of brightly colored shop awnings. "I have a better idea," he said. "Why don't we skip the snorkeling and head over there for lunch?"

Cate shaded her eyes from the bright sun overhead and blinked at the shore. "Smuggler's Cove? You want to eat there?"

"Sounds exciting. Will there be pirates?"

Cate snorted. "Hardly. Unless you call the

tourist-shop owners pirates. Though, they will rob you blind for shell jewelry boxes and shot glasses."

"Sounds perfect. I thought this was an *island* tour, after all. Aren't you going to show me around?"

Cate studied Tack, wary. "There's a nice seafood place there. But it's pricey. All the restaurants in Smuggler's Cove are pricey. It's the gentrified part of the island."

"I'm paying," Tack said.

"I don't need…"

"I *said* I'm paying." Tack grinned, and he could see Cate relenting.

"But I'm not dressed for…"

Tack glanced at the people walking down the small cobblestone streets. "Looks like they're all dressed like us," he said. "Aren't shoes dressing up on an island?"

Cate sighed, and Tack knew then that he had her. She'd run out of excuses. "Fine," she said.

CHAPTER SIX

TACK STEERED A reluctant Cate to the restaurant she'd pointed out, keeping a hand on her elbow in case she decided to bolt. Now that he had more uninterrupted time with her, he wondered what he was doing. *What are you doing taking the prime suspect to a fancy lunch?* All he needed was a DNA sample. Hair, saliva, it didn't matter. Deliver that to Allen. Get Adeeb's visa. All debts repaid. No man left behind in that godforsaken desert.

None of that required glazed scallops and baby carrots. And it wasn't like she was going to flat-out admit to him that she was Cate Allen. Tack knew that. Knew socializing with the woman was a lost cause.

So why am I doing it?

Tack knew why. Because he'd kissed the woman, and he wanted to do it again.

Plain and simple.

He was in dangerous territory. Beyond dangerous. *Careful*, he told himself. *Don't let her pretty smile cloud your judgment.* She was a mark, not a potential hookup.

He couldn't afford to be wrong again, either. He'd sent Allen four DNA samples in the last year, all of them negative. He'd been wrong before. *But he'd never felt this sure.* Still, Allen had made it clear his patience was running out. And time had long since been running out for Adeeb. How much longer could he avoid death? With most of the marines out of Afghanistan, the Taliban was on the rise again. And they had long memories.

"Table for two, please," Tack told the hostess, who sat them with a smile on the open, outdoor table in front, shaded by a banana tree. Cate walked in front of him, her muscled, tanned calves working with each step, and he thought he could watch her walk for as long as she'd let him. They sat down together at the tiny little wicker table, so small their knees bumped beneath.

"Oh, I'm sorry," Cate said, and tried to scrunch to the side, but wound up bumping into another chair at the next table.

"I don't mind." Tack didn't. He could feel her knees against his all day. *What am I doing? Get it together.* "So, you lived in Chicago, right?"

Chicago was where Rick lived.

Cate's head snapped up, her eyes wide. "N-no."

She was like an open book. Amazing, really. How did a woman who manipulated her ex and hatched a grand scheme to forge a new identity lie so badly?

"Are you sure? I thought you said something about…"

"No. Definitely not. I grew up in Minnesota." Cate snatched the menu from the table and stared at it, as if it was written in another language. Absently, she rubbed her finger along the scar on her chin. He studied the small white mark, wondering once more where she'd got it.

"My mistake." Tack smiled, happy to see her squirm. *She's Cate Allen. She has to be.*

"The salmon is excellent here," she said, keeping her eyes fixed on the menu. "So is the shrimp salad."

"I'll have the salmon, then." He didn't even pick up the menu as he kept studying her. "So, how long have you owned the resort?"

She looked relieved for the question that had nothing to do with Chicago. "Two years," she said. "Almost three. Mark's my business partner. We decided we'd had enough of Minnesota winters." She gave a rueful smile. "Mark always said everybody waits until they're old to retire someplace nice, but why not do it when you're young enough to enjoy it?"

"That's pretty great. And lucky that you had the funds to do it." Tack let the words sit there, watching her face carefully for signs of...he didn't know what. Guilt? Remorse? Discomfort? She launched the resort on stolen funds, after all.

Cate glanced back down at the menu. "I was lucky with some investments," she said, noncommittal.

Investments. That's what she called stealing.

"But...I take it business isn't as good as you want it to be."

Cate squirmed. "No. The cruise ships have really taken a bite out of our business, unfortunately, and..." She drifted off. The waitress appeared and took their order. Tack took the liberty of ordering a bottle of wine, to Cate's surprise. If he wanted answers, wine could only help. *In vino veritas.*

"Do you think Mark would try to sell behind your back?"

Cate glanced at him sharply, eyes wary. "Why do you say that?"

"I heard what Terry said." The waitress returned with the bottle, pouring them both a glass and then setting the already sweating bottle of white in an ice bucket on the table. The humidity of the afternoon began to creep into the air, fighting the cool breeze rolling in from the sea.

"Mark wouldn't go behind my back like that." Cate sounded resolute. She stared at him, mouth set in a thin line.

"You sound sure."

"Mark and I...go way back." There was that note of protectiveness again. Were they having an affair? Something about those two seemed more than friends. She took a big swig of her wine, shifting uncomfortably.

"You seem protective of him."

"He's my partner." She glanced away from him. Some tourists in Bermuda shorts carrying shopping bags ambled by the main walk near the patio, and she focused on them.

"More than just a business partner?" Tack leaned forward, taking a sip of the crisp wine.

"What are you implying?" Cate drank some more.

"You know what."

"No. Of course not! He's married!" she exclaimed, looking a little shocked and a bit offended. "I told you."

"As if that ever stopped two people in love or lust before." Tack laughed.

"I don't date married men." Her eyes flashed resolve.

"Okay, okay." Tack raised his hands in surrender. "Look, in my experience, people cheat."

"*All* people? You can't be serious."

"Well, my commanding officer cheated on his wife. Many times." *One more reason Derek Hollie deserved that punch in the face.* He'd take another dishonorable discharge if he could get Derek alone in a room without the MP for five minutes.

Still, why was he talking about Hollie? He hadn't meant for any of that to come up. This wasn't about revealing *his* secrets; it was about *hers*. Yet sitting across from her, he just wanted to share. He didn't know why. Next, he'd be telling her about Adeeb, about the deal he struck with her ex-husband.

"Really?" Cate thought about that. "My ex also cheated. A lot. I know what that feels like."

"I would never cheat on you." *Where did that come from?* It popped out of his mouth completely unbidden. He wished he could say it was a ploy, a way of gaining her trust, but his gut told him it was actually the truth. When did he become such a starry-eyed romantic for goodness' sake? He was a tough-as-nails marine who never talked about his feelings, but sitting across this gorgeous blonde, all he wanted to do was tell her how pretty she was. Clearly, he'd gone soft.

"So you and Mark aren't...that," he said, trying to steer the conversation back to her. "But you sure seem close."

"We are. But I'm close to his wife, too. They're my best friends in the world. You know those people who would do anything for you? No matter what? The friends you could call in the middle of the night, even, and they'd come right over? Mark and Carol are like that for me."

Tack thought about it. He knew friends like that. Like Adeeb. He would jump on a grenade for him. And actually did. Thank God the thing had been a dud.

Tack nodded. "So, Mark wouldn't sell out from under you, but what if he's right and you have to sell?"

"I can't." She shook her head resolutely, wisps of her honey-blond hair coming loose from its ponytail. She swiped back a tendril and tucked it behind her ear.

The waitress came back, setting piping hot salmon dishes in front them. Tack took a bite of the delicate fish, and it melted on his tongue. Cate dug into hers like a starving prisoner. She was either hungry for food or a distraction. Of course, he was the one who ended up distracted, watching her take small bites with that sensual mouth of hers. He remembered the taste of her lips—sweet, like cherry lip balm.

"You said you were lucky in investments. So, why not just dip into those reserve funds?" *The millions you've got stashed away somewhere.*

"I put most of what I had in the resort and the rest in land nearby," she said, flatly, taking another bite and washing it down with a generous helping of wine. "There are no reserve funds."

Tack wasn't sure what to believe. Could that be possible? He didn't see how. Not unless she actually stuffed her money into the walls of the guest rooms. They fell into a short silence, and Tack watched her eat. Maybe her game was to try to lure in new tourists with her sad story. Maybe she fleeced every new guy who came through.

"Interested in any investors?" he asked, testing his theory. "I've done well for myself as a private contractor, and I also know a few friends who have more money than they know what to do with."

Cate shook her head. "That's nice of you, really. But no. I don't want investors." She said it in a way that left no room for argument. The fact that she didn't take the low-hanging fruit made Tack wonder if he'd read her wrong. "Even with Mark, it's a sixty-forty partnership. I have the final say."

The woman clearly liked to be in control. Tack felt his mind wander suddenly to their kiss. He wondered if she liked to hold the reins in bed, too. He imagined her on top of him, and all the many ways she could make him beg for more.

"Why no partners?" *Focus.* "Investors could help."

"I made the mistake once of trusting the wrong person to—" she hesitated "—to look after me." She frowned and absently touched the white line of the scar on her chin. A nervous tick? he wondered. "I'm not going to do that again."

Now he wondered if she was talking about Rick. Sure seemed like it.

"That scar," he said, "on your chin. How'd you get it?"

The question took her completely by surprise. She actually covered her entire chin with the palm of her hand, as if by doing so she could make the question go away.

"What scar?" Her green eyes darted from side to side. Boy, she was a terrible liar.

"The one you keep…touching."

"Oh? This?" She rubbed her finger once more across the small, raised line. "Nothing. An old...accident." She wouldn't look at him and instead focused on the remaining food on her plate. She was absolutely lying to him. But why? Because she probably got that in the struggle. The struggle when she tried to kill her husband. The night she left. Rick Allen had told him all about it. How her well-laid plans had gone to hell.

"You touch it a lot." *Guilt*, he thought. *Pure guilt.*

"I...I do?" Realizing she was just at that second rubbing her finger across it, she quickly thrust her hands into her lap. Then she glanced at her wine and reached for it, taking a long sip. She shrugged and then glanced at her watch. "Oh, we're late!" she exclaimed, desperate to change the subject. "If we leave now, we'll be half an hour late to dock, and I'm sure you had other things to do this afternoon."

He chuckled. "I'm right where I want to be." He held her gaze until she blinked rapidly and looked away. "Let's stay. How about dessert?"

"But... I..." Cate looked like a trapped rat, squirming to get out of a cage. "I should get back to the resort. I've got to do the accounting books today and then talk to Mark."

"I think you've got time for dessert." Tack

nodded toward the waitress, who came over and told them about the dessert options. Tack watched Cate's face as it momentarily lit up at the mention of some chocolate cheesecake. He ordered that and two forks.

"Cate is a pretty name." He wanted to know why she kept it. Why she decided it was such a good idea to keep the first name that authorities and her husband would be looking for. Why was that worth the risk?

"It was my mother's name," she said, quietly. "She died when I was six, and...well, it's one of the few things I have from her."

That information temporarily blindsided Tack.

He'd done his research, sure. He knew her mother was deceased—died suddenly of a rare and aggressive kind of cancer when she was a kid, but it had just been a fact on paper, nothing more. Now, sitting across from her, he realized how the fact affected her in deep ways. How he'd simply dismissed that as a lead he couldn't follow, instead of imagining the human impact of losing a parent so young.

"When she was alive, Daddy didn't drink as much. After she went, he was heartbroken." Cate stared off into space as if remembering an old moment. "I don't really blame him. I missed her, too. If I could've gotten drunk, I would've."

Tack realized how important, how life-changing her mother's passing had been for her. For him, it had been simply a box he'd checked off on his follow-up list.

"I'm sorry," he said, meaning more for just her loss. But also for his callousness.

"She was the best mom," she said brightly. "So gentle and kind. Always laughing. And bubbly. A bright light lived inside her, you know? She made friends everywhere she went." She glanced toward the sea, as if wrapped up in a memory. "When she died, Daddy had trouble holding down a job. We were very poor."

Tack imagined her as a little girl, with a father who couldn't quite keep it together, all while grieving the loss of her mother and probably going hungry. He felt for that little girl, despite all his best efforts not to.

Still, he could see how Rick Allen would've been her lottery ticket—how she would've held on to his money as a kind of comfort. A girl who'd known what it was like to be hungry and abandoned might make sure never to feel that way again. If her husband planned to leave her and leave her penniless, then murder might be her only option.

The waitress came with the dessert and

plunked it down before them, breaking the somber spell. They both dug into the chocolate cheesecake, and Tack let himself simply focus on her full lips, wishing he could taste them once more. The memory of the kiss on the boat hit him, and he felt a warm flush at the back of his neck. He wanted to do that again. He wanted to do *more* than that, and he had sense enough to realize that desire had nothing to do with this case and everything to do with the fact that she was damn gorgeous. She took another bite of cheesecake, enjoying a long pull of her fork as she slowly ate the silky dessert. He took a bite for himself.

"Mmm," she murmured, making his heart speed up a little. The moan was almost the sound she'd made when he kissed her. How he wanted to make her moan like that again. He wanted to make her moan like that all night long.

He realized he'd stopped eating and was staring, because she blinked fast and sat up, swiping at her mouth. "You're staring," she said. "Do I have something on my face?" She anxiously patted her chin with a napkin.

"Nothing on your face," he said, shaking his head. *Nothing but the greenest eyes I've ever seen. And the most kissable lips.* "I'm just enjoying watching you."

She shifted in her seat, looking a little uncomfortable. "Chocolate is my weakness," she admitted.

"Is it?" He grinned.

The waitress brought the check and he quickly paid it, just as Cate finished up the last bite of cheesecake.

"Thanks for the meal," she said.

"You're welcome. Thanks for the company." He held her gaze for a beat and enjoyed watching the slow blush creep up the side of her cheek. She fidgeted and pulled her phone from her pocket.

"Is that really the time?" she gasped. She popped to her feet, the chair screeching back behind her. "We have to get going. I've got another tour later this afternoon."

"Sure," Tack said smoothly, standing.

Cate was already making her way to the door. "You go on. I'm going to the bathroom." He nodded at her, and she scurried out of the restaurant. When he was sure she was gone, he grabbed a Ziploc bag from his pocket and discreetly tucked the fork into it, careful not to add his fingerprints to the handle. Fingerprints could ID her, too. There probably wasn't enough saliva left for a DNA sample, but the fingerprints might still be there. He gently placed the fork in his pocket.

As Cate headed to the dock, he realized it

was about time he focused on why he was really here. He pulled his phone from his pocket and called Allen's private line.

"I think I have a promising lead," Tack said before he could change his mind.

CHAPTER SEVEN

AFTER THEY RETURNED to the resort, Cate pulled the boat to the dock and Tack helped secure it.

"There," he said. "All set."

Those were nearly the most words he'd said to her for the entire trip back. He'd gotten moody all of a sudden, though she couldn't think why. She thought they'd actually connected over lunch, but maybe that had been her imagination.

Cate gathered her gear and made for the back of the boat. Tack was already busy with his own bag, keeping his back to her. It felt oddly...cold.

"Uh...thanks again for lunch."

"Yep." Tack glanced at her, the mirrored sunglasses he wore making it impossible to see his eyes. What was with the monosyllables all of a sudden? He also seemed distracted as he glanced at his phone's face, as if expecting a message. Overhead, the sun beamed down on them, and suddenly, Cate felt sweat trickle down her back.

"Uh, well…I hope you enjoyed the tour," Cate said, wondering where the attentive man from lunch had gone.

"Uh-huh." His focus was now entirely on his phone as he tapped a message to someone. A woman? she wondered, and then immediately couldn't figure out why she cared. She couldn't let a stranger in, and she wasn't even sure she could trust him. He could be a serial killer for all she knew. But honestly, what man *kissed* a woman, took her out for an expensive lunch and then abruptly lost interest?

A man who has a long list of gorgeous women in his phone, at his beck and call.

"Okay, then." The words came out snippy as she turned away from him and headed quickly to the resort. He didn't call after her, and when she glanced back once, he was headed away from the dock and to the resort, presumably to his room. His ignoring her irked her, though she couldn't really explain why.

She ought to be relieved he'd stopped asking her questions. *Chicago.* He'd asked her over lunch if she was from Chicago. Did that mean something? Was she being paranoid or should she be worried?

Cate couldn't shake the suspicion that there was more to Tack than met the eye, though she had no proof Rick had hired him. Besides, why would a man Rick had hired to find her take her to a nice lunch? Or…kiss her?

The memory of the kiss washed over her, and Cate suddenly felt heat rush through her abdomen. The man knew how to kiss. It had been…one of the best kisses she'd ever had, or maybe it was just her mind playing tricks on her. Maybe the fact that she hadn't kissed a man in such a long time clouded her judgment.

Cate tried to leave thoughts of Tack behind as she rushed into the resort and headed straight for the upper rooms, where she knew Carol was watching Avery. Sometimes she picked him up from preschool and spent the afternoon playing Legos, usually, or reading books. Mark and Carol's teenage daughter, Grace, also took turns watching Avery, and between them, they usually managed to keep the resort running and make sure the precocious four-year-old stayed out of trouble.

When she got to her rooms, she swung open the door and called out, but no one was there. Avery's room was empty. *Must be downstairs, outside enjoying this gorgeous day.* It was particularly nice weather for St. Anthony's— breezy, mid-70s and not a cloud in the sky. Sometimes, when the sea breeze died down, the humidity hung in the air like a heavy blanket, but today it was the perfect day to build a sand castle on the beach. But Cate already knew they weren't there—she'd come from that way. The lawn, she thought, and headed back to the grassy patch on the other side of the resort. In the middle of that lay a kidney-shaped pool surrounded by white tile and re-clining lawn chairs.

She looked at the empty pool and sighed. There was a time when the pool teemed with people, gleeful splashing and the low beat of music flowing all afternoon. Now, it looked deserted. She wondered if the visitors would ever come back, but told herself she needed to focus on finding Avery before Carol put him down for an afternoon nap. She saw his pre-school backpack on one of the lawn chairs and decided she was close. Cate rounded the corner of the building and saw Carol and Mark near the patio to the resort's breakfast café, por-ing over what looked like the evening's menu. There was no sign of Avery. Grace must be looking after him, Cate thought, and then felt a momentary flash of guilt for how the little boy was shuffled from one person to the next. Of course the Gurdas were amazing people and treated Avery like blood. To the little boy, they were all just one big, happy family.

Carol's face lit up when she saw Cate. "So? How *was* it?"

"You mean the Tack trap you set up for me?" Cate still felt sore about it. She *knew* Carol had somehow managed to finagle the alone time with the ex-marine, and probably at the expense of other paying guests.

"No need to thank me," Carol said, and grinned as she scooted back her patio chair.

"Tack trap? What's this about?" Mark murmured, looking puzzled as he glanced from one woman to the other.

"Your wife decided to kick everybody else off the morning tour so that I'd spend four hours with Tack."

"*Everybody* else, listen to her!" Carol shrugged. "It was one couple. The other couple already canceled, and besides, I think the honeymooners would be better off taking the tour *tomorrow* and told them so, when the sea will be calmer."

"The sea was *plenty* calm," Cate fumed.

"Oh? It was? Silly me." Carol grinned, and Cate let out a frustrated sigh. She was only trying to help. Cate knew that. But if she wanted to die alone and celibate that was *her* business. "So? Did you two…hit it off?"

Cate thought about the kiss. They did. Maybe too well. Until he rushed off the boat and left without a goodbye. *Why do I even care?*

"I don't know."

"You don't *know*?" Carol looked puzzled.

Cate shrugged. "He's okay."

"He's *more* than okay."

"I'm completely lost," Mark said, scratching his head. "What's going on?"

"Your wife is trying to set me up, that's what." Cate put her hands on her hips and glared at Carol, but she just grinned unapologetically. "*Despite* me asking her not to."

"Well, Carol never takes no for an answer," Mark said, chuckling a little. "I've told her no for twenty years and look where it got me. Nowhere."

Carol gave Mark a playful shove, but Cate just grinned. Even with all the teasing, those two were head over heels for one another.

"So, where's Avery?" Cate asked. "With Grace?"

Carol shook her head. "Upstairs, taking a nap in his room. I just ran down here for a quick minute to give Mark the new menu. I was going to run right back up…"

Suddenly, Cate's blood ran cold. "No, he's not," she said. "I was just there. His room was empty."

Carol frowned, suddenly sitting up straight and putting both hands on the table in front of her. "I only left him a couple of minutes ago.

Not even that. Are you sure he wasn't in your suite somewhere?"

Cate remembered running quickly through every room. "I'm sure."

Carol looked stricken. "But how did he get out of the room? I swore I locked it."

"He's like Houdini," Cate said. "Remember how he undid his car seat last week and he was crawling all over the back seat before I could stop him?"

Carol nodded.

"Well, he couldn't have gotten far," Mark said.

Cate had a sinking feeling in her stomach. She wanted to find him. Fast.

TACK SAT IN his resort room, carefully dusting the fork for fingerprints. He managed to get one partial print that wasn't enough to do much other than say the print *might* belong to Cate Allen. Tack felt a surge of disappointment. He *knew* in his gut she was Cate Allen. Yet he lacked the proof his employer demanded.

Getting a better print would mean spending more time with Cate. As he grabbed his room key and sunglasses, he realized he didn't mind that at all.

Down in the lobby, he realized it was strangely

deserted—no sign of Cate, Mark or Carol. Instantly, his instincts went on high alert. Something wasn't right. Then he glanced out the floor-to-ceiling windows overlooking the grounds and saw most of the staff on the lawn—the cook, a maid and Mark all seemed to be scouring the area for something. Or someone.

Tack felt his stomach tighten. Did Cate bolt? Then he saw her, back to him, blond hair tussled by the sea breeze as she stood near the pool. He headed in that direction. Once outside, the hot sun beat down on his head, causing a single drop of sweat to roll down the back of his neck. He heard a chorus of people calling for Avery.

Cate's little boy.

He was missing?

Cate was beginning to look frantic as she paced around the pool and searched the small changing cabanas. He got to her just as she came out of the last one. She nearly collided into his chest. He put out his hands to steady her.

"Tack!" she cried, her face as pale as the white pool tile. "I...I'm sorry. I don't have time..."

Tack ignored the brush-off. "What can I do to help?"

Relief flooded her features. She was too

panicked to deny him. "Avery's missing. He snuck out of his room about fifteen minutes ago."

Tack glanced around, cataloging all the dangers, his mind awhirl with possibilities. This was where he thrived—in predicting bad outcomes. "Does he like to swim?"

Cate nodded. "He does."

He saw Carol and her teenage daughter walking along the beach, looking for signs of the boy. He hated to ask this question, but knew he had to do it. "Do you think he'd go in the ocean?"

Cate shook her head. "I don't think so. Last week he got dunked by a wave, so now he prefers swimming in the pool. Plus, he says the salt water stings his eyes."

Tack nodded, feeling a little relieved. They both knew if he'd walked in that ocean, he could've gotten swept away by the fast-moving current not too far offshore. They might never find him then.

"Does he have anyplace he likes to hide?"

"Here," Cate said, nodding to the small straw changing cabanas near the pool. "And in the maid's closet, but we've already searched through the hotel. Even the boiler room. He's not there."

Tack glanced about the grounds.

"And if he was still here, he'd hear us calling him." Cate bit her lip in worry. "What if a guest..." She let the words hang there, the horror of the incomplete sentence dangling between them.

Without thinking, Tack folded Cate in his arms, and she didn't resist, slipping her hands around his back. He held her for a second, hoping to calm her, when he felt anything *but* calm. He was always calculating the odds, looking for danger, trying to prepare himself for any contingent. It was that very skill that kept so many of his men alive when they'd served under him. But he was an odds man, and he knew the odds of a random kidnapper snagging Avery in a hotel that wasn't even half full were long at best. Tack knew a lot about fear, and about how it clouded judgment. Sometimes, soldiers were so afraid of the thing that probably wouldn't happen that they missed out on the small dangers all around them.

Tack glanced around him, at the many lush and blooming tropical trees on the resort property. The wind blew the petals of the bright white blooming tree above them. It had knotted branches hung low to the ground, and a bright green iguana sat on a tree branch that was just above eye level.

I didn't know iguanas climbed trees, Tack

thought as he glanced at the lizard sitting in the shade. He remembered how he and his brother used to dare each other to climb to the top of the big oak in the front yard, and how they probably would've scared a lizard to death scrambling to the top branches.

Then it hit him—what if Avery *could* hear them? What if he wasn't *on the ground* but *in a tree*?

"You know," Tack said, releasing Cate. "Is it possible Avery is just hiding from us on purpose?"

"It's possible," Cate said. "He loves to play hide-and-seek."

"Does he ever climb trees?"

"Trees?" Cate asked, surprised. "No! He's too little."

"Is he?" Tack remembered the boisterous boy. If he was old enough to run and swim a little, he was definitely old enough to climb trees. "I started at three. My mom had to get me out of a forty-foot pine before I started preschool."

"Really?" Cate looked skeptical, even as she began to look up, scanning the branches of the nearby magnolia. Tack nodded as he began a thorough search of the back of the property for any trees with branches low enough for a four-year-old to reach.

"I've never seen Avery in a tree," Cate said, following Tack toward the thicket of small blooming trees. A giant poinciana tree, with bright red blossoms, sat in the middle, with a low-lying branch at the perfect height for a preschooler to grab. Tack glanced up and saw the small white rubber sole of a boy's shoe. Almost everything else about Avery was covered in thick blooms.

"There's a first time for everything," Tack said and pointed up.

"Avery!" Cate cried. "Avery! What are you doing up there?"

"Climbing!" the boy declared, sounding proud. "I'm going to go to the top!"

Already, Avery stood on the thinnest branches of the tree, and with each new step he took, the top of the tree swayed under his weight. He was already more than twenty feet up, and headed to thirty. One false move, and he'd come toppling down. He had a fifty-fifty shot of hitting softer green lawn or the hard concrete paved path.

"No!" Cate called. "Avery, stop!"

"I'm going to the top, Mama!" Avery had his eyes pinned upward, to the small, wispy branches with the biggest red blooms. "I'm going to get you a pretty flower!"

"Avery, it's okay. Mama doesn't need a flower!"

"The biggest ones are on top!" Avery said, grunting as he hoisted himself up.

"Avery, you come down right now!" Cate planted her hands on her hips, trying to look stern, but Tack could see the real fear on her face.

"Hey, kiddo. Listen to your mom, okay? Come on down." Tack shaded his eyes from the sun, trying to track the boy's upward momentum. He was a seeker, that kid, and fearless. He had to admire that. Might make a fine marine one day.

Avery ignored them both and continued his ascent with determined, small hands grabbing each new branch. Then he placed his small sneakered foot on a new branch that couldn't support his weight. It didn't crack but bent downward, like a reed in the wind, and his toe slipped right off. For a heart-pounding second, he dangled by two hands and no feet.

"Avery!" Cate shouted.

But Tack was already climbing swiftly upward. He didn't have time to worry about the tree holding both his weight and the boy's. He needed to get there and fast before Avery lost his sweaty grip on the single branch, the only thing keeping him from plummeting to the ground below. He reached Avery just as the boy slipped from the branch.

Below, he heard Cate gasp.

Tack caught Avery awkwardly with one arm, managing to hold the kid roughly about the waist. He squirmed a little but then grabbed hold of Tack's neck, like a baby monkey, he thought. Tack carefully maneuvered downward, the boy clinging to him tightly. When he jumped the last few feet to the ground, he kept the boy secure. Cate rushed to them, peeling Avery off Tack and squeezing him to her chest.

"You scared me!" Cate breathed into the boy's hair. She sat him on the ground and searched his face for signs of branch scratches. "Are you okay?"

"Yeah," the boy said, confused about all the fuss.

Cate cupped her boy's face with her hands. "Did you hear us calling for you?" Avery nodded and tried to squirm away from his mother's grip. "Why didn't you come down?"

"I wanted to get a flower for you, Mama!" he cried, as if that made it all okay.

Tack saw the warring emotions on her face and thought the Cate Allen he thought he knew would yell at the boy, put him in his place. But instead she simply scooped him up in her arms and gave him a big squeeze.

"You're sweet to think of Mommy, but next time, don't sneak off, okay?"

Avery nodded into her shoulder. By now, Mark, who'd seen the last minute of the rescue, hurried over. "Is everybody okay?"

"Fine," Cate said. "Thanks to Tack."

"Fast thinking," Mark said, stretching out his hand to Tack's for a shake. "Nicely done, marine."

Tack shook Mark's hand. "It wasn't anything."

Cate held her boy on her hip. He laid his head on her shoulder. The way the boy clung to his mother told Tack how much the boy depended on her. He could see the strong bond between them, and then he felt a pang of guilt for working for the man who'd rather see the boy away from his mother. Of course, Rick had never said that. He'd only said he wanted to find his boy. But Tack knew it probably wouldn't be so that he could ask the court for joint custody.

Don't think about it. Adeeb is your problem. Adeeb, his wife and his daughter. Cate and Avery are not your responsibility.

"A rescue *and* modesty, now you're just making me look like a chump," Mark said, and laughed. "And you, kiddo..." He tugged on Avery's nose. "Don't go scaring us like that again! We thought the pirates got you."

"There aren't any pirates!" Avery said, looking doubtful as his blond curls fell over his left eye. He swiped them back with a grubby hand.

"Oh, yes, there are! Remember? I told you they buried treasure all *over* this island." Avery giggled, as if that was the funniest thing he'd heard. "Uncle Mark, you're funny."

"Funny looking," Mark conceded, and then gave the boy's nose another affectionate tweak.

Tack glanced at Mark, standing close to Cate and Avery, and thought how solid they seemed, how much like a family. He felt a twinge of guilt as his suspicions rose once more. *Was there something going on there?* The thought kept coming up, no matter how much she denied it. That relationship ran deeper than just a financial partnership.

Avery squirmed in Cate's arms, so she put him down.

"Can I go play, Mommy?" he asked.

"Stay where I can see you," she replied.

"Come on, kiddo," Mark said, taking the boy's hand. "Let's go find Aunt Carol and let her know not to worry about you."

Avery grinned as Mark led him down to the beach.

Left alone, Tack felt a pull to Cate. She met

Tack's gaze and smiled, and Tack felt a rush of warmth run down his spine.

"Thank you," she said, and reached out and took his hand. The gesture surprised him. He put his own hand over hers and fought the urge to pull her into his arms and kiss her.

"It's no big deal."

"It is to me." She held his gaze a beat longer than necessary, and he felt a twinge of guilt. The way she was looking at him now, like he was her hero, made him uncomfortable. If only she knew he wasn't a hero. Heroes didn't leave good men behind.

He wondered what she'd think if she knew he was working for her ex-husband, that he was working for the very man who planned to take her boy from her. Tack felt his heart speed up a little as she squeezed his hand. Everything had seemed so simple when he'd been sitting in Allen's office, when he'd seen the man in his wheelchair. But now, with Cate, things were becoming disturbingly gray. She wasn't the woman he said she'd be.

She was such a good mom, such a loving mom, and he had a hard time seeing her as the coldhearted killer who'd tried to murder her husband and steal his fortune. Tack was a good read of people, and Cate just wasn't the ruthless woman Rick had said she was. The warmth in her eyes and the gratitude right now were real.

I made the mistake of letting the wrong person look after me. That's what she'd said over lunch. Did she mean Rick Allen? Did she mean someone else? Maybe she'd met someone after Rick. Someone who took all the money she'd stolen.

I'm supposed to be doing a job. Yet more and more he found himself wanting to know more about Cate. Not whether she was the woman he was looking for, but just because she fascinated him.

Something in his gut told him there was more to her story. Then again, his gut might just be like the rest of his body—eager to get her naked as fast as possible. And it wasn't just her body, he realized. She was complex, more so than any other woman he'd met in a long time. She intrigued him. He could admit that much to himself.

"No, that was great. What you did. You're a hero." She smiled at him, and he could feel the warmth of it in his toes.

"I'm no hero." He said it gruffer than he expected. "If you knew…" He let the sentence hang there. What was he about to admit to her? The debacle of his last tour of duty? The fact that he was a private eye working for her ex-husband? He felt like he ought to clamp his hands over his mouth. There was something about Cate's open face, her big, green eyes.

"If I knew what…?" she pressed, studying him with an intensity that made the urge to admit everything grow. He'd never felt this way before with a woman, felt that if he told her everything he might be accepted. He'd never had that before.

"I'm just not a hero, that's all." He had to grit his teeth to keep from telling her more.

She stared at him a beat. "Listen, I don't know what happened to you over there, and you don't have to tell me, but I know you, here. And from what I've seen, I know you only meant to do good, so maybe it's time to stop beating yourself up about it."

"There'd never be a time I won't beat myself up about it," he admitted truthfully.

"Well, how about just not while you're here, then? You just rescued a little boy. And by the way, there's only a small outpatient clinic on the island. If he'd really gotten hurt, we'd have to airlift him out of here, so you *did* save him. And you should feel good about that."

"Anyone would've…" She stepped forward and put her finger on his lips to shush him. The warmth of her finger there shut him up instantly.

"No, they wouldn't." She was so close now, he could see the dark green rings around her irises. "Look, take it from someone who's made her share of mistakes, okay? One bad decision doesn't mean you're a bad person. And mistakes are how we grow to be better people."

Mistakes like trying to kill your husband? The thought popped into Tack's mind before he could stop it. Yet for the first time, Tack could see real regret on Cate's face. Maybe she had made mistakes that she regretted. Maybe she wasn't completely beyond redemption. Maybe she had regrets. Just like Tack did.

In his pocket, his phone chimed with an incoming text. He reached into his pocket and glanced at the face of his phone.

Rick Allen had seen the photographs he'd sent and he'd responded.

That's her, he wrote. I want DNA to confirm in 24 hours.

CHAPTER EIGHT

TACK WASN'T SURE he could move that fast. He sat at the nearly empty bar that evening, sipping a beer, brooding as he tried to figure out how the hell he was going to swab the inside of Cate's mouth and send it to Mr. Allen in the next twenty-four hours.

Maybe you could use your tongue, a devilish voice in his head said. No matter how hard he tried *not* to be attracted to the woman, just the thought of her made him think the dirtiest thoughts imaginable.

From his seat, he had a view of the pool, and behind him sat a bunch of empty tables.

Given everything he'd seen, the woman was broke.

That much was obvious. Yet how could she be with the amount of money Allen said she'd stolen? A lot of things were starting *not* to add up about his story.

He'd seen what a great and caring mom she was, had seen her frantic with worry about Avery. That wasn't a woman who saw her child as an accessory. Plus, she'd been so grateful for his help that afternoon, and that wasn't the act of an entitled snob. He knew she didn't have an entitled bone in her body.

Then, there were all the interview—her father, childhood friends and college roommates. They all swore she was the nicest person they knew.

Something didn't add up.

When he'd taken the case, it was all about freeing Adeeb. He didn't much care about anything else.

Tack checked his phone. No new message from Adeeb. But sometimes he went days without answering. Tack sent up a little prayer, hoping his friend was all right.

He took another swig of the beer and frowned as he looked at his phone. Time was running out, and Tack had already wasted so much of it running after Cate Allen's ghost.

Life was so damn complicated sometimes. He almost missed Afghanistan. There, he didn't have a whole lot of time to worry about his feelings or second-guess his decisions. In the moment in war, there were orders and there was enemy fire, and there wasn't a whole lot of thinking.

The thinking came when he got home.

Now he wished he could turn his brain off

again. Just be told what to do, be back in a place where orders were orders.

"Want another one?" Mark, who was working the bar, asked him, startling him out of his reverie. "You look like you need one."

"That bad, huh?"

Mark shrugged. He grabbed Tack's empty beer glass and filled it from the tap. "This one's on me, Marine," he said, nodding to the T Marine Battalion T-shirt he wore.

"Thanks, man," he said, nodding back at the fiftysomething man with the nearly white hair and the Bermuda shorts. Tack still wasn't sure just what his relationship was with Cate, but now was as good as any to find out. "Have you known Cate long?"

"A few years," Mark said, a little guarded.

A few years? Tack wondered if that meant right at the time of Cate's escape. Had she been having an affair with Mark? Had he offered to save her if she stole from her rich husband?

Right. A married man ran off with his mistress *and* took his whole family with him? That might just be the dumbest plan Tack ever heard.

"You guys close?" Tack asked, trying to pry a little more without raising suspicion. Mark dried off a glass, taking a minute to answer.

Finally, he looked up, a knowing half smile on his otherwise no-nonsense face.

"You like her." It wasn't a question.

The comment took Tack off guard. In part, because he realized at that moment he actually did.

"Well…" Tack hesitated.

"It's obvious to me, but probably not to her," Mark said. "Don't worry, big guy. I'm just a friend. Nothing more."

Tack's gut told him the man was telling him the truth.

"She's like a kid sister to me. Or, hell, with my age, my daughter." Mark chuckled to himself as he picked up another wet glass and gave it a swipe with the bar towel. "But I look after her. She's got a big heart, and she's been through a lot."

"What do you mean?"

Mark looked at him a beat and then poured two tequila shots.

"For this, we need a stronger drink."

He slid one shot over to Tack, who took it. He met Mark's gaze and then drank the amber liquid that burned like fire down his throat. He was reminded suddenly of his first free night after boot camp, where he and a gaggle of new recruits had laid waste to more than one bottle of tequila.

"Phew," Mark said, and shook his head. "There we go. That hits the spot." He grinned at Tack. "Another?"

Tack shrugged. Why not? He wasn't going to get a DNA swab this evening unless he rappelled off the resort roof and onto Cate's balcony. He'd have to come up with something tomorrow.

That or Allen could wait.

Mark slid another shot his way, and the two once again simultaneously downed them, knocking the glasses onto the wooden bar with a satisfied *thunk*.

"That's serious business," Tack remarked. He grabbed his beer and took a swig to wash down the tequila. "So what has Cate been through?"

"Her mom died when she was little. Her dad was an alcoholic." All facts Tack already knew. "And she has had some very bad relationships."

"How so?"

"A bad guy, that's all I'll say. Bad in every way."

"What? Did he hit her?"

Mark just glared at Tack, saying nothing and letting him draw his own conclusions, which weren't good. Cate was in a relationship with an abusive man? Tack did a quick catalog of all the people he'd interviewed. She'd had one boyfriend before Allen, a mousy engineer with a nerdy streak who went to Northwestern. Tack couldn't imagine he'd be the violent one. Though, sometimes, you never knew about people. Still.

"Was it her husband?"

"I've already said too much," Mark said, looking spooked and glaring at his empty glass as if it were to blame.

Was Mark talking about Allen? If so, this straightforward case just got a hell of a lot more complicated. If it was Allen, then Tack was going to have to hit someone. Now.

Tack gripped his glass so hard, he thought it might shatter.

"Forget I ever mentioned it," Mark said, and that was the last thing the man would say on the matter. But Tack wasn't finished. He was going to find out the truth, one way or another.

CATE COULDN'T STOP thinking about Tack. Even the next day, as she sat with Mark going over some ideas to revamp business for the resort, he was still in her thoughts. Without him, Avery would've fallen from that tree and broken his arm—or worse. If Avery had fallen out of that tree and broken something, they would have had to take a helicopter to St. Thomas, which had the closest hospital. And what would've happened if they'd double-checked their IDs? Asked more questions than Cate was comfortable answering? Mark had made it clear when she'd run that the best way not to get caught was to stay off the grid. Stay out of hospitals and away from the police. Their fake identities were strong, but why push it? She and Avery had new last names now, but that didn't mean they couldn't be found out.

She was so grateful that Tack had thought to look in the tree and had found Avery. She couldn't help but think it was because Tack was a man, who'd once been a boy. He thought like one. Most days, she had no idea what was running through little Avery's head, no idea how he decided suddenly to climb trees or jump in a pool without his life jacket. He was a little daredevil, a trait he most certainly didn't get from her.

Rick had taken risks, had taken them all the time. He also controlled everything and everyone around him. It was why he was so successful in business and so ruthless in marriage. Her boy was okay, and Rick hadn't found them. Another good day down.

"Earth to Cate. Come in, Cate." Mark frowned at her as they sat on the patio near the pool going over this month's bills.

"I'm sorry, I…"

"Was a million miles away," Mark said, sounding stern. "Am I the only one around here worried about the bills?"

"No. Of course not." She hesitated, realizing that with all the hubbub with Avery, she'd forgotten about Terry Blake. "Hey. I talked to Terry Blake. He mentioned he talked to you about selling the resort."

Mark scowled. "That guy is full of it. Believe me, he knows better than to talk to me. I'd tell him where to go and how to get there."

Cate felt relief. "I didn't think so, but he seemed so sure."

Mark shook his head. "If you want to sell, then we sell. I'm not going to be strong-armed by Terry freakin' Blake. He was probably just trying to get into your head. Make you want to sell."

"That's true." Cate nodded. "It's how he operates."

"So, now that's out of the way, how about we focus on how we keep this place open. How about this new fund-raiser?" Mark tapped the stack of brightly colored flyers he'd drawn up, designed to attract spring break kids from the local resorts.

"I don't know, Mark. Drunk college kids?" Cate shook her head. It wasn't what she envisioned for her resort, which she always wanted to be elegant with a touch of class. The idea of kids—probably most of them underage for the States, though legal here—swigging cheap cocktails was never something she'd planned on.

"Beggars can't be choosers, Cate. We're in the red. We need *something* and spring break won't last forever."

"I know. I know. Okay... I guess, go ahead."

"Good, because we're on for a party tonight." Mark shuffled his flyers.

"Mark! You didn't tell me!" Cate protested.

"I knew you'd have to say yes," Mark said. "We don't have a choice if we want to pay our utilities this month."

Cate sighed. She knew Mark was right. He always was. "Why don't you take these," he said and handed her a stack. "Go put them up around town today."

She sighed again. "Okay."

"I've already gotten the word out online," he told her.

"Mark!" she protested.

"Don't worry—nothing that can be traced back to you or me, okay? I was careful."

Cate suddenly felt exposed. Yet she trusted Mark. He knew what he was doing. She owed her and her boy's life to him, after all. "Okay, Mark. Okay."

"It'll be fine," he promised, and she hoped he was right. "I've got to go check with Carol about the appetizers for tonight." Cate nodded. "And Grace is watching Avery tonight. No buts. She's already on babysitting duty. We'll need you down on the floor. We need all the bartenders we can get."

"Great," Cate said, feeling the opposite. The last thing she wanted to do all night was sling cheap cocktails.

"Remember, it's to save your baby. *Our* baby." Mark spread his arms to encompass the resort, and Cate reluctantly nodded. She knew it was for a good cause. She wanted this to work, too. Something had to.

Cate glanced at the neon-pink flyer in her hand advertising cheap mixed drinks and karaoke. God, she'd officially become one of *those* resorts. She shook her head.

Just then, out of the corner of her eye, she saw a streak of tanned torso.

Tack.

She knew before she turned it was him. After all, who else at the resort had the body of a Viking god? No one.

"Eye candy, huh?" Mark hadn't left, and he was watching her stare openly at Tack, who was currently strolling to the pool wearing only swim trunks and flip-flops, his eyes hidden by aviator sunglasses and his dark hair in thick waves that curled around his ears. She tried to imagine him with a marine's flattop, but couldn't. His hair was too good. It would be a shame to cut it.

Actually, she wanted to run her fingers through it right then.

Or put her hands on his bare chest, which was art worthy. His muscles sculpted themselves.

"Uh, no… I…" Cate suddenly felt flustered. The last person she wanted grief from was Mark.

"Don't worry. I had a chat with your boyfriend at the bar last night."

"What? He's not my…" Cate's neck felt like it was on fire.

"Don't worry. He likes you, too. It's obvious he's got a thing for you." Mark gave her a playful shove with his elbow.

"Why? What did he say?" Cate suddenly felt like a preteen passing notes in class.

"Nothing. I just told him to be nice to you, or I'd beat him up."

Cate burst out laughing. Mark was no match for Tack, and they both knew it.

"Hey, I think he was *mildly* threatened."

Cate squeezed his arm. "You're a good man, Mark."

"Don't I know it? Anyway, I think he does like you. For what it's worth. Most of the time he can't take his eyes off you. Like he's trying to figure you out."

"Is that a good thing?"

"I don't know. Why don't you ask him?"

Cate stared at Mark. "Are you giving me permission to date? Does this mean you've already run a background check?"

If anything, Mark always erred on being overprotective.

"I haven't yet, but why don't I get on that. In the meantime, flirting never hurt anybody." He grinned and headed away from her, whistling as he went.

Cate glanced over at Tack and was shocked to find he was staring straight at her.

Was Mark right?

She glanced away, uncomfortable. When she looked up again, he was still...staring. Almost daring her to come over there. Boy, did she want to. She wanted to sprint over, wanted to feel the thick muscles of his shoulders. He picked a reclining chair near the edge of the pool and sat on it, then stretched his golden body across its blue-striped length. She felt an irresistible pull toward him. But what would she do when she got there? Ask him if he needed help applying sunscreen? She nearly giggled at the thought. She could almost see the next one-star Yelp review for the resort: *Owner sexually harasses pool patrons.*

Then again, he had kissed her on the boat. *Then* bought her lunch. *Then* rescued her son from nearly falling out of a tree.

It's not like he hadn't expressed interest.

So why was he over there? And not here?

He was simply lying by the pool. She felt sure he'd seen her when he'd come out. After all, she was only about thirty feet from him. But why did she get the impression he was taunting her to come over? Daring *her* to make the first move this morning?

It felt like a delicious little game of cat and mouse.

As he shifted his gorgeous body beneath the morning sun, she thought she could stare at him all day. And probably night, too. He was a capital *M, Man.* Like none she'd remembered meeting before. Sure, good-looking guys came in and out of the resort all the time, but one so tall…so decidedly…in charge? Never. She felt a flush creep up her neck as she debated about going over there.

What would she say?

It's not like she had a lot of experience hitting on gorgeous men. Or even ugly men. She had no game. She'd not even considered getting one, not since fleeing Rick. Now, there was Tack, and she wanted *something*, she realized. To flirt? More?

And what did she even *know* about him? Other than he was gorgeous. And smart. And kind. Ugh. She wasn't even over there, and she was already trying to fall in love with the man. What was wrong with her? Cate watched as he sat up and stretched, and she nearly felt her jaw drop open as she saw her answer. One man simply shouldn't have so many muscles.

She gathered her papers and realized she would have to pass by his chair if she ever wanted to leave the pool area. Not that she did right at the moment. Staring at Tack, she forgot what other things she was supposed to be doing right at that instant. Hanging flyers in town? Was that it?

Maybe she should go over and thank him once more for Avery? Then again, that might be overkill. He saved the boy from a tree, not a great white.

Okay. Just go over there. Say hi. Then leave. How hard can it be?

Cate smoothed the folds of her faded blue sundress and walked over to Tack. It all seemed so straightforward—stop, say hi and move on.

Before she could speak, Tack spoke. "What are you doing tonight?"

The offer made her feel all warm inside. Was he asking her out? Then, of course, she remembered her obligations.

"This," she said, and sighed as she held up the garish flyer.

"'Spring Break Fest'?" Tack read aloud and shook his head. "Free mai tais for the ladies?" Tack squinted. "How many people do you expect?"

"I don't know, but Mark hopes a lot."

"Did you hire any security?" Tack glanced around the pool.

"Security?" Cate echoed, puzzled.

"Bouncers. For when the drunk kids get out of hand."

Cate felt her stomach sink. She hadn't even thought of that. "No."

"How about I help out tonight? I've bounced at bars before." Tack pulled himself from his chair and now towered over her. She craned her neck to meet his gaze and had to shield her eyes from the bright sun somewhere above his chestnut brown curls.

"We don't need to card, probably. St. Anthony's drinking age is eighteen," she said.

"Which is why so many college kids like to come here."

"No carding, but you still need someone to keep an eye on the rowdies." Cate knew he'd be a cooling factor. Just having him there would discourage some from getting out of control. Kids would have to be crazy to want to tangle with him.

"But I can't pay you. I'm…" Broke, she thought but didn't finish. She could barely pay the maids and was another month away from having to do the job herself.

"I'll do it free of charge," he said quickly. "*If* you agree to come to my room for the after-party."

Cate's throat suddenly went dry. Was he asking her what she thought he was asking?

"For drinks," he quickly added. "Just a drink. If you feel better staying at the bar, that's fine."

Why did she feel a suddenly clunky disappointment in the pit of her stomach? The bar was a much safer option. She didn't even know this man! Why was she even considering going up to his room?

"So what do you say? A drink?"

"Yes," Cate said, defying all her good sense. "We can have a drink after."

"Good," Tack said and took her hand, sending tiny little electric sparks in all directions. He bent over it and gave the back of it a tiny kiss, never breaking eye contact. "Can't wait for that."

CHAPTER NINE

THE FLYERS AND whatever other advertising Mark put into motion worked. Cate couldn't believe the number of kids—and she definitely thought of them as *kids*, as most of them barely looked fifteen, much less like they should be in college. She nearly bumped into a guy who she could've sworn ought to be in high school.

"Sorry," she murmured, not that she could be heard over the thumping music blaring out over the pool and to the beach. The acne-prone teen just gave her a long, slow once-over. *Oh, no*, she thought. There's no possible way this *child* found her attractive.

He raised his glass and grinned, and she almost expected to see braces. Thankfully, he had none. That didn't make the drunken leer on his face any less palatable, though. She scooted past him even as he sloshed his fruity drink on her stone patio tiles. She wondered how much scrubbing it would take to get all the gunk off. Already, her flip-flops were sticking to the smooth stone, and bright red splatters of spilled cocktails coated most of the tile.

Mark worked the bar, looking red and sweaty. Cate was trying to reach him to help out. She barely managed to get through the throng of thirsty partygoers.

"Whose stupid idea was this?" Mark grumbled, just loudly enough to be heard over the thump of bass from the DJ's speakers. He flashed a wry grin as she slid in back behind the bar to help him.

"At least tell me *some* of these people are paying for their drinks," Cate said. Since two-thirds were the ladies of "ladies drink free until nine," Cate almost didn't want to know how much they were losing on this venture.

"We're making money, we are," Mark said, and nodded toward the overflowing tip jar. The number of dollar bills crammed in there would at least cover the utilities this month, she figured.

"We'd better," Cate murmured as she pushed a few more plastic cups of red liquid into the hands of eager college coeds.

"It was a good idea to hire the muscle," Mark said, nodding toward Tack, who stood arms crossed near the DJ. He scoured the crowd with a stern look on his face. "He already broke up two fights."

"I didn't hire him," Cate said. "He *volunteered*."

Mark laughed and shook his head. "He must *really* have it bad for you, then," he said, shouting even louder as the music amped up. Cate felt her face grow warm and was glad the dim lights of the patio hid her blush. She wondered if he'd managed to dig into Tack's background, but also knew this wasn't the place to ask. Besides, if he did find something, he'd let her know. Mark wasn't one to keep secrets from her. It was one of the things that made their partnership work so well. She could always count on Mark to tell it to her straight. She believed him when he told her Terry Blake had been lying.

Cate poured the last of a pitcher of mai tai into a waiting glass and then turned to Mark, who was busy mixing a new batch. He emptied the rum bottle and glanced up at Cate.

"We've got more in the kitchen," he shouted, indicating the resort with a jerk of his thumb. "Can you go get it? I'll hold off the thirsty ones."

As the press of college kids only seemed to get thicker at the bar, Cate knew she had no time to lose. Rum was needed—stat. She inched her way through the crowd, but found it slow going. She glanced up once and saw Tack studying the dance floor, where one skinny kid in a bright blue Hawaiian shirt was busy trying to do the worm. He'd had so much to drink, he looked more like a slug squirming in the sunlight, but Cate was sure in his own mind he was legendary. She sighed and rolled her eyes, trying to remember her own college days. She'd been working two jobs to put herself through school, so she didn't have time to party. It had only been dumb luck she'd even met Rick. She'd happened to be working in the dean's office, one of her many work-study jobs, when Rick Allen came in. He'd gone to Northwestern, too, and was prepared to give a hefty donation for a new building there.

Somehow, between her fetching him coffee and him approving plans for the building that would bear his name, he'd asked for her number. She'd been so caught off guard, she'd given it to him without hesitation, even though she had steadfastly fought off the boys interested in her. She didn't have time to date. She barely had time to study.

He'd been ten years older than she was and different from any man she'd ever met. Then again, it wasn't every day a girl met one of the youngest self-made billionaires in the world. After that, it had been a whirlwind courtship. How could she resist the amazing gifts? The sudden weekend invites to far-flung romantic locales like Paris and Rome?

He'd been such a gentleman then. Of course, his control-freak self came out in small doses—in his annoyance when she'd even glance at her phone in his presence, his overbearing way of ordering *for* her without letting her decide what she'd eat, even his insistence on picking her last semester's courses at Northwestern. She'd just thought it was his way of taking care of her. She didn't realize that it was all about him *controlling* her.

When asked once by a reporter the one thing that was the greatest challenge about running one of the world's most successful real estate companies, he'd said, "That people have free will."

Everyone thought he'd been joking, but Cate knew the truth. Rick would love the world better if everyone were compelled to obey him. Free will *was* a wrinkle in his otherwise perfect world. He hated that people could defy him.

She shook her head. When were the memories going to fade?

Suddenly, someone grabbed her arm in such a way that she thought, for a split second, somehow Rick had managed to jump from her thoughts and onto the crowded dance floor.

"Where you going, hottie?" Cate turned to find herself smushed against the drunk kid in the blue Hawaiian shirt. He reeked of mai tais and sweat, and he held her arm in an iron grip.

"Let me go," Cate said, trying to sound like the grown-up she was, though the drunk kid was taller than her and probably had about fifty pounds on her at least. When he'd been rolling around on the floor he'd looked smaller, but up close, he was the size of a defensive tackle. She pulled away, but he held her fast.

"Dance with me!" he commanded, breathing sour rum in her face. She flinched and shoved her hands against this chest, but by now he'd wrapped both big arms around her.

"No," Cate growled, now feeling comically small and weak as she fought uselessly against him. She felt that familiar rush of powerlessness, the same feeling she'd felt with Rick, when he'd pinned her to the floor in their living room the night he'd put her head through their glass coffee table. The panic welled up in her throat, and she started clawing at her captor, though he was too drunk to notice the scratches. "No!" she shouted, but her voice was drowned out by the thumping loud bass of the DJ as the kid pressed harder against her, pushing her chest into his. She felt like she couldn't breathe. She was going to suffocate.

"Hey," a voice growled behind her, and without looking she knew it was Tack, could feel his tall presence behind her even before he reached out and grabbed the punk kid's shoulder. "The lady said she didn't want to dance."

The kid stared down at Tack's hand, which held a patch of his cheap Hawaiian shirt. Before he could do more than that, Tack yanked him away from Cate with such force he staggered backward and fell with a thump on his butt.

"On your feet." Even drunk, the kid managed to pop back up. "You're out."

The kid moved as if to swing at Tack, but Tack did a quick move and suddenly had the kid's arm pinned behind his back. "Get moving," Tack ordered, and the kid obliged as Tack pushed him through the crowded dance floor. Shocked, all Cate could do was follow. He shoved the kid past the pool and jammed bar and didn't stop moving until he'd gotten to the edge of the property near the parking lot. He gave the kid an extra hard shove and he staggered, nearly falling before he righted himself.

"You're out," Tack repeated. "If I see you anywhere *near* here again, next time, I won't be so gentle."

The kid frowned and considered talking back, but then he took in Tack's full height, and the size of his enormous biceps and decided against it.

Then, Tack focused on Cate.

"Are you all right?"

Cate nodded. But she felt a little shaken by all the memories of being grabbed and manhandled that had surfaced. The bottomless pit of powerlessness, the hopelessness that strangled her.

"You don't look fine." Tack put his arm around her and brought her around to the lobby of the resort, which was much less crowded. The thump of the music was faded here. "Why don't you sit down?" He guided her to the small love seat in the air-conditioned nook by the front desk. Cate slumped into it wordlessly. When had her legs turned to jelly? Why were her hands shaking?

"Do you need some water?" Tack asked, hovering near her.

"No. Thanks." Even her voice sounded shaky. What was wrong with her? But she already knew the answer. Rick was what was wrong with her. Rick and all the times he hit her. "I'm sorry. I…I just don't like being touched like that."

Tack frowned. "Nobody does," he said. "That kid's a prick, but he's not going to touch you again." The way he said it made Cate feel well protected. She was sure Tack had scared that kid to death. Cate nodded and tried to get her breathing back under control. An anxiety attack now wouldn't help anyone, and besides, she had to get back to that party and help Mark. She'd promised to bring more rum.

Her hands still shook, and she laced her fingers together to keep them from shaking. Tack noticed.

"This isn't about that kid, is it?" Tack said, eyeing her carefully. "This is about something else."

How did he know?

"Why do you say that?" Cate's guard was up. What did he know? Why would he even ask something like that?

"I know what post-traumatic stress looks like," Tack said. "Most of my buddies had it. You show all the signs. Something happened to you that wasn't this kid."

Cate blinked fast, her heart rate shooting up and her breath coming fast. She felt suddenly transparent, as if he already knew all her secrets. She worked so hard to pretend everything was fine, that his calling her out felt like she'd been stripped naked of all her defenses. She knew in an instant that lying would do her no good. Somehow, he'd see through the lie. He seemed to be able to see everything about her in that moment. She wondered how he managed that.

"I…I don't like to talk about it," she said at last.

"Try me." Tack studied her, his brown eyes sincere. She suddenly wanted to share, to unburden herself. How long had she carried these secrets? Even Mark and Carol didn't know them all, didn't know all of what Rick had done to her. All she had to do was open her mouth and let the words come tumbling out. She wondered what would happen then.

But she couldn't. There was Avery to think about it. And the fact that Rick was still looking for her. She didn't know this man, no matter how well-meaning he seemed. She didn't trust him. She didn't know if she could trust anyone.

"I…I can't."

She shook her head and pressed her lips together, as if worried her past might just leap out of her throat without her permission.

Tack looked disappointed, and she hated that look.

"Okay, then. When you're ready," he said, and gave her knee a pat.

I might never be ready, she thought. "I should get Mark more rum." She stood, despite the fact that her knees felt a little wobbly. When she took a step, one nearly gave out, and Tack grabbed her elbow.

"Easy. Listen, go upstairs. Rest. I'll help Mark at the bar."

"But…"

"I can walk you." Tack gently guided her toward the elevators.

"I don't need a chaperone. I'm fine." Cate felt weak-kneed and weak-headed, but she didn't want Tack to know that. She felt like she was a kid being sent to bed without dinner.

"You need to rest," Tack commanded. "Your body's feeling shock, so you need to rest."

"But… I'm…"

"Going to *rest*," he stressed as he pressed the elevator button.

"I don't need to rest. I can help at the party. The resort needs me." The elevator doors slid open and Cate stood her ground, refusing to get in.

"God, you may be the most stubborn woman I've ever met," Tack growled, and then, in an instant had swept her up in his arms. Cate was so shocked, she let out a squeal. A few patrons in the lobby turned to stare, and Cate felt her face flush.

"Put me down!" she cried.

"I am going to *carry* you up the stairs and

to your room unless you get in this elevator and go."

Tack didn't fight fair. She wanted to go back to the party, but she also didn't want the scene of this muscle-bound marine carrying her through the lobby. How would she explain *that* to Mark?

"Put me down."

"*Only* if you agree to go upstairs and get some rest." The elevator doors threatened to shut, and Tack stopped them with one well-placed foot.

Cate saw no alternative. She was beaten, fair and square.

"Fine," she said. "I'll go."

Tack put her down, and she moved reluctantly into the elevator. He reached in and clicked the button for the top floor. "I'll come up and check on you later," he promised as the doors slid shut between them.

CHAPTER TEN

ONCE IN HER ROOM, Cate felt idiotic. She was fine. Sure, her legs were shaky and she felt like she couldn't quite catch her breath, but other than that she was fine. Then again, as the door slipped shut behind her, she felt suddenly light-headed as she sank onto her sofa, knees wobbly. Her head pounded with an adrenaline headache, and her arms felt tingly and strange.

This wasn't the first time she'd had a near panic attack, and probably wouldn't be the last.

Post-traumatic stress. Was that really what this was? She'd never served in combat. Then again, as she remembered some of the nights she spent with Rick, it often felt like war.

She glanced around her living room, which was empty. Carol had told her earlier that Grace would be watching Avery in their suite across the hall, which was fine by Cate. She needed a minute to compose herself.

I'm fine. I'm not hurt. Rick is thousands of miles away. I'm safe. Avery's safe.

She repeated the chant in her head until her

breathing calmed. Then, she got to her feet and plugged in the kettle. Moments later she was sipping a cup of tea, trying to unravel the nerves that had bunched up at the back of her neck. *After this cup, I'll head downstairs*, she thought, but then found herself staring into space, lost in all those many horrible memories of her past.

Rick's temper would always flare up when she least expected it, like a storm out of the blue. Sometimes, she'd get hit before she even realized he was angry. That's how violent his temper became. He didn't even bother to hide his behavior in front of servants. She remembered the army of maids, the butler, the valet and all the people who stoically turned a blind eye. Cate had been surrounded by people, but she'd been anything but safe.

That feeling of being completely vulnerable and alone stuck with her, even now. *I'm free*, she told herself. *I don't live there anymore.*

But the fast rate of her heart told her part of her would always live in that house. She laid down her empty cup and stretched out on the sofa. Without meaning to, she drifted to sleep thinking about her past. She dreamed dark, unsettling dreams until a soft knock on the door brought her to high alert. Her heart leaped to her chest, and for a crazy split second, she thought Rick might be at the door.

Don't be ridiculous, Cate. He doesn't know you're here.

Cate glanced at the clock on her wall and saw it was late. She moved to the peephole and glanced through, and saw Carol standing there. Cate swung open the door and glanced worriedly down the hallway.

"Carol?"

"Tack told me about…what happened. I just wanted to check on you. See if you're okay." Carol bit her lower lip, brow furrowed in worry.

"I'm okay. Really." Cate squeezed Carol's hand.

"Are you sure? You look so…pale." Carol leaned in the open door and gave Cate a warm hug, rubbing her back in the way that always made her feel better. "Do you want something to eat? Or drink? Do you need a shot of tequila?"

Cate laughed a little at her friend's joke. "There might not be enough tequila in the world. Do you have a Xanax?"

Carol smiled and hugged her friend once more.

"You're okay, you know. You're not there anymore. You're here. You're safe."

Cate shook her head. "Why don't I feel

safe?" She couldn't shake the feeling that Rick was closing in on her, that it was only a matter of time before she was found.

Before Carol could answer, the elevator down the hall dinged, announcing the arrival of someone new. Both women turned to look, Cate again feeling an unexplained dread. No guests stayed on this floor, at least not this weekend with the hotel half empty. Soon, they saw Tack's broad shoulders emerge from the elevator. Her heart sped up a little, and her hands flew to her hair. When was the last time she'd combed it? She had no idea. She glanced at Carol, who wore a knowing grin.

"What?" Cate whispered.

"You talk to him." Carol nudged Cate forward.

"But what about Avery?"

"He'll sleep on the couch. It'll be a sleepover. You know how he loves those," Carol said as she slipped across the hall.

Tack was halfway down the hall, a half smile on his face. "Carol, don't...don't leave," Cate whispered.

"Why? He's not here for *me*," Carol said as she opened her door and sneaked in. She poked her head out. "And feel free to stay out *all night*. Seriously. Avery will stay with us."

"Carol..."

But Tack was upon her then.

"Hey." Tack's sensual mouth spread into a sly smile. "Where'd Carol go?" He glanced at the closing door and the half wave from her soon-to-be-fired resort manager. Cate couldn't believe Carol had left her stranded out in the hall *alone with this man.*

"Uh, Carol just wanted to check in on Avery."

"How is he?"

"Fine."

"I wanted to see how you were." Tack studied her face, and Cate felt a rush of heat flood her cheeks. She wasn't used to someone checking up on her. Or looking after her.

"I'm fine. Really." But even as Cate spoke, she couldn't quite meet Tack's gaze. It wasn't a lie, exactly, but it wasn't the truth, either.

Tack put his finger beneath her chin and tilted it upward, so their eyes met. "You wouldn't be lying to me, would you?"

Cate found she couldn't answer him then. She felt mesmerized by the closeness of him, the fact that if she stood on her tiptoes she might even kiss the man.

No. What am I thinking? Kiss him right in the hall?

"Well, if you're *really* fine, then you owe me that drink." Tack held up a bottle of wine and two glasses.

"Well…Carol did say she'd watch Avery." Cate couldn't believe she'd actually said that out loud. She'd meant to keep that thought strictly in her own head, yet it slipped out, unbidden. Tack seemed to have that effect on her. She wanted to simply *confess everything* when he was around.

"Why don't we take this to my room, then?" Tack held up the wine and the glasses.

She wanted to protest, but the fact was, she wanted that drink.

"I promise I won't bite."

But what if I want you to? Cate was simply staring at Tack now, she knew it, the white-hot thought suddenly crowding all other logical ones from her head. Maybe Carol was rubbing off on her. Something seemed to be steering her mind decidedly toward sex. She knew exactly why, too. The man was built like a brick wall, a really sexy, really hot, brick wall.

"Cate?" His deep baritone brought her out of her fantasy. How long had she just been staring at him? And *what* was wrong with her?

"Oh, uh, yeah. Sure. Okay."

Never mind that going to a strange man's room was something *she never did*. But this man rescued Avery. This man saved her from a drunk patron. She couldn't imagine a predator would go to those lengths just to take advantage of her.

And could he take advantage if that's exactly what she wanted him to do?

They rode the elevator down two floors, and all the while all Cate could think was how close his elbow was to hers, how immensely tall and broad he was in the small space of the elevator.

"I don't usually do this," she blurted.

"What? Ride elevators?" Tack's sensual mouth spread into a sly grin.

Cate laughed. "No. Have drinks. This late." *In a strange man's room.*

"You don't usually stay up past ten thirty? Really?" Now Tack seemed to be calling her bluff. The elevator doors dinged, and Tack held them open for her as she scooted out, feeling flustered and off balance. Suddenly, she also wondered what she was agreeing to by going to his room. Did he expect to kiss her? More? Did she want him to?

She glanced back at his dark eyes, which seemed to be able to read her mind. *Oh, yes. Yes, she did.*

Tack slid his key card into his door, then pushed it open with one beefy shoulder.

"After you." She went and she could feel his gaze raking over her. She wondered if he approved of the capri yoga pants she'd hastily thrown on this morning. She'd been going for comfort. She hadn't expected a date. *Was this a date?*

The clink of the wineglasses reverberated in the empty but tidy room. Cate was suddenly all too aware that the only real place to sit was the queen bed, made up in the colorful floral aqua pattern.

This might be more than a date.

Tack flung open the glass door patio, letting in the warm sea air. "Sit outside?"

"Uh…yeah." Cate nodded, feeling relief and disappointment all at once. She took her wineglass and followed him out to the small patio dinette. She noticed that Tack had gotten the seaside room with one of the best views in the resort. The moon hung over the Caribbean, bathing the water in a glistening silver light. This might be less overtly sexual than the bed, but it was no less romantic. Tack uncorked the wine with a reassuring-sounding pop.

"How did…the party go?" Cate asked.

"Mark was pretty happy about it," Tack said. "But I'm guessing you're not going to like the state of the pool tomorrow. You might need a sledgehammer to get up all the spilled mai tais."

"That bad?"

"Worse. And some kids broke a few poolside chairs. Turns out the recliners weren't meant to be danced on."

"Oh, no." Cate pinched her nose, trying to hold a stress headache at bay. "That sounds like a disaster."

"Oh, it absolutely was." Tack grinned as he took a sip from his drink. "And Mark wants to do it again."

"Lord help us." Cate shook her head and took the glass. "Won't you be gone by then?"

The realization that his week would be up by then hit her like a ton of bricks.

"Maybe I could extend my stay," he said and her stomach did a little flip. "To your resort." He raised his glass. "I hope it's back on its feet soon, so you *won't* have to throw any more parties."

Cate clinked glasses with him. "Cheers to that." She took a sip. "Thank you. Again."

"For what?"

"For…looking after me tonight."

Tack studied her a moment. "My pleasure," he said after a beat.

They slipped into small talk for a bit. The wine was going down far too fast, but Cate didn't seem to mind. Tack refilled her glass even before it was empty, making it even harder to keep track of what she'd drunk. The cool breeze off the sea ruffled her hair, making her feel relaxed for the first time in a very long time. The stress of the day seemed to melt away a little, and she wondered if this was what contentment felt like.

"Do you want to talk about it?" Tack asked after a moment.

"What? The drunk kid who got handsy?" Cate shrugged. "It was nothing. I just...overreacted."

"No, you didn't." Tack glanced at her, leaning forward on the small table, placing his strong elbows on the glass top. "There's something you're not telling me."

Cate laughed a little. "How do you know that? You don't even know me." The wine made her head feel light, but even so, she knew better than to just talk freely. She glanced at the sea, hoping she'd find a change of subject out there on the waves.

"Let's play a little game," Tack suggested, his low voice sending a shiver through her. She suddenly felt a wild hope that the game might be strip poker.

"What kind of game?" Cate asked, cautious. In the silver moonlight, she could see the challenge in his eyes.

"Five Questions."

"Isn't it supposed to be Twenty Questions?"

"Not this game. This game, we get to ask

each other five questions. If you refuse to answer, then you have to drink half your glass of wine. If you lie, you have to drink your entire glass of wine. If you tell the truth, then *I* have to drink my entire glass of wine."

"That's a lot of drinking."

"That's why there's just five questions." Tack grinned.

Every fiber in Cate's body told her not to play this game. It was dangerous, and foolhardy, to say the least. And her head was already buzzing with the little bit of wine she'd already had.

"Come on, Cate. What are you afraid of?" Tack leaned in and gently drew a line down the back of her hand. She watched the tip of his finger, mesmerized. She knew exactly what she was afraid of. *Him*.

"Nothing," she said.

"Then let's play."

"Fine," she said, and decided then and there she'd just lie. How would he know the difference?

"Okay, then. Ladies first. Ask me the first question."

"So, what's the worst thing that happened to you in Afghanistan?"

Tack froze, hand on the stem of his wineglass. "I don't like to talk about it."

Cate leaned in, feeling giddy. "Are you refusing to talk about it? Then you'll have to drink half your glass."

Tack shook his head. "God, you don't pull any punches. Go straight for the jugular."

"I like to win."

A small smile tugged at the corner of Tack's full mouth. "I get that about you."

"So? Are you refusing to answer?"

Tack glanced at her, seeming to weigh his options. "I left someone behind. He was a local translator, saved me and my soldiers more than once. He was a brave man, a good man, and..." Tack paused, and swallowed. "And because of the help he gave us, the Taliban vowed revenge. He was supposed to get a visa to come to the US. He didn't."

"And...?" Cate got the impression he wasn't telling her the whole story.

"And I've been trying to get him over ever since. Lobbied my senators, wrote letters to the president. Still working on it, and he's still over there." Tack sat back in his chair and folded his muscular forearms across his chest.

"I'm sorry," Cate said. "Do you know if he's okay? Do you talk to him?"

Tack stared at his wineglass. "When he can talk, when he gets access to Wi-Fi, which isn't often. He's got a little girl now, too. Her life is in danger until I can get them all home."

"Is there anything more you can do? You wrote your senator, but maybe there's something else you could try?"

Tack hesitated a moment. "I've tried," he said. "It's like banging my head against a concrete wall. Veterans can barely get funding for benefits, and so getting anybody to care about the people who helped us who aren't citizens is a tough sell."

"Surely, someone would listen. After everything he did to help you."

"I'm still trying," Tack said, and Cate believed him. "I can't live with myself if he dies. The man put his life on the line and we left him alone with the wolves. Some thanks."

"Don't give up. It's…it's not right he can't come here," Cate protested, slamming her open palm on the glass tabletop, making the wineglasses rattle.

"Well, the good news is, you can drink away your indignation." Tack nodded toward her wineglass. "I answered your question, so drink up, girl. The whole glass."

"No!"

"Yes. Them's the rules." Tack grinned, confident in his victory. "Or you lose, Miss 'I like to win.'"

Cate felt a competitive spirit rise in her. She wasn't bested yet. "Fine." Cate took her glass and finished the rest of the white wine in it, coughing a little at the end as she sucked in a breath of air. "That is the fastest I've ever drank a Pinot Grigio."

"Always a first time. How are you feeling?" Tack studied her.

"A little drunk." That was the truth. No lie there. The instant the wine hit her stomach it seemed like it took the express veins straight to her brain. Losing came with a high price. Still, the alcohol loosened the stiffness in her neck, the anxiety that she'd held there since the kid tried to grab her on the dance floor. It felt…good. Maybe this game wasn't so bad, after all.

"Now it's my turn to ask a question," Tack said as he refilled her glass.

"Good. I'll be as deliberately vague as you were. Then it'll be your turn to drink."

"We'll see about that." Tack scooted his chair closer to hers, so their knees touched, and Cate felt the impact, the warmth of his legs near hers. His proximity made her head swim even more than the wine as she tried to focus on him. His dark eyes were all challenge.

"Where…" he began and paused.

"Where what?" Now she couldn't wait to have the question out there. What would he ask her? She held her breath, wanting it to be over with already.

"...did..."

His eyes never left hers.

Now she was starting to forget about the question and being on the spot, and all she could think of was how dark his eyes were. She could barely see his pupils.

"Where did what?"

"Where did you..." He was almost nose to nose. She glanced down at his lips. Was he going to kiss her? There was nothing in the rules about a stolen kiss. Her body came alive at the idea.

"Where did you get—" then he reached up just as her mouth gently parted "—that scar." His gentle caress on the old wound on her chin made her flinch ever so slightly as she realized that he did not plan to kiss her at all. He'd asked her a question. A devastating one. The scar.

God, the scar!

She'd like to forget she ever had it, but it's not like she ever could. It stared back at her every morning in the mirror. Rick's mark.

She remembered the screaming that night, the fury in Rick's eyes. *No one leaves me. No one ever leaves me.* Him grabbing her by the hair, then smashing her downward. The horrible crack of the glass coffee table. Her mouth filling with the copper taste of blood.

How did Tack know the perfect question to ask?

"I don't talk about that scar," Cate said, which was the truth.

"Does that mean you're not answering?" Tack scooted her wineglass closer to her. Her head already swam. No way could she down another half glass. Not this soon.

"No," Cate said. "I'll answer." She tried to focus on what she could say that was truthful without actually giving anything away. She felt that once she started talking about Rick, she might never be able to stop. With the amount of wine swimming in her brain, she feared revealing more than she intended. Best not to reveal anything.

"I..." She was about to say *I fell.* It was the standard abused woman answer, wasn't it? She'd used that same lie a dozen times when people asked about bumps or bruises. But now, with Tack, she didn't want to use that same old lie. She was *tired* of lying. Why did she always have to take the blame? The *I fell* was just *one more way* she let Rick off the hook. It was *one more way* she'd blame herself for what was clearly *his* fault. The cover-up of the abuse was almost worse than the abuse itself. At least when she was being hit, she *knew* it wasn't her fault. Covering up for him *made* it her fault. Made her culpable, because *she* was the one who took the blame in public. He had to take the blame only in private, when he asked for her forgiveness in tender moments of regret. And she forgave him so many times because she already thought, *It's partly my fault, anyway.*

And she was done with that. She'd been done with that the night she fled. She didn't know *why now*, if it was the wine, or the way Tack was looking at her, but suddenly she wanted very much to stop covering up for a man who didn't deserve it.

"Someone threw me down against a glass coffee table. It broke. A shard cut me," Cate said. And as soon as the words were out of her mouth, she felt such an enormous sense of relief. The truth was so freeing, so powerful, that she wanted to say it again and again. *I didn't fall. It wasn't an accident. An asshole who weighed seventy pounds more than me shoved my face into the glass. That's how I got this scar.* Anger washed through her, anger and outrage.

And it seemed to run straight to Tack. He

went stock-still. The color drained from his tanned face. "Someone *did* that to you? Who?" he demanded, looking like a cunning predator, all shrewd aggression. If this was what the enemy faced on the battlefield, she imagined they'd run for cover.

"That's a separate question," she said, only just managing to keep her head in the game.

"Cate," Tack growled, all mirth gone. "Tell me who did that."

"After you drink."

"We're not playing the game anymore." Tack shook his head. "Tell me."

Cate suddenly had the feeling if she told him, Tack might jump on the next plane and go beat the hell out of her ex. She almost would pay to see that. There was such urgency in his voice, he seemed *far* too attached to her answer. Did he like her so much?

"That's not fair." Cate's head swam. And Tack had barely touched his wine.

"Tell me." Tack took a deep breath and grabbed her hand. "Please."

Cate had a hard time focusing. Two glasses of wine in a relatively short time frame made her feel light-headed. The answer popped out almost before she realized she'd said it out loud. "My husband."

Tack let her hand go and jumped up from

the table, his metal chair falling back with a screech and a clang.

"Tack!" Cate cried, surprised at his outburst. He'd turned his back to her and was staring out at the moonlit palm trees on the beach.

"Was that the only time?" Tack's voice was so low, she thought she might have imagined it.

"No," Cate admitted. The cool ocean breeze died, and the air around them had gotten thick suddenly, hard to breathe.

Cate still felt confused by Tack's reaction. Why was he taking this so personally? She was flattered he was so angry on her behalf, but it just seemed an overreaction.

"Why…" Tack took a deep breath, clutching the railing before him. Cate sat, uncertain. He seemed like all coiled energy. She wasn't sure if he was angry or…something else. "Why did he do it? The coffee table?"

"He was angry because I'd accused him of cheating. He'd strayed before in our marriage, and I found a text message, and I wanted to leave…" Cate let out a long breath. "The guiltier he is of something, the more he took it out on me."

"Not right. It's just not right," Tack murmured, shaking his head.

Cate agreed. None of it was right. When she caught Rick doing wrong, his temper was by far the worst. She *knew* this, too, and yet she couldn't help it. She'd found the text messages on his phone, the *pictures* the woman had sent him. The invitation to come back to her bed. It was obvious what was happening. Despite all he'd done to her, Cate still found it in her to be angry about the betrayal. Though now, looking back on it, she wondered why she bothered to care.

It was probably because afterward, he'd be so apologetic, so sweet. She soldiered through the abuse because he was always so certain that he could hold in the monster inside him that it wouldn't get free next time.

"Things got out of control." That was the understatement of the year, she thought, as she remembered his white-hot fury, Rick grabbing a fistful of her hair. The screaming. *Her* screaming. The hard crunch of glass against her face.

"It's the reason I..." Cate was about to say *took Avery and left.* She was about to say too much. *What am I doing? Admitting to what I did?* She let the sentence just hang there. Her cover story was that she left after her husband died, not before. That was always supposed to be the story. She had a flash of the last time she saw Rick's face. The shock, the terror in it, before he fell. She shook herself. *It was an accident, nothing more. No more than an accident.* She never meant to hurt him. She only meant for him to stop hurting *her.*

Tack turned and looked at her for the first time, his dark eyes unreadable. "Did you go to the police?"

Cate threw back her head and laughed, a bitter cackle. "No."

Tack crossed his arms, confused by her laughter. "Why not?"

"My husband owned the police. He owned everybody. He was very rich and very powerful. He golfed with the mayor and the chief of police. One call from him and the charges would be dropped."

Tack frowned. "How did you know?"

"I tried once," Cate said, remembering the time she worked up the courage to head down to the local police station. How the sergeant there was concerned as he examined the fresh bruises on her arms and neck, even took down her statement vowing to follow-up, only to have the chief of police call Rick the very next morning. Rick had been furious. So angry, in fact, he'd made sure she couldn't move from bed the next morning. She never went to the police again. "Let's just say I learned that was a very bad idea."

"He paid them off." The words came out flat, angry. Tack's full attention was on her now, and she could see the vein in his forehead twitching.

Cate nodded.

Tack clenched his fist and looked away from her again, out to the beach bathed in moonlight.

"It wasn't every day…he got physical," Cate felt the need to say. "And when he did, he was so apologetic, so deeply sorry… Well, I know there's this perception that abusers are just evil people all the time, but…it's not like that." Instantly, she regretted it. Why was she defending the man who'd treated her so miserably? "It was very hard to leave."

"Did you try?" The question hung there without judgment. Tack turned to look at her with an intensity that made her a little uncomfortable. She finished the last of her wine, and Tack quickly poured more into her glass. Before she knew it, she'd taken another deep drink, her head swimming with alcohol and bad memories.

"I tried once." *One time before I actually succeeded*, she thought, but didn't say. Cate stared at the white liquid in her glass and swirled it around the edges. "He caught me before Avery and I had even made it to the state line. Then he had the nanny take Avery and fly him to a penthouse in New York. He wouldn't let me see him, wouldn't let the security of the building let me through. I didn't see Avery for two whole months. He told me if I ever tried anything like that again, he'd make sure I'd never see my son again."

"There are laws. The courts. He wouldn't be able to do that."

Cate shrugged one shoulder. "He said he'd tell them I was unstable. He'd have witnesses and the best attorneys money could buy. I knew I had no chance at winning that battle."

"So you ran."

"So...I..." Alarm bells went off in her head. How did Tack know she ran? She never said she ran. "Why do you say that?"

"You live here now. I just assumed..."

Cate stared at Tack a beat, but the wine clouded her ability to process her suspicion. She shook her head, hoping to redirect the conversation. "I know all this sounds crazy. I should've left him before...before things got so bad."

The muscles in Tack's jaw flexed. Cate could feel his anger. "No man should ever hit a woman. Period."

"But if I'd left him earlier..."

"No man should ever, under any circumstances, *hit* a woman. It's not okay. It's never okay. This is not about what you should or shouldn't do, this is about *him* being an asshole." Tack squinted. "But it's wrong. What your husband did to you. I...I hate men who hurt women." His fist tightened more, and he glared at it. "Someone should do something about it."

"It's no use. He's..." Cate stopped herself in the nick of time. Her husband was supposed to be dead, and she'd almost admitted he wasn't. She'd almost given away her whole cover. "He's gone."

"Right. You said he died? Car accident?"

Cate nodded. She wanted fiercely to change the subject. The lie felt all wrong now after sharing something so raw and so real. She wanted to tell him the whole truth, but she knew she couldn't. Not with Avery's safety at stake.

Then she wondered why she'd shared any of it. She stared at her wineglass, feeling the heavy weight of regret. She'd nearly blown her cover. And Avery's. To a man she barely knew all because of some stupid drinking game she was too old to play, anyway. She felt a rush of emotion—the fatigue of living a lie, the fear of being found out. She was so very tired. It was all too much.

She glanced at Tack and saw a flash of pity in his eyes. That was the last straw.

She shouldn't have shared so much. Not only was sharing dangerous, but now Tack thought of her as a pitiful thing—an abused wife. Was there anything more pathetic? She wasn't a victim, she wanted to shout. She'd fought back. She'd made a life for herself. She hadn't just sat back and taken what Rick had dished out. She'd left him. The triumph she'd felt minutes earlier of admitting the wrong he'd done to her melted away now as guilt crowded in—she was the one who still had so much to lose.

She shot to her feet. "I…I need to go."

Tack reached out then and grabbed her wrist. He gave a gentle tug and suddenly she was in his lap, their faces dangerously close.

"Don't go," he said in a gravelly whisper. He put his arm around her, and he felt so big and strong and steady. She wanted to lean into that strength. Be protected. When she met his understanding eyes, she saw compassion, not pity. She also saw want. She'd forgotten what that felt like. To be seen and understood. She'd been living her lie of a life for so long, with only Mark and Carol knowing the truth. And they hardly ever talked about it.

Cate's head spun a little with wine, but she knew exactly what she was doing when she leaned forward and kissed him.

CHAPTER ELEVEN

THE MINUTE HER lips met his, Cate felt the entire world melt away. It was all Tack, his soft but firm lips pressing against hers, his hands tightening possessively around her waist. His lips parted and she tasted him, their tongues meeting in a delicate dance. God, she wanted this man. Everything about him drove her crazy—the taste of him, the strong muscles in his legs that she could feel pressing against her backside, the thickness of the back of his neck as she wrapped her arms around him.

The kiss turned deeper, more insistent, and so did Tack's hands. Suddenly, she wanted them everywhere. Pure instinct took over as she hungrily devoured his mouth. She'd forgotten what this kind of passion felt like. Now, it all came roaring back, as if she were sixteen again, caught up in the throes of her first crush. Her hands roamed down his impossibly broad shoulders, down to his solid biceps. The man was a walking wall of muscle. She felt so little in his lap, so girl-like. The feeling gave her a little rush.

Cate felt his lap come alive. And in an instant thought, *Nothing small down there. Or soft, either.*

The wicked thought pushed her on and deepened the kiss. God, was he the best kisser on earth? It sure seemed that way.

He broke from her and she gasped for air, shocked by how he muddled all her senses. All she wanted to do was taste him again.

"Should we take this inside?" he asked her, and all she could do was nod. Speech was beyond her. Cate straightened as if to slide off his lap, but Tack had other ideas. He simply swooped her into his arms and stood, his mouth meeting hers once more. She had no time to think about how easily he carried her, as if she weighed nothing, or where he was leading her. Before long, she felt the soft comfort of bedding beneath the small of her back. Tack laid her down, mouth still on hers. He broke free long enough to look at her.

"This okay?" he asked. The question was open-ended, but Cate couldn't imagine saying no to anything he wanted to do to her right in that moment. She wanted it all.

"Yes," Cate managed to say, grabbing the front of his shirt and pulling him down on top of her. He came with little resistance, and she soon felt his sweet weight on top of her. She ran her hands under his shirt, her fingers exploring the tight muscles of his chest. They were so hard and so…defined. She circled his chest with her hands, and he moaned beneath her touch. Her breath quickened.

It had been so long since she'd been with a man, she wondered if she could remember what to do.

She could feel him stiffen on top of her. *She* was having this effect on him. The thought made her feel giddy with power. He wanted her. Cate let her hand slip down between them, feeling his growing hardness through the front of his shorts. The unmistakable bulge felt large in her small palm. Turns out, his shoulders weren't the only thing broad about him, she thought with a wry grin. He responded instantly to her touch and groaned once more, a husky kind of growl into her mouth.

Turned out, she did remember, she thought. She remembered what to do just fine.

His hands roamed beneath her shirt, cupping her lacy bralette, massaging her. Now it was her turn to feel a rush of heat, to moan beneath his gentle touch as he gave her a tender squeeze. God, so good. It had been so long since she'd been touched like this. She never wanted it to stop.

He broke free of her mouth, studying her face as if he wanted to remember it forever. "You're so beautiful, Cate. So very beautiful."

The sincerity in his eyes drove her wild. She met his mouth once more, hungry for his touch, for more. She went for the front button of his shorts, but he grabbed her hand.

"No," he murmured. "No…not yet."

Before she could question him, he'd run his hand up the side of her leg, rising all the way to her deepest center. He slipped his hand inside her lacy underwear, and she gasped.

"Oh, Cate. You're so…wet," he murmured into her mouth, surprise and awe in his voice. It drove her mad. She kissed him fiercely. *He'd* made her that way. Hot and trembling with need.

He touched her gently, delicately, driving all the nerve endings in her body to the very brink. Just when she thought she'd fall over the cliff, he stopped. She burned with a desire she'd never felt before, like an addict in dire need of a heroin binge. She just wanted… more.

"Please," she murmured against his mouth. She wanted him inside her. She wanted to feel him in the most intimate way possible. Once more, she grabbed for the waist of his shorts, but once more, he moved out of the way.

"Ladies, first," he said, and his magic fingers went to work again. They drove her wild with want, with desire. She arched her back, desperately wanting more. He stoked the flames expertly. Before she knew it, she was tumbling wildly, hopelessly over the edge.

She came in a strangled shout as a wave of pleasure nearly knocked her against the bed. Her heart thudded in her chest, and she felt like she would never be able to catch her breath.

"There, that's better," he murmured against the hollow of her neck, laying gentle kisses as he withdrew his fingers. She felt so spent, so entirely wrung out. Yet she wanted *him*, wanted him to have the same pleasure. Cate reached out for him, but again, he stopped her.

"I'll get mine another time," he said. "I'm in no hurry."

She should've fought him, but her arms felt like jelly. She'd never come so hard before, at least not like that.

"You...know what you're doing."

Tack grinned. "I told you, I'm good at tactical maneuvers." He laid a gentle kiss on her nose.

Cate giggled. "I can attest to that," she murmured, her eyes suddenly feeling impossibly heavy. It was the wine. She wasn't used to drinking so much, so fast...or having amazing, mind-blowing orgasms, either. The toxic combination of feel-good hormones and alcohol made fighting sleep a losing battle.

"Rest," Tack commanded, pulling her into his arms. She'd never felt so cared for, and so safe. She found herself drifting off in the warmth of his embrace.

TACK HELD CATE, listening to the sound of her delicate breathing. He tightened his grip on her, and she let out a delicious, satisfied little moan. He'd never seen a woman so open before, so willing to come for him in a way that left nothing behind. She'd been the most beautiful woman in the world when she'd orgasmed, and all he wanted to do was make it happen again. His groin stirred with frustration. He wanted *inside* her, in the worst possible way, but he also knew it wouldn't be fair to her. Not when he was still working for her ex-husband, not when she didn't know why he was really there.

God. How was he going to tell her? He wasn't. He couldn't. He could never, ever let her find out. He'd been so wrong about her. About everything. Mark had been right about a terrible man in her life, and that man was his own *boss*.

He looked at her sleeping peacefully in his arms, so amazingly trusting, so free. Her mouth fell open ever so slightly. He could get a DNA sample right now. It would be so easy.

So he could hurt her again?

Tack stared at the scar on her chin and felt the anger rise in his belly. He'd believed her, every word she said. There was a brutal honesty about it, a core truth that even he could see. And this truth made him furious.

He'd been working for the wrong side.

All this time he thought he'd been doing the right thing, bringing a greedy and potentially dangerous woman to justice, reuniting a boy with his caring father, saving Adeeb. He'd been on his high horse, believing he was so very right. But now that Tack knew his boss was a scumbag, he'd clearly made the biggest mistake of his life.

He berated himself for not asking Allen more questions, for not being more skeptical of the story of the homicidal socialite. But he had just wanted to fulfill the promise he'd made to the man who'd saved his life. He didn't want to turn over any rocks, find any worms. He wanted a clean-cut and simple mission. No complications.

He was usually so good at seeing all the angles, but not lately. Not in a long while.

How could he have been so blind? Why didn't he see the possibility before? Cate hadn't been a killer. She'd been a victim. It all made sense now—when Carol had seemed hesitant at the mention of Cate's ex. Now he knew why. Because the son of a bitch had been beating the hell out of her. He knew men like Rick Allen. Knew how they thought the world belonged to them, dripping with entitlement, because the rules simply didn't apply. They didn't live by a code, they only lived to get what they wanted, and they didn't care how they did it. Or who got hurt in the process.

Tack felt anger rising like bile in his throat. He wanted badly to teach that man some manners, but how?

Cate snuggled into him, and all he wanted to do was protect her from her ex, from anyone else who'd ever try to hurt her again. He stroked her hair and realized he'd made the worst mistake he could—he'd fallen for this beautiful woman.

But what happens when she finds out I've

been working for her ex? Tack already knew. She'd hate him. She'd see it as the ultimate betrayal, because it was. He wanted her more than he'd wanted any woman he could remember. But he couldn't take advantage of her like that. It would be the worst kind of violation.

Yet how could he ever admit the truth? He didn't know if he could. What would he even say? *Hi, Cate, I'm working for the monster you managed to escape. Wanna date?*

And what *really* happened that night she left? The night she almost killed her husband? Now he wasn't so sure. Was it self-defense? Or did she just snap?

Either way, this mystery was far from solved.

The fact remained that Rick Allen was in a wheelchair and Cate put him there.

The phone on his bedside table came to life with a low beep. From where he sat he could see a text from his employer.

Time's up.

His stomach sank.

He wished he'd never taken this job. It was going to cost him. It already had.

How could he decide between Cate and Adeeb?

Adeeb was like a brother.

Cate just might be…someone he could fall in love with. Maybe he already was falling in love with her. But Adeeb… If he or his family died, Tack would never forgive himself. But he wasn't going to hand Cate over to this monster, either.

He needed more time to figure another way out, more time to figure out what to do next.

He wanted Adeeb to be safe.

But every bone in his body wanted to protect Cate, as well.

How could he possibly do both?

The wheels of his mind began to turn. How would he fix this? He'd have to think of something.

His phone lit up with an incoming text from his boss.

Tack glared at his phone.

You took too long to get the sample. I sent someone else. Already en route.

Allen was supposed to give him twenty-four hours! He hadn't reached that time limit yet, but apparently, the real estate mogul didn't mind changing rules mid-game. It was one more thing he hated about the man.

Wait. I can still do this, he typed.

You want your visa? Better get the sample first.

He felt his palms sweat. He'd have to derail the new guy. But then what? Allen would be relentless. There'd be another one after that, and another. Unless they could get a bogus sample and convince the mogul this was a dead end. It was their only shot.

But first he'd have to figure out who the new detective was and intercept him. At the airport? The hotel lobby? It wouldn't be the first time he'd have to run an op that required him to be in two places at once.

CATE WOKE UP to an empty room. She sat up in bed, startled as if from a bad dream, and glanced around for a second, not knowing where she was. Then she saw Tack's seabag at the foot of the bed. *Tack's room. God! What did I...*

Then she remembered. The wine. The kissing. Tack and his magic fingers.

And then she'd fallen asleep? In his bed! What was wrong with her?

She waited for any sound in the room or adjacent bathroom, but heard nothing other than the distant sound of waves crashing on the beach. Quickly, she scrambled out of bed. She checked the clock by the bedside table. It was three in the morning. She hadn't meant to stay this long.

Where is Tack?

Cate wondered if this was his polite way of telling her he'd had his fill? That somehow, she wasn't welcome anymore? She didn't know of many men who'd leave a willing woman in their beds and then *hoped* she disappeared while they were gone, but then again, she didn't know what to make of the fact that he wasn't here.

And Cate was 100 percent sober. All traces of the wine had fled and now she felt the violent urge to flee. The panic rose in Cate's throat. A pulse thrummed in her temple that started an uncomfortable rhythm she knew was the beginning of a headache, probably from the wine she'd now handily metabolized. She jammed her foot into one of her flip-flops.

She had to get out of there. She marched to the door to his room and opened it, ducking her head into the hallway and doing a quick check. Only empty white tiles stared back at her. No sign of Tack, or any other guest for that matter. Thank God. She hurried out, wearing only one flip-flop and marched down the hallway to the elevators. She pressed the call button and waited, wondering if she ought to make a beeline for the stairs.

Come on, elevator! The resort is half empty, so you can't seriously be in use right now.

What seemed like an eternity passed before the light flicked off, and the loud ding of the incoming elevator blared through the hallway. Cate cringed at the sound, glancing around once more as she slipped into the elevator and quickly pressed her floor number. Breathing a sigh of relief, she slumped against the wall. As the doors closed, she felt a small twinge of disappointment. Had she wanted to be caught? Wanted Tack to drag her, caveman style, back to his room and finish what he started?

God, what he started. Cate's cheeks flushed with heat as she remembered how deftly his hands had explored her body. How every light caress sent her barreling closer to the perfect peak of ecstasy. Would she want that again? *Yes, please.* Not to mention the impressive bulge she'd felt in his pants. Her mind whirled with the delicious possibilities of what they could do together, but she had no condoms. She wasn't on the pill. Why would she be? It seemed an unnecessary expense for a single mom not planning to date. Was she just going to hope Avery didn't wind up with a little brother or sister?

She felt like she'd been hit with a cold splash of frigid water. How could she even think about being so reckless? What would happen if she were pregnant *and* essentially a fugitive on the run? No. She could not let that happen. No way.

The elevator arrived at her floor, and she dashed out as well as she could maneuver with one flip-flop and quickly reached her door. She slid her key card in the lock and swung it open, only to have the door behind her open and Carol pop out. Had the woman been waiting to hear the lock beep?

Cate whirled. "Carol, God, you scared me!"

"Back already?" she asked, grinning.

"It's like three in the morning!" Cate murmured, quickly kicking off her one flip-flop behind her and into her suite. No need for Carol to see she'd come home wearing just one.

Carol perked up at that. "It is? Oh, then…"

"What are you doing up?"

"I fell asleep on the armchair, and when I heard your key, I had to say hi." She glanced at Cate, taking in her full rumpled appearance. "Looks like *someone* got what she needed?"

Cate's hands flew to her hair, and she realized she was probably a hot mess. She hadn't checked her appearance in the mirror before she'd left Tack's room. She could only imagine what she looked like—wild sex hair, smudged mascara, the works. "I…" Cate trailed off. What *did* happen in Tack's room? She'd gotten something. But had he? He seemed particularly fixed on *not* getting any himself. She wondered what that meant.

"Well, I…I…"

"You're actually stammering." Carol beamed. "My girl got laid!" Carol bounded over and gave Cate a huge hug. "I'm so glad for you."

"You sound like I just won an Olympic medal."

"Well, for you, you kind of did. I was beginning to wonder if you'd ever get back up on that horse again."

"You know that's not my focus. I need to be here for Avery."

"And you are. We *all* are, but you also need to have a life, Cate." Carol grabbed her shoulders and shook her a little. "You don't deserve just to waste away here, trapped by your past."

"But aren't I, though?" Cate thought about what it would be like to level with Tack, to tell him the truth: she wasn't who she pretended to be. She was in fact a fugitive. What kind of man would ever agree to be with a woman if they'd have to run from the authorities their whole lives? Would he turn her in? She thought about his reaction to news that her husband had hurt her. Could he protect her from him? She shook her head. No one could protect her from Rick. No one.

"At some point, you're going to have to let someone in," Carol said.

"I've got you. And Mark. Avery and Grace."

"Someone besides us. We can't be all of what you need." Carol let her hands drop from Cate's shoulders. Part of her knew her friend was right, and yet the other part was scared blind. How could she trust a near stranger with that secret? How could she trust anyone?

"You know Rick has that reward. How can I...I mean, how could anyone turn that down?" The last Cate had heard, Rick offered a ten-million-dollar reward for anyone who could find her. One million for a simple lead on her whereabouts. In a world where money talked, Rick shouted. Loudly. Who could keep a secret when there was that kind of money at stake?

"Money isn't everything." Carol patted Cate's arm. "And don't worry about Avery. He's fast asleep on my sofa. Mark or I will get him to school in the morning." She yawned. "Probably Mark! I'm going to go to bed. I'm glad you had fun." She grinned.

"I didn't say I had fun." Cate crossed her arms.

Carol just chuckled. "You didn't have to."

CHAPTER TWELVE

CATE WOKE UP feeling a little like the whole evening might have been a dream. Had she really let Tack touch her…everywhere? She got up, threw on a sundress and was thankful that Carol had gotten Avery off to preschool that morning, wondering whether she'd see Tack that morning, wondering if it would be awkward… After all, maybe he'd taken one look at her old stretch marks on her lower abdomen and thought, *No, thank you!* Maybe that's why he didn't want to…get naked with her? She loved what he did to her, and yet she wondered why he wasn't taking any pleasure for himself? Tack puzzled her.

And part of her wondered what he'd thought when he'd gone back to his room and found it empty. Was he disappointed? Relieved? Did she want to know if it was the latter? She couldn't concentrate on anything all morning, her focus worse than a toddler's as she headed down to the front desk to relieve Mark from night-desk duty.

"About time," he grumbled when Cate arrived at five past nine. "Carol's already called three times, just so you know."

"Did she tell you about..." Cate suddenly felt so incredibly embarrassed. Having Carol celebrating her reentry into the world of sex-having adults wasn't exactly the kind of thing she'd *like* to share with Mark.

"Yes, she did." Mark eyed Cate with some degree of judgment.

"Well, I..."

Mark held up a hand like a crossing guard. "Oh, no. Don't tell me details. Carol told me *enough*." He rolled his eyes and made a sour face as if reliving an unpleasant moment. "I don't want to know *any* more."

Cate blushed pink. "I...I..." She took her seat, arranging her long skirt around her and studying it a bit too long to avoid eye contact with Mark.

"You're a grown woman. It's *none* of my business. Of *our* business, and that's what I told Carol." Mark picked up his clipboard. "Just be careful, okay?"

Cate nodded. "I'm trying to be."

Mark stopped at the edge of the check-in desk and leaned one elbow on the counter. "What do we know about this guy?" Mark sounded protective and territorial, like a dad.

Cate shook her head. "I don't know."

Mark grimaced. "I need to run that check like I promised. I'll have some of my people check into him, okay? I'll get the scoop for you. He might be a felon. You never know."

"That would be just my luck." Cate sighed.

"I'll figure it out. In the *meantime*, we need another one of those parties like last night's. We brought in more than enough to pay the mortgage this month."

"Seriously?"

Cate rolled her eyes. She didn't want a repeat of last night.

"Seriously. Better get the mai tais ready for the next one."

"Ugh," Cate groaned, but Mark just laughed as he made his way to the elevators. Cate glanced out the window to the pool and saw Paulo, their best maintenance worker, cleaning up the broken chairs and the mess the college kids left. He had two enormous trash cans full of beer bottles and was working on filling a third. Bottles didn't lie; the kids did turn out their pockets the night before. And would probably do so again the next weekend, and as long as the steady stream of spring breakers came through. Was this their answer for saving the resort?

Cate shuddered at the thought.

"Penny for your thoughts?" Tack had somehow managed to sneak up on her, and she whirled around, shocked to find the six-foot-four marine hovering near her shoulder. How did he move so quietly? Like a damn panther.

"Where'd you come from?" she squealed in surprise.

"Iowa, originally," he answered, and grinned. "By the way, I believe you left *this* in my room last night?" He held up her missing left flip-flop, and Cate felt her cheeks turn a shade redder than a tomato.

"Oh, uh… Yes." She grabbed the shoe from his hand and stashed it on her lap.

"I found it *in the bed*, under the covers." He grinned that beautiful, sexy smile, and Cate felt her insides turning to melted goo. Why'd he have to be so damn gorgeous? It would be easier to tell the man no if he had some hideous flaw. But he had none. He leaned closer to her, dipping his head so it was close to her ear. "I wish you had stayed in my bed last night."

His words sent a shiver of delight down her spine. She wished that, too. God, did she!

"You disappeared." She couldn't quite keep the accusation out of her voice. After all, she had woken up to an empty room.

"I went in search of a late-night snack. Thought you might be hungry, too, after all that...work." He let the word linger between them, his meaning clear. He smiled once more, and she thought it was the most enjoyable "work" she'd had in quite a long time. "Then, imagine my surprise when I come back and find you've made a run for it."

"I didn't run." She did, actually.

Tack just shook his head. Then his attention seemed to focus on a couple walking down by the pool. He studied them a moment before turning back to her.

"Well, maybe next time I'll have to make sure to keep my eyes on you." The way he was looking at her made Cate want that very much.

She was about to tell him they ought to skip the formalities and just go to his room *right now*, but the phone she carried in her back pocket rang. She pulled it out and checked the number.

Avery's preschool.

"I've got to take this," she told Tack. She pressed the phone against her ear. "Hello?"

"Hi. Ms. Dalton?" a worried-sounding voice said from the other end.

"Yes." Cate swallowed the fear that suddenly threatened to close her throat. "Is Avery okay?"

"He's…" The woman paused. "He's…uh… missing."

"What do you mean he's missing?" Cate's voice went up an octave. Tack, now fully invested in the conversation, stepped closer to her.

"We believe he took an unsanctioned walk away from the playground, and we currently have several teachers looking for him."

"When did he go missing?"

"About a half hour ago."

"A half hour?" Cate spat, her insides suddenly turning to ice. Thirty minutes was an eternity. She knew Avery liked to play spontaneous games of hide-and-seek, just like on the hotel grounds the other day, but for *thirty minutes*? She glanced at Tack, whose face looked solemn. "Did you check any trees on the property? He likes to hide in trees."

"We'll do that, yes, and maybe you should…"

Cate didn't want to let her finish her sentence. "I'm coming. I'm coming right now." She clicked off her phone and glanced at Tack.

"I'm driving," he said in a voice that left no room for argument.

TACK GRIPPED THE steering wheel of one of the hotel's vans and glanced at Cate, who looked pale and uneasy, in the passenger seat. Anxiously, she nibbled at the end of her index finger, a jittery habit he thought she probably wasn't even aware she did. All he could think of was how royally he'd screwed up. What if Mr. Allen's new man took Avery? What if he was too late?

He'd spent most of the night trying to figure out whether any planes had landed on the island, and the rest of it watching the hotel lobby for any signs of strangers. He'd been so certain Cate was the target, he hadn't even thought the boy would be in danger. Besides, his employer never made a move without thinking about a hundred steps in advance, so Tack just didn't think a snatch and grab would be on the menu.

"The preschool is right downtown, not too far from the grocery store. Do you know that street?" Cate asked. "If you go left here…"

He turned, even though he already knew where to head. The island was small; he'd remembered passing the grocery store on the way in.

"Between the tiki bar and the grocery, right?" he asked and she nodded. "I think I know it."

Tack's mind spun as he drove, trying to figure out all the angles. He wasn't sure he could. Maybe he ought to tell her the truth now. Lay it all out there, let the chips fall where they may. Then she'd have all the information. She'd hate him, but she'd have the information she needed to make the decision about next steps.

If they found the boy safely, then Tack had no doubt Cate would run. If she knew her ex was this close to finding her, she'd run. What choice did she have?

"You think he's okay?" Her voice broke his concentration on the road. He glanced over at her, managing to notice that she looked stunning in that sundress she wore, a faded gray that somehow made her eyes look even greener. She swiped a bit of hair from her face, and he noticed how perfect her skin was without makeup, even in this light. He felt guilty for noticing that at a time like this, but then again, he was just a man. And she was a damn fine woman. He couldn't help *but* notice.

"I hope so," he said noncommittally, wishing he could provide more comfort. But he'd lied to her enough. He thought a few white lies now just added insult to injury.

Cate reached out and touched Tack's forearm. He nearly jumped from the contact.

"Thank you," she said, her eyes moist and her voice trembling a little with emotion. "I...I just appreciate you coming. You didn't have to, but it means a lot to me."

Tack felt a sharp prick of guilt, like a sour taste in his mouth. *Of course I had to. I might be the one who caused this.*

But he couldn't say that, could he? Not now. Not when they didn't know if Allen had a hand in this.

"Avery likes to wander off," Cate said, almost as if trying to convince herself there was no foul play. "But he's never left preschool before."

"Why weren't they watching him?"

Cate shook her head. "I don't know."

They arrived at the small school, driving through the parking lot of the aquarium next door. The palm trees provided ample shade as they dipped into an empty parking spot. Cate sprang from the van, hardly waiting for Tack to turn off the ignition. She was through the glass double doors as Tack trotted to catch up with her. An iguana scurried out of his path as he strode through the doors. Tack wondered if being here at the school was a waste of time. Maybe he ought to take that van and head straight to the airport. If this was a kidnapping, if Mr. Allen intended to swipe his son, that's where they would be.

Cate was already talking to the distraught

teacher who'd lost Avery. She was a plump woman with silver-gray hair woven into a French braid. She twisted her hands and looked visibly upset.

"We normally do a head count *twice*, and I don't know how we missed him on the way in," she said. "Well, I do think I know what happened. The children were lined up, but we were missing one. Avery's friend, Pete. He went to look for him, I think, but I didn't realize he had gone. And now, with Pete back in line…" The teacher bit her lip. "I didn't count again. That was my fault."

"Are you sure that's the last place you saw him? In the playground?" Cate asked.

"Yes. He was on the swings."

Tack glanced at the swing set, which happened to be near the small wooden fence that surrounded the little play area. A sidewalk lay on the other side, and lush, pink tropical flowers bloomed there. The fence was low enough that an adult could've reached over and helped little Avery over it.

"Did you see any strangers near the playground? Any adults?" Tack launched the question, wanting to get to the heart of the matter as fast as he could. His gut told him this woman probably had no idea what had happened or any clues that could help them.

Cate, however, looked stricken at the very mention of a stranger, her thoughts obviously going to the darkest places imaginable. Tack hated to scare her, but he needed information. A description of the stranger. A car. He just didn't believe that this time Avery had wandered off. He knew he was jumping to conclusions without a lot of evidence, but he had a very strong feeling he was right. It was too much of a coincidence that Mr. Allen undermined him by sending a second detective and that Avery went missing the same day the scout was supposed to arrive.

"I don't think so," the teacher said, frowning. "But… Wait… There was a delivery truck parked near there. A brown one."

"Did you see the delivery driver? Was he in uniform?"

"I don't remember seeing him," the teacher said. "Just the truck."

Tack was almost positive somehow that the delivery truck was the key. He needed to get to the airport. To the cargo section. He had a hunch the boy would be there.

"Can we help you look?" Cate asked, biting her fingernail and looking as if she was going to have a nervous breakdown. Her concern for Avery was written all over her face. Tack hated that he'd likely caused that worry. Why hadn't he stayed at the airport last night? He should have. He thought monitoring the resort would've been enough. But he hadn't counted on Avery being a target. The old Tack would have. He was losing his edge.

"Absolutely," the teacher said. "Let me just call the other aides that are out looking and see where we should focus our attention." The teacher ducked back into her office.

Tack knew he needed to act. Time was running out.

"Cate, I'll be back," Tack said, knowing he had to get to the airport, and he had to do it now.

Cate whirled. "Where are you going?"

Tack opened his mouth to lie. He wanted to keep Cate out of it. He did. But he also knew it wasn't fair to her to keep her in the dark. Not about this.

"I'm going to the airport," he said.

"You think...Avery was taken?" Cate looked inconsolable now, all her worst fears playing out in the panic he saw in her eyes.

Please don't ask me how I know this. Tack wasn't sure he'd be able to lie. Not now.

"I think that's where we need to look," he said, turning to leave, keys in hand. "You stay here. I'll go."

"Absolutely not," she said, grabbing his elbow. "You're not going without me."

"Cate…" He wanted to tell her to stay. Her coming would just make things worse, would play right into Rick Allen's hands. She'd be walking into more trouble than she knew. "You shouldn't go. It's a long shot. I just want to—"

"You think my son's been kidnapped and you want me to stay here?" Cate tightened her grip on his elbow. "I'm his *mother*."

"Okay," Tack said, wondering when the next question would come, when she'd ask him *why* he suspected her boy might be at the airport. He knew he should tell her. In that moment, he knew it was the time to let her know. And yet fear strangled him. *Once she knows, she'll hate me forever. Any chance I'd have with her will be gone.*

So, he let the moment pass. Either way, he knew he'd regret it. Telling her or not telling her, he couldn't win.

"Let's go then," he said as they both darted to the van. "Can you look up flights to the mainland? I'll drive."

Cate pulled out her phone and anxiously fiddled with her skirt as Tack fired up the engine. "Looks like the next flight out is in an hour. There was one before that, but it was at six in the morning. No private planes that I know of."

Tack knew that six would've been too early. Avery had been missing only thirty minutes, anyhow, at least that the teachers knew.

"Thank God for this being a small island," he said. Small airport, fewer flights. "We have a chance, then, to catch them."

Tack turned onto the narrow, two-lane costal highway and quickly passed a slow-moving truck filled with bananas.

"Tack," she began, voice anxious. "There's something you should know."

Tack glanced at Cate. Did she know already? Had she guessed his secret?

"What is it?"

"I'm…I'm not who you think I am." Cate bit her bottom lip.

Neither am I, he wanted to shout. But now was not the time. How could he admit the truth to her now? That he might have upended her whole life? Put her boy in danger?

He shook his head. No, now was not the time to confess his sins. Or to make his conscience feel better. Now was the time to get Avery back.

An old hatchback cut out from a driveway in front of them, causing Tack to slam on the brakes and honk. He swerved around the vehicle and hit the gas. He needed to get to the airport.

"Cate, I know you," he said. He thought about the kindness he'd seen the last few days, the way she opened herself up to him when she laid in his bed. No, he *knew* her, probably better than she knew herself.

"But I haven't told you the whole truth. About me."

"It doesn't matter. I *know* you." And he did. So much better than she thought. He didn't want her to have to confess her sins to him, not when his sins were that much greater. Not when he'd put Avery in harm's way.

"Avery probably was kidnapped," she said. "But not by a stranger."

Tack just wanted this conversation to end. "His father is still alive," he said, not meeting her gaze as he kept his focus on the road and the approaching airport sign.

"How did you know that?"

"Let's discuss that later." Tack was already out of the car and happy to put off her question. He grabbed her by the hand and they trotted to the airport, sliding through the automatic doors and into the lobby that had only a handful of ticket counters. The sleepy tropical airport was open-aired at the side, the baggage claim having one entire wall open to the palm trees. A small baggage vehicle came and dumped a load of suitcases on the rotating carousel.

A small metal detector was set up in the middle, and a few people lined up to go through for the next flight. The airport only had three gates, so it wouldn't be hard to find Avery. Tack glanced at the security and noticed nobody was checking for tickets. St Anthony's island wasn't worked by the TSA, after all.

"Come on," Tack said, and they headed for the metal detectors, easily getting through because neither one carried a bag. Cate glanced anxiously back and forth, looking for her son.

After a second, she froze, tugging on Tack's arm. "There!" she murmured.

Tack turned in time to see Avery sitting on a chair at Gate 2, swinging his small feet and looking anxious, but calm. The boy was clearly scared. With him was a man he'd never thought he'd see again.

Derek Hollie. His former commanding officer. The one who'd made sure Adeeb's name was not in the running for the last of the visas. The man responsible for his court-martial.

Now, here he was, with Avery, working for Rick Allen.

Cate was already moving toward them, and had already called Avery's name. The boy jumped up when he saw his mom and started to run, but Derek grabbed his shirt, alarmed. He turned just in time to see them both.

"Tack Reeves," he said, a smug grin tugging at the corners of his mouth.

CHAPTER THIRTEEN

"DEREK HOLLIE," TACK SAID, his muscles tensing for a fight as he took in his former commanding officer clutching Avery's shirt. The boy wiggled and tried to reach his mom. Tack kept Cate behind him with one firm arm. He didn't trust Derek. Not as far as he could throw him.

"That's Captain Hollie to you, First Lieutenant."

Rank didn't have anything to do with where they were now, but there was no telling Derek that. He didn't deserve his silver bars.

"You *know* this man?" Cate's fingers dug into Tack's arm.

"Oh, we go *waaaaay* back. Third Battalion, the Fighting Ghosts, right, First Lieutenant?" Tack frowned as Derek grinned. "But that was a long time ago. Before we *both* worked for your husband, Cate."

Tack glanced over and saw all the blood drain from Cate's face. He himself felt like he'd been hit in the gut, all the air knocked out of him. This wasn't the way he wanted her to find out. He desperately wanted to explain, but he also knew he couldn't. Not now. Not with Derek here, holding on to Avery, not with the boy in the balance.

"I don't understand," Cate murmured in shock as she pulled her hand away from Tack's, moving away from him as if betrayal could be contagious. "What's he talking about?"

"Cate..." Tack wanted the one word to convey everything—how sorry he was, how wrong he was to ever doubt her, how he planned to return every dime he'd been paid. He reached for her arm, but she yanked it away.

"Don't touch me," she growled.

He knew words didn't matter now. He could tell by the look in her eyes, the heartbreak, the hurt, that no amount of explaining would probably ever help. He'd lost her. Probably forever.

"Oh, don't tell me." Derek shook his head. "Did you go falling for your mark? I see you still have trouble keeping your personal feelings out of the mission. You always did get too attached to the natives."

"No. I'm loyal to those who deserve it. Unlike you. You don't know what loyalty even means."

When Adeeb had needed him most, Derek had turned his back. And it had all been because he didn't like Tack. Never did like him the second he set eyes on him, probably because Tack questioned almost every decision Derek made. It went against the chain of command, but Tack wasn't going to be silent when mistakes were being made. Derek made it personal. And because Tack supported Adeeb, Derek was going to make sure that the translator didn't make it out of Afghanistan.

Cate glanced at Derek, the wheels in her mind clearly turning, and jumping to all the wrong conclusions.

"Give Avery to me," Tack told Derek, suddenly wanting nothing more than his old commanding officer to give him a reason to punch him in the face. Avery struggled against Hollie's grip, and he let out a whine. Soon, he'd be crying.

"This boy and his mom are worth a cool *ten* million. No way I'm handing him over. Why don't you give me her, and we'll split the fee?" Derek wore his hair close-shaven like he was still in the military. He still acted like a commander, too, one who never got tired of ordering everyone else around. "I don't know why *you're* being such a fool. Unless you want the money for yourself."

"I don't care about the money."

Derek laughed. "You always were a Boy Scout, but never did have any brains, Tack."

"Derek, give him back to his mother."

"Or what?" Derek wasn't as tall as Tack, but he was just as meaty. Tack knew already that the man fought dirty. Not that Tack would mind another go-round.

"Or I'll make you."

"You remember what happened last time you tried that?"

Tack remembered the day he'd found out Adeeb had been left off the visa list. Tack had marched into Derek's command center and punched the man in the face.

The court-martial came after that. And he'd do the exact same thing again if he could. Only this time, he'd hit him more than once. And harder. Much harder.

"Here you don't have any stripes on your chest," Tack said. "No MP to protect you, either." *No MP to pull me off you once we start. I will demolish you.*

"Mom?" Avery whined, scared, the boy not even squirming in Derek's grasp. He sensed something was wrong. The tension of the adults wasn't lost on him. Tack glanced at the boy, the innocent boy, and wondered how long Derek was going to use him as a shield.

"This boy is going back," Derek said. "You

should've done it, but since you wouldn't, now it's up to me."

"You're not taking that boy back. He belongs with his mother."

"That's not what the laws of the United States say, friend." Derek smirked and gave Cate a slow once-over, in a way that Tack didn't like. He seemed to enjoy watching her squirm. "That little island babe is wanted for felony kidnapping and attempted murder. Do you want me to go on?"

Cate visibly flinched. Tack resisted the urge to comfort her, to reach out and touch her.

"We're not in the United States, so you're going to let that boy go, or I'm going to call the police and *you'll* be arrested for kidnapping."

Derek paused a second, considering. "You want to involve the police? You sure about that?"

That would mean Cate's true identity would come to light. It could mean bad things for her and Avery. Tack glanced at Cate. "I'm sure," she said, through gritted teeth. "Give me back my son."

Derek glanced down at the boy and then at Cate. Tack wasn't sure what he planned to do. Fight? Run? Either option would be stupid. The man had to know he was painted into a corner. There wasn't a way out, not now. Tack was not going to let him get on that plane, and there was no way the local police would buy his story, not without proper paperwork, or an order from a US judge.

Tack glared at Derek, trying to read the man's twisted mind but couldn't. Eventually, however, he saw reason and let Avery go. The little boy ran into the waiting arms of his mother and squeezed her tightly. Tack heard a sigh of relief escape her lips, and she covered her boy's face with kisses, murmuring how much she loved him. Tack stayed back, making sure Derek didn't follow.

"Now we're going to leave," Tack said. "And you're going to stay away from us."

"Run, but you can't hide. That's ten million you're sitting on, and I plan to cash that in. No way you can keep your lotto winnings to yourself, bro. I'll be there. When you least expect it, I'll come to take it from you."

Tack knew it wasn't an idle threat. Derek didn't make idle threats. He glanced beside him, but Cate was gone. He turned and saw her rushing toward the exit with Avery. He wouldn't expect anything less. Fortunately, Tack had the keys to the van in his pocket.

"You're working for the wrong side." Tack backed away slowly.

Derek grinned, an evil confidence in his

face. "I'm working for *me* like always, brother. That's never the wrong side."

Tack moved to the exit, but never lost sight of Derek, who stood with his hands casually tucked in his pockets, making no move to pursue. Not that he'd need to. *He knows where his target lives and works*, Tack thought. He trotted through the automatic doors in time to see Cate slip into a waiting cab, Avery already inside. Their eyes met one last time. He wasn't sure what she was feeling. Anger? Fear? But what he did know was the look on her face meant goodbye.

CATE HUGGED HER son to her chest, feeling a rush of emotions—shock, anger, betrayal. She couldn't believe she'd been so blind. Of course Tack had been working for her ex-husband. Of *course* he'd been playing her from the start. Why else would a gorgeous ex-marine even be interested in her? How often had her ex told her that she wasn't naturally pretty? That it was all about the makeup and clothes she wore? The clothes *he* bought her. That she was naturally a skinny, flat-chested thing, a woman no one would be interested in, not without his money.

She'd actually allowed herself to think Tack had wanted her for *her*, and wanted to believe that he'd felt the same primal attraction she'd felt the moment she laid eyes on him in the airport. She thought their connection had been real.

Sitting in the cab and holding her son close to her side as the ocean breeze ruffled her hair through the open window, she felt a pang of hurt that went deeper than she ever could've imagined. She'd only known Tack a short time, and yet now she felt like her heart had been ripped out of her chest. Without even realizing it, he'd wiggled his way into her hopes and dreams, and while she'd never in a million years thought she'd imagine a future with anyone, she had let herself envision, just for an instant, a real connection with someone.

Now that was all shattered.

It was all a lie. A horrible lie. The worst kind of lie.

She felt her face burn as she remembered how she'd let herself go, how she'd *come* for that man, all pent-up passion as she lay in his bed. Now she understood why he'd chosen not to sleep with her. *He finds me repulsive, probably. He just flirted with me enough to get what he needed: information.*

The thoughts felt like ice picks through her brain.

She felt hurt and so horribly embarrassed.

Had he been laughing at her the whole time? Pitying her? Did he plan to take Avery for himself one night when she was passed out cold in his bed?

He belongs with his mother.

Tack had said those words just now in the airport, but how could he possibly mean them? If he had, then he never would've brought Rick Allen to her door.

Cate ran a hand through her hair as she stared out to the palm trees whipping by the window of the cab. She'd been so stupid. She almost lost her *son* because she'd let herself flirt a little, let herself believe that a man could be interested in her for *her*. She'd let down her guard *one time*, and now everything might be lost forever.

Rick knew where she was.

The thought terrified her. To get her son back, he'd kill her if he had to. *Or he'd see me rot in jail.*

Cate hugged Avery tighter. She couldn't let that happen. Or let Rick raise Avery. Would he become another abuser? Would he be abused himself? Cate didn't want to imagine those possibilities, didn't even want to let them in. She was going to keep Avery away from all that. At all costs.

But how?

She knew now how hard it would be to escape. How nearly impossible it would be to hide again.

I did it once, she thought. *I could do it again.*

"Mommy?" Avery whined next to her, glancing up with his big, innocent eyes. "Where are we going?"

She wanted to tell him *home*, but she knew now that the resort wasn't going to be home to them anymore. They didn't have a home. Not now. Maybe not ever.

She grabbed her phone from her pocket and dialed Mark. She had no idea what to do next, but she knew she needed to find the fastest way off the island. It was then that she realized he'd been trying to call her. He'd left two voice mails already.

He answered on the first ring.

"Cate! God! Where are you? Don't trust Tack. I just found out he's..."

"A private eye working for Rick," Cate finished.

"I was just going to say a private eye, that's what my sources tell me, but you're sure—he's working for Rick?"

"I found out the hard way." Cate sighed, her head suddenly throbbing, and her eyes welling up with tears. Why had she been so trusting? Why hadn't she asked more questions?

"Cate. What happened? Are you okay? Is Avery with you?"

"We're fine. For now, but…"

"Is Tack with you? Is he following you?" Mark sounded anxious, fearful even.

Cate whipped around in the cab, glancing out the back window, but didn't see the hotel van. No sign of Tack.

"No. We gave him the slip at the airport, I think."

"Thank God. Cate, he's dangerous." She already knew that, as he was working for Rick and it didn't get more dangerous than that, but she had a feeling Mark meant something else.

"Why do you say that?"

"The man has a dishonorable discharge. The man was *kicked out of the marines*."

Cate felt blindsided. Was everything she ever knew about Tack a lie?

"What for?"

"Assault. Nearly killed his commanding officer."

Cate felt her pulse speed up as sweat broke out on her lower back. Tack nearly killed *his commander*? In the military that was about the worst thing you could do. There wasn't an excuse for it that Cate had ever heard of.

"Doesn't look like he's Mr. Good Guy,"

Mark said drily. "A man like that doesn't have morals. Stay as far away as you can from him."

Cate felt sick suddenly. Yes, she'd been betrayed, but she'd thought it was all about money. She couldn't imagine Tack...violent. He'd talked to her son. He'd been with her alone. What if he had a hair-trigger temper like Rick? What if he was just as bad as Rick? And he was probably looking for her right now.

"We have to leave the island. We've got to go tonight. Rick knows we're here. Tack is looking for us." Cate felt the panic rising in her throat. Already she felt trapped, the small island shrinking every second. She felt so exposed, as if every car they passed on the small two-lane road might hold someone sent by Rick. She glanced behind them, out the rearview mirror of the cab, frantically searching for any sign of Tack. Was he following her? She didn't see the old hotel van. She hoped they'd lost him.

"He already sent another person after us, and you know he won't stop there," Cate said, thinking about Derek at the airport. *Had that been the man Tack almost killed?* That would explain the hostility between the two men.

Mark let out a low groan. This was bad news for him as well as her, and they both knew it. Rick didn't know Mark, but he would after this, and he'd dream up a way to make Mark's life difficult, too, Cate had no doubt. And he had a family to think about.

"Maybe you and Carol and Grace should go, too. Take what's left of petty cash. I know it's not much, but it might have to do."

"No, Cate. We're not going to run. I'm staying. Let him do his worst. I'll make sure the resort is kept running for you, or sell it if you need me to."

"Mark. No. You know this man. He'll ruin you." Cate couldn't believe Mark was even considering staying. He must be out of his mind. Rick had trumped up false charges on enemies before, sent them to jail, or worse.

"He'll try," Mark scoffed. "I'm not afraid of bullies."

"I know, but…" How to explain that Rick Allen wasn't just a run-of-the-mill bully? He was something far, far worse.

"Cate, what can the man do to me? I'm already running a failing resort, and I've got a *teenage daughter*. Believe me, she can do worse to her old man with one eye roll than Rick ever could."

Cate laughed a little, warmed by Mark's levity, and hoped he was right. It was too scary to think about what might happen to the Gurdas if he was wrong.

"Don't worry about us, okay?" Mark's voice

sounded solid and reassuring. "We're going to get you and Avery to a safe place right now. That's mission critical."

Suddenly, Cate felt a rush of gratitude—for Mark and Carol, for her true friends. They gave her a little bit of hope.

"What do I do?" Her mind whirled with fear and panic. She wasn't even sure of the right course of action. Go back to the resort and get their things? Hide out somewhere else?

"Tack knows the resort," Mark said. "Don't come here. We'll bring the papers and your bags to you. Do you have a place in mind?"

She thought about the island, and everywhere she could go just seemed too visible and required cash that she didn't have. She knew it wouldn't be safe to use her credit card anywhere, and she couldn't figure out how she'd get another hotel room, or even a booth at a restaurant, without one. Besides, the idea of sitting in a bar with Avery somewhere just didn't seem right. Nor did walking around a small strip mall.

She racked her brain, trying to come up with places that Tack wouldn't look for her.

"I know exactly where to go," she finally said.

TACK DID HIS best to keep Cate in his sights, without getting close enough to tip her off that he was following. He managed to drop back eight cars, and the curves along the cliffside highway would also help him blend in. Following her wouldn't be that difficult, but he knew catching her would be. The woman had a talent for disappearing, and he had a feeling she was planning to do that right now. She was in full-on flight mode, and it was all his fault.

He'd betrayed her, and he knew she'd never forgive him, but he only hoped she'd listen to him. He could help her. But running was a bad idea.

He knew Rick Allen, and knew that the best way to deal with a bully was head-on. Running only made things worse. Right now, there was a very real possibility Cate would face jail time for kidnapping her son, and the attempted murder of her ex-husband. Tack didn't know exactly how to ensure that Cate didn't go to jail and Avery could still see his mother, but he knew he could figure something out. If only he could think long enough about all the angles. He could find some way forward. But not if she ran.

If she ran, she was very likely to be caught. And that meant jail. And no more Avery.

Then again, if she stayed put, it might also mean jail. Tack wasn't blind to the reality of the situation. She'd taken her child out of the country for three years. And her allegations of abuse would be his word against hers, since the local police incinerated that report she filed all those years ago. Still, Tack would figure it out. There had to be a way to prove she was abused. Witnesses at the police station, maybe. *Witnesses who weren't in the pocket of Rick Allen?*

Even he had to admit that things looked grim for Cate.

And I'd been the one to paint her in this corner.

He didn't know how he'd make it up to her, but somehow he would.

He watched as the small taxi made its way around a truck turning left. He noticed that the cab drove past the turnoff to the resort, and Tack wondered what game Cate might be playing.

Tack gripped the steering wheel. Whatever it was, he would find out.

Tack checked his own rearview mirror, to see any cars that might be tailing him. He didn't trust Derek. Not at all. The man was probably the worst captain in the entire marine corps. The rules never did apply to him. He never cared about loyalty. About even his own men, just his own future. He wanted to be promoted more than he cared about what happened to anybody around him. Even now, Tack could feel the anger bubbling up in him, the righteous indignation. The man was an asshole, and now he was working for an even bigger one.

Tack didn't see Derek following him. He probably planned to stay right at the airport. *If I were him, that's what I'd do.* The quickest way off the island was by plane.

Tack looked ahead and saw Cate's taxi turn toward the green-blue water.

Scratch that. The best way off the island might just be by boat.

CHAPTER FOURTEEN

THE TAXI STOPPED at St. Anthony's Marina, and Cate leaned over and paid the driver the last of the cash she happened to have in her wallet. She grabbed Avery's hand and led him gently out of the cab as they walked along the dock.

"Boats!" Avery cried in little boy delight as Cate steered him along the row of impressive fishing boats and yachts.

Cate steeled herself. She couldn't believe she was considering doing this, but she also knew she had no choice. She and Avery passed by Terry Blake's obnoxious party boat, and she let out a long sigh. She had to be desperate to come groveling to *that* man. But Rick had found her. She was that desperate.

She pulled open the double doors of the marina's office and felt the cool air-conditioned air sweep over her. Terry owned not just the party boat, but the marina, as well. It was why he'd been so interested in buying the resort, less than half a mile down the road. With it, he'd wind up owning a fifth of the island. She saw Terry standing behind the counter, talking to his pretty receptionist, who was wearing one of his neon-green party-boat tank tops tied up under her bikini top.

Terry looked up, saw Cate and a smile broke out on his ruby-red face. His eyes were bloodshot, even though it wasn't that late in the day.

"Cate! So good to see you. What can I do for you?" He wiggled his massively overgrown eyebrows, making sure to make the innuendo obvious. God, was she really going to sell to this man?

I don't have a choice.

She took a deep breath and tried to send him her best smile, despite the fact that his overgrown gray chest hair stuck out of his button-up Hawaiian shirt.

"Could we...talk for a moment?" Cate glanced at the receptionist with the orange tan and the bleached blond hair, tied up in a messy ponytail. She was young and curvy, and seemed sweet.

"Who's this little guy?" the receptionist cooed as she eyed Avery. She swept around the counter in flip-flops and bent low enough to give Avery a little pinch on the cheek. "What's your name?"

"Avery," he said, shyly clinging to his mother's legs.

"Avery, do you like to draw? Want a coloring page?"

Avery looked at Cate, and she nodded, figuring the young woman was harmless. The receptionist grabbed a printout from the top of the counter along with a pack of four crayons. Avery grabbed them quickly and with excitement tottered off to a seat near Terry's office to color.

"Avery…" Cate called.

"He'll be fine there," Terry said. "Casey will watch him, won't you, hon?"

"Sure thing!" Casey cooed.

Cate hesitated. Terry leaned over and put his arm around Cate's shoulder. "I think we need to leave the grown-up talk to the *grown-ups*, you know what I'm saying?" Terry moved his arm down a little, and placed a suggestive hand on the small of her back. She nearly jumped out of her skin and bolted straight out of there right then. She didn't know what *he* expected, but Cate was going to keep this *all* business.

"Terry, I'm here to talk business."

Terry didn't lose a beat. "Good! Good. Then step inside," he said as he nudged her forward with his hand.

Cate glanced at her boy and figured he was right outside the office. Maybe it was best he stayed there. The less he saw of Terry, probably the better.

Terry pointed to a chair and Cate slid into it. Terry, however, sat at the edge of his desk, giving her a full-view of the strained buttons of his blue Hawaiian shirt, which seemed in danger at any moment of pinging off and hitting her in the eye. She tried to avert her gaze, as she was pretty sure if she stared, she'd be able to see belly hair poking out of the gaping holes.

"What can I do for you, honey?" Terry asked.

"This is all about business," she said.

"And wouldn't I like to *give you the business*." Terry snorted at his own joke and then shrugged. He had to have been drinking, Cate thought.

"Terry. I'm here because I want to sell you the undeveloped beachfront property."

Terry raised his eyebrows in surprise. "Really?"

Cate nodded.

"What about the resort?"

Cate thought about Mark's share of it. She couldn't sell that without talking to him first, and he'd said he wanted to stay. "No," she said, shaking her head firmly. "Just the beachfront property. It's right next to your marina. You could expand, or build your own resort right there."

They both knew that the beachfront was

what he really wanted. The parcel lay between the marina and her resort.

"How much?" Terry asked her, suddenly all business, all sexual innuendo gone.

"I just want a catamaran," she said, simply.

Terry blinked fast, as if she'd thrown cold water in his face. He couldn't have looked more flabbergasted. "But that's $350,000 at most. Your land is worth three times that."

"Are you going to take the deal or not?"

Terry squinted at her, clearly trying to look for an angle. "What's the catch?"

"I can't wait for a close on the land, and all the paperwork and everything else." Cate wanted to keep to the truth as much as possible. She needed Terry to go for this deal, and she needed him to do it quickly. Every second ticking by was one she couldn't afford to lose.

"What? Got the police after you?" Terry laughed, because the island police were notoriously slow to do anything. There were only four police cars and eight officers for the whole island.

"No," Cate said. *I've got someone way worse after me.*

"What about the deed and title?"

"Mark is bringing it."

"Now?" Terry hopped off his desk, as if he thought Mark might stride through his office doors at any second, which Cate really hoped he did. She'd told Mark on the phone to bring the deed, their suitcases and whatever food or supplies he could fit in his car. Terry paced a little, thinking.

"Just a catamaran? Which one?"

"How about the *Sweet Pea*?" He owned two catamarans, one yacht and a party boat. The catamaran she wanted was the newer of the two. It wouldn't be the easiest to maneuver by herself into and out of port, but she didn't have much choice at the moment. His yacht was too big, and the party boat wouldn't set out to sea.

"The deed to your beach property. For the *Sweet Pea*." Terry said it slowly, as if waiting for Cate to tell him it was all a practical joke.

"On one condition."

Terry looked wary. He was waiting for this. "What is it?"

"That I take the *Sweet Pea* today."

Terry relaxed. "That's it? Boy, you are in a hurry, aren't you?"

He had no idea. Cate felt antsy. Too much time was ticking away, and Terry needed to just get on board. "So, do we have a deal?" She offered him her hand.

Terry looked at her and suddenly joy spread across his face. "You bet your sweet ass we've got a deal." Terry grabbed Cate's hand and shook it with such force Cate's teeth rattled together. She might hate Terry on principle, but at that moment, she came dangerously close to wanting to hug the man. Of course, one whiff of his cheap cologne instantly dislodged that notion, but still. Terry and his gold-chain-wearing, hairy self might've just saved her life.

Cate checked her phone and saw a message from Mark.

I'll be there in two minutes.

Cate felt tears sting the back of her eyes. How grateful she felt at that moment to have hope.

TACK PARKED THE hotel van in the marina's parking lot. Thanks to the view of the boats and open water, he'd know if a boat left. And then what? Hijack a boat like he was in the middle of a spy movie?

Maybe.

He weighed his options. He could rush in and demand to speak with her. Try to get her to see reason?

I don't even have a plan. What am I going to tell her? Just face the music and hope for the best?

Even he knew that sounded ridiculous.

He knew the facts: she'd taken her boy away

from his father and out of the country. It was parental kidnapping under Illinois state law, which made it illegal for a parent, even if he or she was legally married to the other parent, to conceal a child from his or her spouse for more than two weeks. It had been close to three years, so he was fairly sure she'd violated that law, and probably a dozen others that Allen's lawyers would cite. But surely there was a defense? He'd reached out to a family law friend he knew from high school who'd gone on to law school. He glanced at his phone to see if his friend had a chance to respond. Just then, his phone dinged with the answer he was looking for.

If your friend was fleeing domestic violence, which is hard to prove, she could use an affirmative defense. Sometimes this works.

Tack quickly texted back. No jail time?

Not if the judge believes the mother and son were really in danger. But you'd need proof. Police reports. Restraining orders.

Tack winced. He already knew there wasn't a paper trail for the abuse. Cate had said Allen had the local cops in his pocket.

Not to mention, aside from the kidnapping charge, there was the money Cate took. Though proving that wasn't joint property since they were married at the time would be hard for Allen to do.

Still. There had to be a way of proving her abuse claims. Tack might even be able to talk some sense into his former boss. At least, he'd be willing to try. It would be easier to negotiate a truce if Cate didn't run. If she gave herself up.

Still, if he were honest with himself, at this moment all he wanted her to know was that he was sorry. That he didn't mean for any of this to happen, that if he'd known the kind of man Allen really was, he would never have led him straight to her.

But he had. He knew that. He'd have to work to make it right somehow.

Walking away was simply not an option.

Tack saw another car drive up to the marina, and he saw Mark Gurda get out, then pull several suitcases out of his trunk. His wife, Carol, was with him, too. He watched as Cate and Avery emerged from the office of the marina, and Carol embraced Cate in a long hug. He couldn't tell from here, but it looked emotional and intense.

Tack sat upright.

She was going to flee now. Tack knew he had only minutes to catch her before she'd sailed off to God knew where.

He watched as Mark helped Cate load her suitcases on a catamaran moored to the dock, and saw him toss tote bags full of supplies onto the waiting deck. Mark pulled out a manila folder from one of the bags. Cate nodded, and they exchanged a few words that Tack couldn't make out. He never was a good lip-reader. Then, Mark, Cate and Avery marched back into the marina.

Tack launched himself out of the van and made his way straight to the catamaran, with a quick glance about to make sure no one saw him. He hopped onto the boat and made his way to the lower decks, slipping inside the first cabin door. Inside, was a small queen-size bunk—must be the master suite—flanked by the boat's likely only working toilet. He slid the door closed again and waited.

"YOU BE CAREFUL, NOW," Mark said, giving Cate a big hug on the dock as they stood beside the massive boat. Carol stood with them, shading her eyes from the bright Caribbean sun.

"I will," Cate said, turning back to see her

son happily sitting on the bench bolted to the deck, wearing an oversize bright orange life preserver. Seagulls circled above them, their high-pitched calls sounding like an invitation to the sea. White clouds covered most of the blue sky, but none of them looked too threatening. Not that she had a choice on the matter. She'd sail, rain or no rain.

"You sure you don't want to stay?" Carol asked, frowning. "We can fight him."

"How?" Cate already tried fighting Rick. She remembered her futile trip to the police station. *How do you fight a man who owns everything...and everyone?*

"I don't know. But we can fight him together. It's not right what he did to you...and it's not right for you to spend your life running for a crime *he* committed."

"I know what I did." Cate wasn't innocent, either. She couldn't pretend that.

"Rick deserved what he got." Mark wouldn't be swayed. Cate could see that on his determined face. "Any reasonable judge would think so."

"Reasonable or not, the law is the law." Kidnapping, attempted murder, theft. She was sure Rick had a laundry list of charges on an indictment ready to file the second she stepped back on American soil. She wasn't going to spend her life in jail, away from her son. She'd run now and keep on running if it meant keeping her son safe. The idea of him in Rick's control made her flesh crawl.

She glanced at Mark and saw his ruffled, not-recently-combed silver-white hair and his rumpled Hawaiian shirt. She looked at Carol, too, her best friend and confidant. Cate felt a strong pang suddenly. What if she never saw this couple again? They were more than her best friends. They were family.

Cate gave Mark a big hug. She released him and felt teary-eyed. "Don't go crying on me!" he commanded. "Then I'll start crying, and I'm ugly when I cry."

"Believe him," his wife said and chuckled a little. "Oh, sweetie." Carol squeezed her tightly. "Be safe."

"I'll figure out a way we can be in contact," Mark promised her.

Cate nodded and then got on the boat, her feet feeling almost as heavy as her heart. Mark undid the rope latching the boat to the dock and tossed the slack up to her. She grabbed it and waved at him.

"You sure you don't need any help getting this monster out?" Mark called.

"I've handled worse," she said, thinking she'd have to learn to make do. She was once again alone. It was her and Avery against the world, just like the night she'd fled Rick's mansion with her boy in her arms.

As she pushed out to sea, she turned back to see Mark and Carol waving to her from the dock. She threw up an arm, and then she focused on steering her boat. She broke free of the little inlet, and not too long after found herself on open blue-green water, the waves mostly calm as they lapped against the side of the boat. She felt a weight lift off her shoulders as she put space between her and the shore of St. Anthony's. She glanced at the lush, green tropical place she once called home and wondered if she'd ever see it again. She'd become attached to the island, and the people there. That had been her mistake. She couldn't afford to let anyone close to her, not when she had to keep one step ahead of Rick.

She'd have to keep everyone away from them.

Especially men like Tack.

The very thought of him made her tighten her grip on the wheel.

The island grew farther in the distance, now just a little green-and-brown clump. She steered east, and with any luck, in a day they'd arrive in Aruba. Then, she'd have to make contact with Mark's friend at a marina there. It wouldn't take long for Rick to find out she'd bought the *Sweet Pea*, and once he did, he could probably track them through ports around the world. She'd decided to get a different boat, downsize to one she could more easily manage. Then she'd stock up with more supplies and head out into seriously open water.

Avery happily watched the waves as the sea spray misted them both. The wind kicked up a bit, and Cate altered her course, even as the waves grew choppier. Avery nearly toppled off the bench as Cate reached out a steadying hand. As they got farther from land, the clouds above them grew darker and more menacing. She checked the radio, but found no warnings of an extreme storm. The burner phone Mark bought her told her the weather report for the day was scattered storms, but nothing too serious. If they kept sailing, it would probably just be a little bit of rain. At least, she hoped so.

"Hang on," she told Avery and he nodded, all seriousness. She was about to take him belowdecks, tell him to wait it out in the cabin if it got worse, but just then the wind whipped the rigging hard. A latch flew loose, a rippling sail suddenly flapping precariously in the wind. The boat dipped sharply to the right, and Avery gave a little shout as he hung on with his little fists. The big boat was unwieldy for one person, but she also knew she had no choice in the matter. She would trade the boat in at Aruba, but in the meantime, she needed to get there. And she wouldn't do that with a detached sail.

She clicked on the autopilot and ran to the front of the boat, careful to hold on to the rigging as she went, always aware that one false step could send her into the sea. She couldn't afford any mistakes. Cate reached out and tried to grab the flapping rope and latch. It must not have been properly secured in the first place to come ripping out like that. She focused all her attention on the latch as she went about attaching it once more, and securing the sail. That problem solved, she thought, just as an eight-foot wave collapsed into the side of the boat, sending it careening off to the left.

Cate lost her grip and went flying backward, and in a heart-stopping moment, frantically grasped at air. A shout escaped her lips as she sailed away from the deck, hitting her head on the steel railing with a clunk. She bounced to the deck, landing awkwardly on her wrist, and the rocking boat nearly slid her straight into the water. But Cate managed to frantically grasp the railing, though one wrist seemed not to be working quite right. She could only really hold the railing with one hand. And one hand wasn't going to be enough as the boat once more bucked under her. Salt water sprayed her face, drenching her entire left side. She shook the water off her face and tried to grip the rail with her other hand, but it seemed to uselessly flop. What was wrong with her wrist? She had to pull herself up.

"Mommy!" she heard Avery cry from the wheelhouse in distress. She wanted to tell him to stay, not to worry, but she got another face full of salt water. The water drenched the railing, and it became slippery beneath her fingers. She wasn't sure how much longer she'd be able to hang on.

Then she felt a strong hand grasp her arms.

"I got you," a familiar voice boomed over the rush of the waves. She thought for an instant she was imagining it, but then he pulled her aboard, and in an instant, she was inside Tack's strong embrace. "I see you're still as accident prone as ever. You okay?"

She coughed, salt water stinging her throat

as she fought to get away from him. "Where did you…"

The boat lurched again, sending her into his chest. The rest of her words were muffled in his muscles.

"Let's get you and Avery belowdeck," he said.

"No!" she shouted over the wind as she shook her head fiercely. "No, I'm sailing this boat." He would probably take the opportunity to turn them around and head right back to St. Anthony's, and probably to Rick's private jet, which would take her straight to jail.

"Your wrist—" he nodded toward it "—might be broken."

"I'm fine," she said, though a slow throb had begun deep in the joint. She didn't have time for injuries now. She had to get them to Aruba. That's all she cared about.

"Let me help."

Cate eyed him warily, wondering what he planned to do. Hit her over the head? Tie her up? Had he already radioed information to that Derek guy? She almost expected a helicopter carrying her ex to make an appearance at any moment.

Small drops of rain hit the deck. The sea remained choppy, and the fact was, she didn't have time to worry about any of that now. Given the storm above them, Rick would probably not be risking a helicopter ride. At least that was a small consolation.

"Okay," Cate said. Better to have Tack in sight at all times than out of sight and sabotaging the boat. She let him steer, but kept a close eye on the compass, making sure they were headed in the right direction. He took direction from her without question, quietly going about the work of tightening rigging and securing the sails as they moved through the storm.

Cate glanced at Avery, who sat quietly, watching the two of them, as if having Tack appear on the boat was exactly what he'd planned. Every once in a while, Tack would check in with the boy, make sure he was okay or ask him if he needed to go down belowdecks. The gesture would've been heartwarming except for the fact that Tack had lied to them, was probably still lying to them, and nothing he said or did could be trusted. Anger simmered in Cate as she watched Tack take on the role of Boy Scout. He wasn't one of those.

The rain stopped, and the clouds above them began to part as a little bit of sunlight filtered through. The seas calmed, as if nothing had ever been amiss. It was amazing how quickly storms blew in and then evaporated once more out on the ocean. She felt grateful for the respite from the weather, but as she watched Tack talk to Avery, she knew they were far from out of the storm.

CHAPTER FIFTEEN

THE THREE OF them sat in the small galley belowdecks, eating a simple dinner of canned
soup while the autopilot steered the ship into
the evening. Cate and Avery sat tucked on one
side of the table, and Tack, with his impossibly
tall frame, hunched on the other side. The close
quarters made Cate more than aware of Tack's
broad shoulders, which seemed to take up all
the space—and the air—in the tiny cabin.

What she wanted more than anything was to
yell at Tack, confront him about his betrayal,
but she couldn't do that. Not with Avery there.
She didn't want to worry her son.

Cate would have prefered a solemn, angry
quiet to the meal, but Avery couldn't seem to
ask Tack enough questions. Tack, for his part,
answered them patiently. He hadn't yet tired
of the Boy Scout act, Cate thought bitterly.

Her wrist ached, and she had to eat with her
left hand, which proved challenging as a bit of
soup dribbled down her chin.

Avery, for his part, couldn't keep his eyes

off Tack. "What's that for?" Avery asked Tack, who wore a T-shirt with a logo from his marine regiment and division.

"It's the group of marines I served with in Afghanistan."

"You were a marine? Does that mean you've killed people?"

"Avery!" Cate scolded.

"It's okay," Tack said, holding up a hand. "We can talk about that when you're older."

This didn't end the boy's fascination. "You shot a gun?"

"Yes."

"You own a gun?"

"Yes, three." Tack gave the boy an amused smile. He was taking the fifty questions like a champ, but Cate wasn't happy about it. She wanted to tell him to stop encouraging the boy. *After all, you want to take his mother away.*

"What kind?"

"Well…a rifle for hunting and…"

"What do you hunt?"

Cate began to tune them out. She hated guns and had always made sure Avery stayed away from them. If she were honest with herself, her dislike of weapons was her ex's doing. He had an extensive gun collection, an entire roomful, and enough ammunition to survive a zombie apocalypse. She never liked the way he used guns, either. The threat of them always seemed to lie between them. When he got angry, and sometimes when he hit her, he'd tell her, "You're lucky I'm not the kind of man who'd shoot you," as if that was any consolation, as if that should make her feel better.

Once, after a particularly bad blow up, Cate woke up the next morning to find a loaded pistol lying on Rick's pillow, the barrel of the gun pointed at her. The safety off. Rick was nowhere to be found, but the gun spoke volumes about exactly what he intended to do if she didn't get in line.

Of course, Rick denied it later.

I just forgot to put it away. You're blowing things all out of proportion. As usual.

But Cate wasn't stupid. She knew he'd put it there on purpose. He'd put it there to remind her who held the power in the relationship.

Cate did everything she could to make sure Avery stayed away from guns, and now, here Tack was talking about them so casually, as if they were Lego blocks, or any other toy a boy might be interested in. It made her furious.

She didn't want Avery even thinking about guns. His interest in them made her worry. Was he like his father? Did this mean he'd grow up to be just like him?

Cate swatted the thought away. Avery was

nothing like his father. He was sweet and giving and loving. He was no monster.

"Let's talk about something other than guns," Cate said, not looking up from her bowl.

"Mommy doesn't like guns," Avery proclaimed to Tack.

"I think we can figure out something else to talk about," Cate said, taking another sip of chicken noodle soup. Her left hand wobbled, but she managed to get the spoon to her lips this time without spilling any. She cradled her right wrist in her lap. It had begun to throb and swell a little. She hoped it wasn't broken.

"Sure we can," Tack agreed. "I have an idea. Let's talk about where we're going."

Cate nearly spit out her soup. She coughed, a noodle wanting to head down the wrong way, and wheezed. Tack easily reached over and patted her on the back, and she was too shocked and angry to do anything but let him.

"Mommy, you okay?" Avery asked, concern on his adorable face.

When she finally recovered, she took a little sip of water. "I'm fine," she muttered, but she had no intension of telling Tack where they were headed. So he could bust out a satellite phone and call her ex so that he'd have an army waiting for them when they docked?

No.

Cate planned to keep her eye on him the entire time they were on the boat. If he tried to relay a message, she'd...what? Tackle him? She glanced at his size once more, looking like a giant at doll's table. She could not take him on. Not directly.

"So where are we going?" Tack pressed. He studied her, and she could feel the weight of his gaze as his dark eyes never left her. She squirmed uncomfortably, wishing he'd just let it drop.

"It's a surprise," Cate said, trying to keep the anger out of her voice, though the words came out tight.

"I love surprises!" Avery declared and then, suddenly, he yawned, a big gaping one. He usually lost steam around this time, and he was getting sleepy. Cate was grateful for the distraction.

"I think it's time to get ready for bed, young man."

"Mommy!" he protested. "I'm not even tired." Then, of course, he yawned again. She knew tired when she saw it. She worked on getting her boy ready for bed while trying to keep Tack in sight at all times. Tack cooperated, sitting at the table, casually sipping at his can of Coke.

Within a few minutes, Cate had Avery tucked into one of the bunk beds, a grand adventure for the four-year-old. "This is the best bed *ever*," Avery declared as he rubbed his sleepy eyes.

She tucked him in with his favorite stuffy, Mr. Cuddle Bear. As she kissed him on the forehead, she sent up a silent prayer that she could keep him safe, that Tack stowing aboard the boat hadn't ruined everything. Then she turned back to Tack, who watched her slide the cabin door shut. He'd been rummaging through the cooler and managed to come up with a sealed bottle of *blanco* tequila from the cupboard.

"You came prepared."

Cate shook her head. "That must be Terry's."

"Well, in any case, I need a drink. Do you?" Tack asked as he worked on loosening the top.

Anger still rumbled in her chest. *How dare Tack act like everything is fine? How dare he act like the two of us are casual friends grabbing a drink?*

"Don't make me drink alone." He flashed a brilliant smile, and Cate hated the power it had over her. *I still care.* She hated to admit that, but it was true. She was still attracted to the man who'd betrayed her in the worst possible way.

Her wrist ached, and she didn't have any Advil. Tequila might be the next best thing.

Though I need to keep my wits about me. No drunken mistakes this time. I want to be perfectly sober so I can defend myself if the real him shows up. The violent one.

Cate worked hard to keep on her poker face. She knew all about walking on eggshells, making sure not to trigger someone's temper.

"Let's have that drink above deck," she suggested, nodding upward. She didn't want Avery to overhear anything.

Tack quirked an eyebrow. "You going to throw me overboard?" His wry smile told her he was kidding, but the serious look in his eyes said he wasn't taking anything for granted.

"I might."

"Let me have my last drink first," he said as she ducked into the stairs and followed he followed upward. Topside, a brilliant full moon hung in the dark sky. A million stars glimmered, crowding the sky like pinholes of light through a sheet of dark paper.

"Wow," Tack said, glancing up. "I haven't seen that many stars since…Afghanistan." He sighed. "I did bad things there. But nothing as bad as when I took Rick Allen's money. Cate… you have to believe me, I'm sorry. I have a reason. I do. If you'll just hear me out."

The apology took her by surprise. Cate wasn't expecting it, and it deflated her anger a bit. Then, she realized, he could just as easily be lying. It could be another manipulation to get into her good graces, to use her once more.

Cate remained silent, not sure if she wanted to hear more or if she wanted to push him into the water. Part of her wished he was still *in* Afghanistan, then he wouldn't be here, messing up her life.

"Cate, I know you're angry. I know you…" He seemed to search for the right words. Then he took a swig of tequila. He offered her the bottle, but she refused. *I have to keep alert. Be ready. For when Mr. Hyde shows up.*

"*Angry* doesn't even begin to describe it." She crossed her arms and sat on a bench, glaring at him. How dare he upset her up-until-then perfect life? She probably shouldn't provoke him, but she couldn't help it. She was angry. "Avery and I were happy. Carol and Mark and Grace…they were our family, and now we might never see them again."

The hopelessness of that fact spoken out loud suddenly hit her. She might never see Carol or Mark *again*. She and Avery were truly alone. Alone in a dangerous world. She glanced at the bottle in Tack's hand. Now she needed it.

She gestured for it, and he gave it to her. She took a drink, the liquor burning her throat all the way down to her stomach.

"I didn't know. You have to believe when I took this job that your ex was very persuasive. The things he said..."

"What did he say?" Cate really wanted to know.

"He said you tried to kill him. He said you stole millions. He said you were a sociopathic social climber who only cared about money and who stole his son from him."

Cate took another deep swig of tequila, welcoming the burn as it slid down her throat. Pretty soon, she wouldn't be able to tell what was anger and what was tequila.

This was reckless, but she couldn't help it. *He's dangerous*, her mind screamed. Why was she being careless? Because everything seemed so hopeless.

"Of course he did," Cate said, sounding bitter. "He loves to play the victim."

"And he also told me he could help my friend, the interpreter, Adeeb. Remember him? He has a wife and a daughter, Cate. They're stuck in Afghanistan, hunted by the Taliban, because I got crosswise with Derek, the man you saw today. He made it his mission to screw Adeeb to get to me, but Adeeb is a good man and didn't deserve that. He sacrificed so much for me and my marines, and all I want to do is give him the fresh start he's earned with his blood and tears."

Cate had nothing to say to that.

"Rick promised you a visa," she said, realizing that this had never been about her at all, or even money, it had been about Tack's friend. About not leaving him behind. About keeping a promise.

"Yes," Tack said and nodded.

He could've been lying. Hadn't he lied about the dishonorable discharge by failing to mention he'd gotten kicked out of the marines? He hadn't retired. Not by a long shot.

"Was Derek the officer you attacked? Was he why you were court-martialed?" Cate couldn't keep it back any longer.

Tack's head shot up, surprise darting across his face. "You know about that."

"Mark found out. Was it true? Did you nearly kill your commanding officer?"

"Derek exaggerated," Tack said, frowning. "I hit the son of a bitch all right, but I didn't try to kill him. But he wanted me to hit him. He was baiting me. It was his plan to have me court-martialed. That's why he refused to help Adeeb."

Could that be true? It sounded plausible. Cate relaxed a little. She felt relieved, she realized. Relieved there was an explanation. Then the reality of the situation sunk in.

"Now, you have to choose between me... and your friend." Cate already realized the outcome of that decision. How could he pick her over him? She hadn't saved his life. She'd not served beside him in a war zone.

"I don't want to choose," Tack said. "There has to be another way."

Cate knew he'd have to choose. Or maybe she'd make the choice for him. By running as soon as she could.

"Tell me what really happened. The night you left Allen." Tack slipped the bottle from her hands and took a sip.

"Are you trying to figure out if I'm a killer? If I'm somehow less redeemable than Adeeb?" Cate wasn't proud of the words coming out of her mouth, but at least they were honest.

"You know I don't think you're a killer. I just want to know your side. I've heard Allen's. I want to know everything that happened *because I care about you*."

"Do you care about me? You weren't honest with me."

"Cate, I couldn't be. I wanted to be honest with you, but I just couldn't. I owe Adeeb. I thought...this was the only way for him."

"Isn't it still?" Cate hadn't seen how anything had changed.

"I don't know. I hope not. Maybe not." Tack reached out and grabbed her hand. "Will you tell me what happened that night you left? I just want to know."

Cate stared up at the thousands of stars and listened to the soft lap of water against the hull of the boat. Everything seemed so calm now, so unlike the storm just hours before. She felt that if she could stay at sea, she could find peace. A real sanctuary. She didn't want to relive that night at the Allen mansion.

"I don't owe you an explanation."

"That's true. You don't." Tack took another sip of tequila. "But Rick said you tried to murder him. That you lured him upstairs, and then you shoved him when he wasn't looking. He said you laughed while he fell down the stairs, that you left him for dead at the bottom. Did you?"

Rage burned in her chest. How dare he? Is that what he'd told the police? A bitter laugh tried to work its way out of her mouth. He wasn't the victim. Far from it.

"That is not what happened."

"Then tell me."

She felt herself right back in that moment. "I told him I wanted a divorce, that I was done.

He hit me so hard, I fell to my knees in the kitchen."

Tack visibly flinched, his jaw tensing, but he remained silent.

"He'd pulled me up by my hair," Cate continued, her voice sounding detached, cold in her ears. These were facts, nothing more, almost as if they happened to someone else. *You can cry about it or you can get over it.* Her memory of it wasn't even her memory; it was as if she was floating outside her body, watching him take her hair in his fist, whip her head up. She cried and begged him to let her go, but he would never do that. She realized that in that very moment. He'd never let her go. He'd kill her first. "I had no choice but to follow him up the stairs. He told me I could never leave him. He told me I belonged to him."

She could see herself in her mind's eye, crying, mascara running down her face. She wore a bright blue taffeta gown, blood from her face dribbling down on the front. He'd been in a tux. There'd been a time when she'd blame the alcohol for outbursts like this, but now she knew the alcohol just brought out his true self. His mean self.

She'd been angry with herself for bringing up the divorce then. She should've known what would've happened, but part of her couldn't put it off any longer. She'd endured the long limo ride home and a laundry list of his complaints about her behavior during the evening. She'd just had enough—of his never-ending list of criticisms, of all the ways she failed at being perfect, of all the ways she continuously disappointed him, when *he* was the disappointment. *Not* her.

She remembered Mark and Carol, and how kind they'd been to her, and she'd begun to see with perfect clarity that she wasn't the one who deserved this. She was done with him putting all the fault on her, when *his* glaring faults were never up for discussion. She was tired of taking the blame.

"He kicked me at the top of the stairs, hard. Knocked the wind out of me," she said, continuing her story as Tack stared grimly at her. "I rolled down the first step of the landing. He lifted his foot to stomp me. Hurt me some more." What happened next came from pure, protective instinct. "I reached up and grabbed his foot. I twisted it. He lost his balance."

"He fell."

"He tried to grab the railing, but..." She shook her head, remembering how she'd flung his foot away from her, a purely instinctual move. Had she realized he'd fall? She didn't know. All she knew was that she wanted him away from her.

It had been enough to topple his equilibrium. She still remembered the look of shocked surprise on his face as he tumbled, his hand just missing the railing as he snatched thin air.

"Did you want to kill him?" The question hung in the air between them.

"I...I didn't think about that. I just wanted him to stop hurting me."

"So you did what you had to do." Tack nodded. "Sometimes, the worst option is your only option."

"I didn't mean to kill him. But..."

"You didn't call for help, either."

Cate shook her head. Tack handed her the bottle of tequila, and she took a deep drink. "I knew... I just knew when he woke up, he'd kill me. There's no way he'd let me live after...I hurt him like that. I just knew, beyond a shadow of a doubt, he'd kill me. So I got Avery, packed a quick bag and left."

"And the millions?" Tack leaned forward on the bench, resting his forearms on his knees.

"I took my jewelry, which he kept in his safe. Technically, it was mine, though he'd bought it. It would be cheaper for him than a divorce. He didn't sign a prenup with me. It was one of the reasons he could never let me leave him. I'd take half his fortune."

Cate glanced up at the stars again, half hoping she'd find a different reality there. If she'd known money would cause her such problems, she would've insisted on the prenup in the first place. Then maybe he wouldn't have hit her.

Then again, she thought sourly, he probably would've hit her, anyway.

"Wait…" Tack sat up, his back ramrod stiff. "Allen told me he had an iron-clad prenup. That the only way you could get his fortune was by killing him."

Cate shook her head. "He's lying. No prenup. You can check with his attorney, if you want. He told everyone in his life he didn't need one. That he knew what he was doing. That men who had prenups weren't real men because they couldn't 'handle' their wives. It was a whole control thing with him. As long as he kept me in line, then everything would be fine. And when he couldn't keep me in line anymore…"

"He'd kill you." Tack slapped his knees in anger. "Son of a bitch."

"My thoughts exactly." Cate laughed a little. She relaxed a bit. A little voice in her head told her if she'd been Tack, she might have believed Allen, too. Why wouldn't she? Rick Allen was a persuasive man, and very good at pretending to be something he wasn't.

"The crazy thing is, he can't even let me get out of jail," Cate said, shaking her head sadly. "When you think about it. When I got out, I'd still be entitled to half his fortune. If I go to jail, I'm almost certain I'm never coming out. He'll see to that."

Tack stood, clasping and unclasping his fists, as if looking for something to hit. She'd wanted to spare him the truth, but Adeeb's fate and hers weren't that far apart, really. They were both marked for death.

"If he wasn't dying, I'd kill him myself," Tack murmured.

Cate went stock-still. "Say that again?"

Tack glanced at her, his dark eyes widening. "You don't know. Then again, why would you? The man keeps everything a secret."

Cate still wasn't sure she'd heard him right in the first place. Her heart sped up. Could that be true? Could he really be…?

"That's why he hired me, why he's so determined to find you, and find you now," Tack said. "Rick Allen has only a few months to live."

CHAPTER SIXTEEN

CATE FELT HERSELF REELING, and it had nothing to do with the gentle lilt of the ship beneath her feet.

"He's…dying?" She'd never in a million years imagined he'd die before she did. He was always such a huge, looming figure in her consciousness, a kind of malevolent force that would live forever. She felt shock. No matter what Rick did to her, she'd never wish death on anybody.

Yet this changed everything. Would it be possible? A world without Rick Allen? A world without her looking over her shoulder every other minute, without wondering when he'd catch her?

"What's wrong with him?" Cate couldn't imagine what could fell such a determined and stubborn man. Cancer?

Tack's eyes widened. "You don't know what happened when you left?"

Cate felt like she was suddenly trapped in a small tunnel, the walls closing in on her.

"When I left? I know he lived…" He survived a fall that should've killed another man. One of the many reasons Cate had started to feel he was indestructible. She'd tried to find out more, but the stubborn recluse didn't reveal anything. He never gave interviews to the press, and he was nonexistent on social media. All she knew was that his new real estate deals proceeded as usual and there was no obituary, so he'd lived.

"The fall down the stairs," Tack continued. "It paralyzed him. Severed his spinal cord."

Cate felt like she'd been sitting next to a grenade when it detonated. "He's…"

"In a wheelchair," Tack said. "And his lungs aren't working properly, as well as the muscles that help him breathe. He doesn't think he has much time left."

Cate felt all the air whoosh out of her lungs. As much as she hated the man, she never meant him that kind of harm. She felt a wave of guilt wash over her. And then, came fear. She'd taken away his legs, his dignity…not only would he kill her. He'd be sure to make her suffer. *Maybe even make Avery suffer, too, for her sins*.

Cate popped to her feet and began an anxious pacing. "I d-didn't know. I didn't mean to…"

Tack stood, as well. "I know you didn't," he

said in a calm and reassuring voice. He moved in front of her. She stopped and looked up at him, his dark eyes studying her in the moonlight. The twinkle of a thousand stars were just beyond his head. How she wanted to trust him, to believe in him at this moment. How she wanted to walk into his arms and be comforted... And more. Yet she couldn't.

"You're working for him," she said aloud, finding courage deep within her to say the truth she knew had to be said. *In fact, Rick could've hired him to kill me.* The thought sent a cold shiver down her spine. It made perfect sense. Why even bother extraditing her? Why bother with sending an assassin to jail to shiv her in the shower, when he could just get rid of her on this very boat, right now, in the middle of the Caribbean.

Sure, it would leave Avery an orphan, but knowing Rick he'd prefer Avery raised by one of his cousins than her, or even a paid guardian.

"I'm not working for him anymore." Tack put his hands on her shoulders. She tried not to back away from him. *Stay calm*, she told herself. *Nothing will help by panicking.*

"You have to help Adeeb. I know that's why you're doing this," she said. He might not want to kill her, but what if it literally came down to her life…or his friend's? What would he do?

"Just be honest with me, did Rick send you to kill me?" she asked him, unable to hold back anymore. If death was coming, she wanted to know it and look him in the eye. She wanted to be ready.

"Why would you say that?" Tack looked taken aback as he dropped his hands from her shoulders. Shock flicked across his face. "No. Of course not. My job was just to find you. I don't…I don't kill…" He stopped, suddenly, turning his back on her, flustered, as if he'd just remembered he did. Then, she remembered Afghanistan. He'd been evasive when Avery had asked him. That meant he probably had.

"I just… If you're going to do what you have to do, I just… I want you to promise me to keep Avery safe."

It seemed like a ridiculous request. Asking him for mercy, but still. Maybe Rick planned to keep his son and only heir alive. She hoped he was good enough to do that. She wanted Avery with her, but if he couldn't be, then all she wanted was for him to be safe.

"I'm not going to hurt you, or your son," Tack said, turning and meeting her gaze with a stoic look of his own. "I promise you that."

His brown eyes offered loyalty, and maybe even something more. Either that, or he was an amazing actor. The way his dark hair curled down across his forehead made her want to sweep it away.

Tack took another step closer and suddenly they were toe-to-toe. Her fear fled, and the uneasiness she felt turned to something like anticipation. She felt the danger like static electricity between them, or was it primal attraction? She had to crane her neck to look at him, and all she wanted to do was kiss his sensual mouth. God, he was such a good kisser. The memory of his hands on her made her feel hot all over, tingly. Was she attracted to the man who might end her life? She might be too far gone to save.

He took both of her hands in his.

"Cate, I know I've betrayed your trust. I am so very sorry. I didn't know. I never would've accepted this job. I would've found another way for Adeeb." His eyes never left hers, and she felt spellbound for a minute. He was saying everything she wanted to hear. Her heart sped up. "I think I'm falling for you."

For a full minute her heart seemed to stop. He was falling for her? As in *in love*? Then her brain kicked on like a rickety old air-conditioning unit, blasting through her hope.

He's still playing me. A second ago, I thought he was here to kill me, and now I'm supposed to believe he's in love with me? Even worse, he's going to sacrifice his friend for me? How can I live with that?

"But you can't abandon Adeeb. You can't choose me over him." The thought made her sick to her stomach.

Tack shook his head. "I'll just have to find another way. Maybe ask my senator for help again. Maybe, if he lives past the election, there will be changes to the immigration law."

"No." Cate couldn't live with that. Or could she? If it was her and her boy up against someone halfway across the world that she didn't know? Would she really choose the man she didn't know? She felt overwhelmed and confused.

"Cate, I want to be with you."

"But Rick will never stop until he gets me. He won't ever stop. Even if he dies, he'll make sure his estate keeps after me. Somehow. That's just how he works. His revenge will outlive him. There's no reason to be with me, Tack. I bring nothing but baggage."

"Cate, there's every reason to be with you. You're gorgeous, kindhearted, brave and smart. You're everything a man could ask for."

Why was he so persistent? She was on the

run and had next to nothing, except the ring and this boat.

"But I'm not rich."

"Who cares? I've got some money saved. I can care for us."

"What?" Cate couldn't believe what she was hearing.

"And even if I didn't, I can work. We can both find work somewhere. We'll make do. I know we will. All you have to do is trust me."

Could she do that? She badly wanted to. Standing before him now, the gentle sway of the deck beneath their feet. All she wanted to do was believe him.

"But how long before you start resenting me for Adeeb? What if he dies before you can help him? You'll blame me and Avery for his death, and you'll be right."

"No."

"Why should I believe you?"

"All I can do is show you that it's the truth."

Tack pulled her closer to him and dipped his head, covering her lips with his. For a frozen second, she stood stock-still, unsure of what to do. But feeling his warm body against hers, his tender lips gently kissing her, her body took over. She kissed him back with an enthusiasm she forgot she had. Despite all the insanity around them, despite all her doubts, it felt like the most natural thing in the world, and oddly, the most dangerous. She deepened the kiss, and the fire in her belly grew, but also, so did his passion, as she felt him harden through his clothes against her belly.

"Oh, God…Cate," he murmured, leaning into her touch. She kissed him and then broke away. "Cate, I want to be inside you," he groaned, the need obvious in his voice. For a golden moment, she thought, *I want that, too*, before reality crashed into the moment.

She couldn't do this. Not here. Not now. Maybe not ever. She couldn't trust him. As much as she wanted to. She couldn't.

He tugged at her clothes, but she stepped away, releasing him. He let out a moan.

"I…I…just can't."

Tack nodded, as if he understood. "You can trust me, Cate. I promise you that. I'll spend the rest of my life proving it to you if I have to."

The rest of his life? Cate's heart leaped at his words. How could he promise that? It sounded like he was proposing. *He'll say anything to get back into my good graces, and he might be delusional now, but how long before the guilt about Adeeb catches up to him?*

For a second, her will wavered. Her arms already itched to be around the back of his neck, her body pressed to his. No matter what had happened between them, she had to believe the spark between them was real.

But were his words real? Could they really make this happen? Could *she* live with blood on her hands? Adeeb's blood? His young daughter's? She didn't know.

Yet she wasn't sure. Might never be sure he was telling her the truth.

She took another step back, the boat beneath her feet rocking gently in the waves as the autopilot took them into the night.

"I don't know, Tack. I just..." She badly wished she could erase the last twenty-four hours, go back to the simpler time when he was just a sexy tourist who'd taken an interest in her.

I should've known then something was wrong. Why would someone so amazingly sexy be interested in me? It's just like Rick said. I was a nobody.

She hated that Rick's criticisms still rang true after all this time. Her insecurities welled up, and she started to feel the wave of worthlessness that always washed over her anytime she let her ex into her head.

"We both know you wouldn't have taken a second look at me if I wasn't your assignment." Cate hugged herself as she spoke, bracing herself for the inevitable confirmation in his eyes.

Tack shook his head. "That's not true," he said. "You're a stunningly beautiful woman, Cate. You turn heads everywhere you go."

"No. That's not true. I'm plain." Rick told her that. Cate's father, too, back when she was a lanky, awkward teen.

"Who thinks you're plain? Whoever said that needs their eyes checked." Tack gently laid his hands around her arms and squeezed. "You're gorgeous, Cate. I fell for you nearly the moment I laid eyes on you, *despite* all the reasons I shouldn't have."

He moved closer to her, and once again she felt his magnetic pull, the charisma that she found nearly irresistible. This close, she wasn't sure if she'd be able to resist him. All she wanted to do was feel his mouth on hers once more. What did that make her? Desperate?

It was all a lie.

"You were assigned to follow me. Take an interest."

He sighed heavily. "Yes, you were my mark," he admitted, nodding. "I was supposed to keep a level head, but I never could. Not with you."

"That night…in your hotel room…" Cate almost couldn't get the words out, her humiliation burning in her throat. She remembered his hands on her, how he'd taken her to places she hadn't been in years. How he'd made her feel completely out of control.

"Everything I did, I did because I wanted to. It wasn't a ploy."

"But you…you didn't want to…" *Have sex*.

Understanding finally dawned on Tack. "I didn't want to take advantage of you. Not without you knowing the truth. I thought if I did, you'd never forgive me, and frankly, I might not have forgiven myself. I wanted…"

"If I came, it would be less of a betrayal?" She thought about how vulnerable she'd felt in his bed. Would she have let him touch her if she'd known the truth? No.

"I'm sorry, Cate. I'll keep saying it as long as I need to." He lifted his hand and stroked the side of her face. "You're so gorgeous," he murmured. "And you're even more beautiful when you come."

No man had ever told her that before. She wanted to believe it. She desperately did. Cate felt herself once more hesitating, once more wanting to put down her doubts, give him a second chance.

"I'm sorry I didn't tell you before. But we can find a way forward. You and I."

"How? I just don't see how."

Cate turned to examine the autopilot controls, checking their bearing and their coordinates. Tomorrow they'd arrive in Aruba. Then it would be up to her to figure out how to lose Tack. She couldn't let him make this sacrifice for her. But then again, could she run knowing that doing so would take another's life? She didn't know. It had been her and Avery for so long, she couldn't imagine fighting for anyone else.

"Running won't do much except buy you a little bit of time." The deck beneath their feet rocked a bit as Cate studied the controls.

"A little bit of time is a little bit of time. You said it yourself, he's dying. If I outlast him, then I'll have all the time I want."

Tack put his hand on her shoulder and she felt the weight of it, the power. "You'd risk going to jail? Being pursued by authorities long after he's gone?"

"That's better than going to jail now."

"Let me talk to Allen. Let me reason with him. I can be very persuasive."

Looking up at Tack's broad shoulders and his intimidating physique, Cate had no doubt he could be. But this wasn't a normal man, and Rick had never been intimidated by muscle. He was a man who spent his life perfecting the art of being a bully. He also let his money do all the talking for him. There was always bigger and badder muscle he could buy. Cate knew this for a fact.

Tack wouldn't be able to negotiate with him. No one could.

"Maybe he'll drop the charges," Tack pressed. "And even if he doesn't, you can argue to a judge it was self-preservation. He was going to kill you. Maybe we can still somehow free Adeeb and you at the same time."

Cate shook her head. "Rick won't let that happen. No judge would believe us," she said, remembering how quickly the local police had turned on her when she'd asked them for help. They'd probably even testify that she was a crazy woman, or that he was an upstanding citizen, or that they'd never heard of any trouble before. The police chief would happily sit on the witness stand and praise Rick's character. The thought made her stomach turn.

"Cate, I know it seems like you can't win. That he's got all the aces in his hand, but he doesn't. First off, he's dying. I really think that all he wants to do his see his son. He might be willing to negotiate."

Cate shook her head. She knew him better than anyone, and Rick Allen didn't negotiate. He didn't back down. He never conceded anything. "He doesn't want to see Avery. He wants to punish me."

"Are you so sure about that?" Tack pressed. "Maybe he's changed. Dying can do that to a person."

Cate couldn't imagine Rick changing. That would require him admitting that something needed to be changed, and he'd said more than once that he didn't need fixing.

"I'm better off running. He hasn't forgotten what I did to him. He'll want me punished." She knew it to be true. He'd search for her right up until the day he died, and even after, he'd instruct the trustees of his estate to pursue her. Rick Allen didn't forget...or forgive.

"Let me talk to him. I can persuade him to see reason. He's Avery's father."

A creak near the stairs drove Cate's attention to the small hallway that led belowdecks. Avery stood there, hair askance as he clutched the railing with his small hand. He looked bewildered and confused, and she had a horrifying thought in that moment: How long had her boy been standing there? What had he heard?

"Are you talking about my daddy?" he asked.

CHAPTER SEVENTEEN

TACK WATCHED ALL the color drain out of Cate's face, and he realized things had just gone sideways. The boy didn't even know his father was alive, much less that he was actively searching for him.

"Avery, it's time for bed." Cate's voice was firm, but not too firm. She clearly did not want to discuss this now, but eventually, she had to. Even Tack knew that, and he wasn't a father. At some point, the boy would need to know the truth. He still felt that Cate wasn't right in keeping this from the boy. No kid should be told his parent had died, when the parent was very much alive. Even if that parent wasn't the most stellar guy on the block. A boy needed his father, even if his father was...well, Rick Allen.

"But, Mom... Daddy?" The simple words seemed to cut through Cate like a knife. She hesitated, glancing at Tack. He tried to keep his face neutral, but the boy needed to know his father was still alive. He'd know soon enough, anyway. No matter how good Cate was at running, he knew the odds were not in her favor. Not now, not with Allen so close to her. It wouldn't take Derek long, either, to figure out Cate and Avery left on this boat. Then it would be a matter of tracking it to Aruba. She had a chance to get away, but not a very good one. "You were talking about Daddy," Avery said, his little brow furrowed in confusion. Poor kid.

Cate dropped to her knees in front of the boy. "We'll talk about it tomorrow, okay, kiddo?" She put her hands on his shoulders and pulled the little one in for a hug. She met Tack's gaze from down on the deck. "We'll talk about it tomorrow."

Avery yawned, too sleepy to argue as he let his mother lead him back down the stairs and to his bunk belowdecks. When she emerged once more, she carefully secured the gate and latch, so that they wouldn't be so easily overheard. He wouldn't be peeking his head up unless he'd figured out how to unlock a door.

"You have to tell him," Tack said, voice low.

Cate glared at him. "He's not your concern." She tried to edge past him on her way to the wheelhouse.

"Sure he is." Tack blocked her way. "Cate, I...I want to do right by you. And by him."

She hesitated. "But what about Adeeb? You can't abandon him."

Tack's heart was ripped in two. He was torn between loyalty for his brother in arms, and love for the woman who'd turned his life upside down. How could he possibly choose? Yet right now, with her, he couldn't let her suffer. He had to save her.

"I'll find a way to save you both."

"That's not how the world works." Cate looked despondent. "You'll have to choose, and in the end, you'll side with him. Because you've known him longer. Because he's done more for you. He's a hero. I'm no hero."

"You are to me." It was true.

Tack desperately wanted to find a way where he wouldn't have to choose. In the meantime, his entire focus was on making sure Cate didn't run. If Cate ran, she *and* Adeeb lost. He wouldn't be able to save either of them.

He'd do what it took to save them both. He wasn't a quitter. Not in high school football. Not when he volunteered for the marines. Quit didn't live in him.

"You might not know it now, but you will. I'll prove it." Tack towered over her, and she seemed so small and delicate, a woman who desperately needed protection. His protection.

He wanted to care for her, and for Avery. He wanted to keep her safe, and he wanted her to know that, too. He realized he was falling in love with her.

"What if I never believe you?"

"Then I've got a long road ahead of me," Tack said and cracked a grin. Cate resisted smiling, but eventually her mouth twitched.

"I bet you'll get tired of convincing me before we get to Aruba."

"Oh, no, ma'am. I don't have quit in me. I survived basic training, and way worse. You'll have to really bring the pain if you want to get rid of me."

Cate eyed him with suspicion. "Okay, so if I can trust you, if you really do have my best interests at heart, then tell me, what do you think I should do? Turn myself in?"

"No," Tack said, and shook his head. "But I think you should let me try to negotiate with him. Let me bargain and try to get him to drop the charges. I know it's a long shot. I know the man is…stubborn." Cate let out a derisive snort. "Okay, more than stubborn. Pigheaded. But we've got to try. Maybe I can make him see reason. Maybe he'll give up that visa, too. Crazier things have happened."

Cate looked doubtful.

"When we get to Aruba, I say we hide you and Avery. Let me try to talk some sense into Allen. If I can't, then we can run."

"We?" Cate arched an eyebrow.

"Do you think I'm letting you go? I told you, I'm falling for you. That doesn't happen often. You're a special woman, Cate. Worth fighting for. Worth sacrificing for." Tack had never felt so certain of anything in all his life. He suddenly felt invigorated with purpose. He had a reason to get up in the morning that had nothing to do with turning a quick buck, or desperately trying to right past wrongs. He realized how deeply he'd missed that, and how much he'd taken it for granted when he served Uncle Sam, until right this moment.

Cate hesitated. "You're really serious, aren't you?"

"As serious as a jail sentence, which is what you'll get if I *don't* try." Cate grew solemn, her pretty green eyes darkening with worry. He reached out and gently touched her arm, feeling her extra-soft skin beneath his fingers. All he wanted to do was hold this woman for the rest of his life. The intensity of the feeling startled him, and yet it all just felt…right.

"Even if they don't catch you," he said softly. "Do you really want to spend the rest of your life running? That's a different kind of sentence. You run and Adeeb dies. At least my way, I can try to save you both."

"You can't really think that will work. Rick is not a reasonable man."

"Maybe he's found Jesus on his deathbed."

Cate snorted. "The man doesn't have a humble bone in his body."

"You'd be surprised how powerfully persuasive the possibility of imminent death can be."

Cate bite her lower lip. Tack pulled her closer and she let him, and moments later, he'd wrapped his arms around her tiny frame. The woman was so slight, he felt like he could wrap his arms around her twice. She needed him. Avery needed him, and he wasn't going to fail them. One way or another, he was going to find a way out of this mess.

"I nearly killed him…" Cate whispered.

"What he did to you was wrong. He was wrong, and you did the only thing you could do. You fled. That took courage." It did, and her standing up for herself and her son was one of the many reasons Tack had fallen for this woman.

"I should've done it years before. Maybe even before Avery. But for so long, I was afraid." The words came out so low against his chest that he almost thought he hadn't heard them.

"I know you were." Tack squeezed her tighter. "And if you'd run earlier, you would've never had Avery, and he's a blessing. So you have nothing to beat yourself up for."

She nodded against his chest as he sank onto the small bench on the deck and pulled her to him. "I wouldn't trade him for the world."

"Exactly. So you have nothing to regret."

"I hadn't thought about it like that before."

"Well, now you should start." Tack rested his chin against the top of her head, and felt like nothing could be more perfect than having Cate in his arms, her legs pressing against his on the small bench.

"True, but…all those years. All that time… being afraid. I think I'm still afraid," she murmured, her voice choked with emotion at the confession. He hugged her tighter.

"We all live with fear."

"Do you?"

He thought about Adeeb, and about all the regrets that weighed so heavily on him. "Every day."

"What are you afraid of?"

That I didn't do all I could to save the one man who'd saved me.

"That I'll fail someone I care about again."

That was the truth.

"So why did Derek hate you? Why didn't he help Adeeb?"

"Because I lodged an official complaint against him. I jeopardized his promotion," Tack admitted. He didn't like talking about it, because he regretted doing it. "I should've just kept my mouth shut. Kissed the man's ass more, but the fact was, he was making calculated political decisions, rather than thinking of the mission. Or his men." Tack shook his head. "I also thought he might be taking bribes from someone in the Afghan government. Never had any proof, though."

"Then you should've reported him. You did the right thing," Cate said.

"No. If I'd kept my mouth shut, Adeeb would be home by now," Tack said. "Derek knew how I felt about him. He screwed Adeeb just to mess with me. That's how petty the man is. I knew that, too. I knew when I filed that complaint there'd be repercussions. I just thought they'd be on my head. Not Adeeb's."

Cate cuddled into him. "We all make mistakes. I stayed with Rick too long. Does that mean that everything that happened to me was my fault?"

Tack shook his head. "Hell, no."

"Then maybe you should start giving yourself a little bit of a break."

Tack knew logically what she said made sense, but it just didn't jibe with the feelings in his heart. It might never. He couldn't lay down the guilt, not yet. He might carry it until he died. He blamed Derek; of course he did, because if he hadn't been such a monster, then Adeeb and his family would be safe. But mostly, he blamed himself because he always knew what kind of man Derek was. An ambitious sociopath.

He marveled about how open Cate's heart was, how forgiving. With her, he felt like a better man, his best self. He wondered if he might find some measure of peace with her. Maybe if Cate loved him, he could. She looked so damn beautiful in that sundress, showing off her tanned shoulders and thin frame. Even now, he wanted to whip it off her, just as he had that morning when he'd seen her in it for the first time.

He glanced down and saw the small scar on her chin and felt anger rise in him again as he flicked his thumb across the thin line. He never wanted anyone to hurt her again.

"I'm never going to let anyone touch you," Tack growled. "You know that?"

"Good," she said.

Anger boiled up in him. Anger at Rick Allen.

"I want to kill him," Tack said.

"I tried, I guess, but look where that got me." Cate chuckled darkly into his chest. He had to laugh, too, a little. Sometimes, things looked so bleak that the only viable options were laughing or crying. On deployment, gallows humor was nearly the only kind of humor. "You really think you can talk to him? Rick?"

"Believe me, the last thing I want to do is negotiate with that scumbag. But I don't want him to keep hurting you, and that's what he'll be doing if you keep running. He'll keep on hurting you forever."

Cate pulled away, blinking, and in the moonlight she looked deliciously kissable. All Tack wanted to do was make her his in every possible way.

"Let's try it my way, okay? Let me see what I can do. It might be a long shot, but at least it will be a chance that you can live your life free of him."

"I'm scared." Cate flinched a little as she said that, as if she were ashamed.

"I know," he said. "You've got every reason to be. But you are brave. And strong, and I know you can do this. You've already been through so much worse. This is a piece of cake."

Cate took a deep breath, her chest rising, then exhaled slowly.

"There's no other way?"

"I think it's our only shot. Unless you're secretly hiding millions and plan to disappear to Bora Bora."

Cate laughed ruefully. "I wish."

"Then we've got to try."

Cate studied him. She was so close all he wanted to do was kiss her once more, kiss her and feel her body cave to his, the want in her mouth like a fire that burned him from the inside out. He moved closer and she didn't back away, so he bent his head and kissed her. Passion suddenly took control. He'd never felt so drawn to a woman before, so captivated. He wanted her more than he'd wanted any woman in his life. The want scared him, but it also drove him. He wanted to make her his.

She melted into his body like she belonged there, and he wrapped his hands in her long hair and gave it a little tug. She drew back, breathless, her pupils dark circles in her eyes.

Blood pooled in her cheeks, and all he wanted to do was bite her full bottom lip.

"I want you," he growled, a guttural sound of need.

She ran her slight hands up the front of his shirt, and he nearly lost it right then. He was holding himself together by the tautest piano string, and he knew any little thing would be his undoing. If she kept touching him like that, he'd have her on the deck of this boat.

"I want you, too," she murmured softly, looking down at her feet. Was she suddenly shy? Now, when she had him in the palm of her hand? When he was little more than putty in her fingers?

He ran kisses down the side of her neck, and she moaned, a sound that nearly undid him as he moved down the soft skin of her throat. They stumbled backward together, and suddenly he had her pressed against the main mast. She wrapped her hands around his neck, but the touch of her fingernails against his skin made him wild with desire, and *he* wanted to drive this boat. He whipped her hands together above her head and held them there as he laid a trail of kisses along the neckline of her sundress. Her skin tasted so sweet, with just a hint of sea salt. He glanced up and saw her head thrown back against the mast, her blond hair almost silver in the moonlight.

She raised a leg and wrapped it around him, and he pressed into her. He ran his leg up the side of her leg, pushing up her hem, kneading the firm muscle there. God, this woman was a pure high. He couldn't get enough of her. He doubted he ever would. She kissed him with a ferocity that made him mad with desire. He needed this woman. Now.

He swept her up in his arms, and she clung to him, wrapping her legs around his waist. She kissed him, her hair falling across his cheek as he held her up. With no bed to take her to, he settled on the next best thing: the trampoline across the stern of the boat, stretched taut and strong enough to hold them. Or so he hoped. He laid her down on the steely fabric, and she went willingly. He whipped off his shirt, and she glided her fingers down the front of his chest appreciatively. Her light touch drove him crazy with want.

He pushed the skirt of her sundress aside as he ran his hand between the fabric and her skin, touching the softest part of her. He found her ready for him, more than ready, as she moaned and leaned into his touch. He tugged down the silky thong she wore, and suddenly she was bare and wanting. He wanted to make her come again, like he had in his room, but this time, he wanted to come with her. Tack hesitated, wondering whether this was the right thing to do, here on this boat. Did she even want him? But she was already fumbling with the front of his shorts, freeing him.

"Cate…" If they kept on, he wouldn't be able to stop. He knew that. "Cate, I…"

"I want you to," she said, voice deep. Then she was on top of him, showing him exactly how much she wanted him.

For a second, Tack couldn't speak. He couldn't even breathe. It was all too good.

"God, you feel…amazing, Cate. Simply… amazing." It was true. No one had ever felt like her before. A distant part of his brain told him this was insanity. Doing this—without protection!

But then she ground her hips against his. In no time at all, she'd climaxed, tightening and flexing around him. He told himself he'd need to hold it, but he couldn't. She had him in a viselike grip, and she wasn't letting go. He couldn't fight her. He didn't want to fight her. It was just too good.

"Cate…I…" It was coming now. "Cate, I…I love you."

And then, he came.

CATE FELL ON top of Tack's chest, a sweaty mess, wondering if she'd just heard him right. Did he say he loved her? That couldn't possibly be right. The man who'd worked for her ex-husband...*loved* her? Part of her thought it was just another con, another lie, yet the way he said it, *how* he said it, his dark eyes brimming with beautiful truth, told her the words weren't faked.

Tack Reeves loved her.

Part of her felt giddy.

The other part felt nauseous. How could she be with him if doing so asked him to give up the life of his best friend?

Plus, she was likely going to go to jail the second they landed in Aruba, because Rick Allen would have the entire island on lockdown probably, so what did it even matter daydreaming about being with anyone? Her future probably included a cell mate named Ironfist.

Well, you did just have sex with him. Unprotected, extremely irresponsible sex, a nagging little voice in her head told her. *Clearly, you feel something for him, too.*

Cate wasn't sure how that had happened. One second, she was her rational self, and the next, Tack was kissing her and she was taking off all her clothes and *mounting* the man.

Good Lord. *Then again, I haven't had actual, biblical sex in years.* Apparently, she was a woman with needs, and those needs had finally completely taken over her life.

We just had sex. On the boat. With... Oh, God. With Avery sleeping below!

She glanced at the locked door of the cabin and breathed a sigh of relief. At least she'd locked the door. But still. What on earth had she been thinking? She hadn't, that's what. Sure, she could try to tell herself she was happily playing Tack, trying to distract him, or win him over, or whatever it was that poised seductresses did to undercover agents, but she wasn't that kind of girl. Never had been. Frankly, she'd just been hot for this man and hadn't been able to put the brakes on in time. That was the sad, honest truth of the matter.

All of this ran through her mind as she lay on Tack's chest. His ample, muscular, bare chest, and even as she told herself all the reasons this had been a terrible mistake, part of her wondered if she could somehow manage to repeat this mistake again. Maybe right now.

"You're amazing, Cate," he murmured in her hair. His chest rose and fell softly in the moonlight, the sea breeze ruffling the small hairs on his muscled forearms as he hugged her tightly to him. "I've never met a woman like you."

"I've never met a man like you." That was the God's honest truth. He was built like an action hero, but had the heart of a romance-novel hero. *He just told you he loves you.* But Cate wasn't ready to say that back. She wasn't sure if she'd ever be ready. How could she trust this was real? Everything in her history told her to never ever believe in happy endings.

Thoughts swirled in her mind as the boat glided beneath the stars. Would she really try to let Tack negotiate with Rick? Would that even work? Or would the best course of action be to try to lose Tack the second they docked and hope for the best? Or…should she turn herself in? Maybe Rick would give the visa to Adeeb if he thought Tack was still working for him. If he thought Tack had been the one to bring her in. But what about Avery?

God, she didn't know what to do.

"I want to spend my life with you, Cate."

"You don't even know me," she murmured, tracing the line of his abdomen. "How can you say that?"

"Because I know you. I know what a big heart you have. What an amazing mother you are. I know you're brave, and you keep on fighting even when there's no fight left. You're everything I want in a woman. Besides, I told you that I'd spend the rest of my life making you trust me again, and I plan to do just that."

Cate felt overwhelmed and confused. Could this be real? Could he mean it?

"I'm not sure how I feel about that." Cate pushed herself up on her elbow and glanced at Tack's chiseled face, lit by the moon above them.

"Don't you feel this between us? This... pull?"

Did she? It's why she was half naked and nearly hanging off the edge of a catamaran right now.

"Of course. But...what if that's just physical?" *What if the second I give you my heart, you turn into a terrible person. Like Rick did.*

"It's not," Tack said. "It's more than that. The physical wouldn't be so good without more there. You're the one for me."

How could he know that? How could he be so sure? Cate thought Rick had been the one, but look how that turned out. She felt gunshy, and worse, like she wasn't able to trust her own instincts. Tack had betrayed her— granted, for a reason she could understand— but still, could she trust him from here on out? Could she trust any man?

"Tack… I just…don't know."

"Sweetheart, you don't have to know. You don't have to believe in me. I believe in us, and I'll be here when you *do* realize you love me, too."

Uncertainty swirled in her mind.

"Tack…" She shook her head. The whole notion was crazy. How could someone fall in love so fast?

"I'm a patient man. I'll wait." He hugged her close. "How about this, for *this* one night, right now, because we're stuck on this boat, how about you don't worry about what happens tomorrow?" Tack murmured in her hair. "How about for just tonight, you trust me?"

"Okay," she agreed, because what harm could it do?

He kissed her, and all thoughts about the future left her mind, and suddenly she was in the here and now, exactly where she wanted to be. She didn't have to worry about what happened when the boat docked, or whether she could trust Tack. Right now, it was just her and him and the sea. Simple and uncomplicated.

CATE WOKE THE next morning belowdecks in the small bed she shared with Avery. She'd set the autopilot and had decided to trust Tack wouldn't change it. Cate yawned as the night before came tumbling back to her—the fact that they'd stayed on deck for hours, not sneaking back downstairs until the wee hours of the morning. She'd only gotten maybe an hour or two of sleep, as the gray light of early morning filtered into the window.

A rustling at the foot of the bed caught her attention.

Avery was already awake and puttering about the small cabin, opening empty cabinets and peering in, entertaining himself. As she watched him, the boy so full of determination and curiosity, her heart filled with love. Tack had been right last night—every decision she ever made about Rick she'd do all over again if it meant that Avery was here by her side. She was so grateful for him, and she couldn't imagine her life without her little boy.

Then she thought about going to jail and possibly never seeing him again, and a chill ran through her. Even if Rick was dying, Cate knew he'd somehow make sure she never got out of prison, or if she did, she'd never see Avery again. He'd probably poison the boy against her.

At least that's one thing I never did, Cate thought. She could have, easily. She could've told the boy the unvarnished truth about what kind of man his father was, but she thought it was kinder if he thought him dead.

Tack, of course, thought differently, but now Cate wasn't sure how to break the news to her boy that she'd lied to him. The last thing on earth she'd ever wanted to do was hurt Avery. All she'd done, she did to protect him.

Would she risk *him* just so Tack could try to talk to a man that Cate knew couldn't be reasoned with? She already knew what kind of man Rick was. There was no way he'd let go of his vendetta. Tack might yet get Adeeb's visa, but if Cate stood by and waited, she'd be in jail. Her boy in Rick's care... And then, after he died, raised by some coldhearted nanny most likely, set up by Rick's estate. Cate had relatives, yes, but would they have enough money to fight Rick in court? It would take tens of thousands of dollars to wage a custody battle, and she had a feeling they'd lose. That made her feel even worse.

Cate cared for Tack. She felt horrible about Adeeb, but when it came down to it, could she risk her boy's happiness?

"Mommy!" Avery called, seeing her watching him. He bounded toward the bed and launched himself on it, tackling her in the process. He was a ferocious little ball of energy from the time he woke up until he conked out at night. Cate wished, not for the first time, she could plug into his little always-on-the-go battery.

"Morning, sweetie," she said, returning his tight hug. "Did you sleep well?"

"We're still on the boat!" he cried, delighted, and it made Cate giggle, because where else would they be? But a little boy's imagination probably included being beamed off the sailboat in the middle of the night.

"That's right," she said. "Just a few more hours, and we'll be to a new island."

"Are we going to live there?" Avery asked.

"No, sweetie," she said, keeping her voice a low whisper as she motioned for him to come even closer. "Can you keep a secret?" she asked him.

He nodded solemnly.

"We're going to get another boat and go sailing some more," she murmured, so quietly that even if Tack had his ear pressed to the cabin door he wouldn't be able to hear her. "Would you like that?"

"Yessss!" he cried, pumping a tiny fist in the air.

"Remember, it's our secret," she cautioned him, and he instantly grew somber.

"Secret!" he murmured, and nodded gravely.

Cate heard the creak of footsteps above their head, and padded to the small door and slid it open. She glanced down the hall and saw Tack's bunk open and empty. He must be on deck.

"Avery, stay down here," she cautioned the boy, and he nodded, happily banging another cabinet door shut. Cate climbed up the small steps barefoot, in the same sundress she'd worn to bed. Her hair was a holy mess, but she didn't care. She had to make sure Tack wasn't leading them off course. She'd made the decision to trust him, but now she was doubting herself again. Had it been the right choice?

The sun on the horizon hit her face, and she felt the warmth of the morning on her shoulders as she stepped onto the deck. Around her, glistening blue sea stretched for miles. She saw Tack right away, shirtless, leaning against the wheelhouse, one tanned hand shading his eyes from the sun as he glanced at the horizon. She stopped in her tracks as she watched the curve of his back in the morning light. God, the man was a work of art—all perfectly cut edges. Her heart sped up, even as she tried to squash her inward girlie excitement at seeing him turn and meet her gaze. He grinned, and her stomach flipped. Lord, that man had an insane power over her. She could feel the tug to him from across the boat, as if she were a fish on a line being reeled in.

"You're up," he said and looked genuinely happy to see her, and not at all like a man who'd been sabotaging the steering, or putting the autopilot off course. She moved closer to him, and he gave her a warm hug in his big arms. She couldn't help but feel safe there.

What am I doing? I can't let my guard down. I've made my decision. I've got to stick with it.

She cleared her throat. "Everything okay up here?"

Cate tried to get a look to the side to see the autopilot controls, and saw the compass, which told her they were still on a straight course to Aruba. Why would she think he'd try to change them?

"Everything is fine now that you're here," he said, resting his chin on the top of her head. Cate might never get used to that. She was five-eight, and had never been with a man so tall to make *her* feel short. Yet she liked it, feeling small in his muscled arms. She closed her eyes and squeezed him a little tighter.

What's one more hug? What's a tiny little moment where she could let go of her suspicions and just *be* in this gorgeous man's arms. She thought about the night before, how absolutely reckless she'd been. What was she thinking? Unprotected sex under the stars? She was not the kind of woman who ever threw caution to the wind like that. In fact, she'd have to get her hands on some plan B contraceptive the second the boat docked, she thought, her mind already ticking through all the worst-case scenarios. She'd become so distracted she forgot to enjoy the embrace, and when Tack stiffened and backed away, she was so deep in her own thoughts she almost missed the change in mood.

"We've got company," Tack announced, a guttural growl that put every one of her senses on high alert. She whipped around to glance back the stern and saw a small dot of a sailboat in the distance.

Breath caught in her throat. Could it be Rick? Had he found her somehow?

"Do you think they're following us?" she said, her heart wanting to leap into her throat and out of her body altogether. *Please, God, let it not be one of Rick's lackeys.*

Tack reached into the wheelhouse, grabbed the binoculars from the upper shelf and scanned the horizon.

"Can't tell who's on the boat from here," he said. "We'll just have to wait and see."

Cate nibbled on one of her cuticles. "What do we do if they are?"

"We'll find out what they want," Tack said. "But it'll be better if we dock in Aruba first. Meeting at sea is never a good idea. People drown that way. Boats go down. Besides, that boat is smaller than ours. I don't think they'll catch up to us on wind power alone."

"Maybe I can outmaneuver them."

Tack glanced at Cate. "You into racing, now?"

"I'm into anything that makes sure I don't have to answer more questions than I want to."

Tack grinned and shook his head. "You are a woman full of surprises."

CHAPTER EIGHTEEN

TACK WATCHED IN awe as Cate took the boat off autopilot and took control. She ordered him about, telling him which ropes to pull and which sails to heave, and soon enough, the boat caught the wind. It lurched abruptly to the side, almost coming out of the water, and a canister near the wheel toppled to the ground, spilling out a book of matches and a couple of safety pins. Tack grabbed the items and stuck them in his pocket right before the ship lurched again and he caught hold of a nearby railing. The canister rolled past his feet and off the edge of the boat into the blue-green sea. *That had almost been me.*

He righted himself as Cate flashed a sheepish grin. *Sorry,* she mouthed as she turned the wheel once more. The boat trailing them grew smaller and smaller in the distance until Tack couldn't see it with his binoculars. Cate was a woman of many talents, and she seemed always to impress him. A woman who could sail *and* who didn't know the meaning of the word *quit*, well, she was a woman after his own heart. Tack could see just how perfect they were for each other—both unyielding, both stubborn and both fiercely protective of the people they loved. She was loyal, despite what Rick said. He could see that in everything she did for her son and for her friends, too.

They were perfect for each other.

Except for the fact that I picked the wrong team from the get-go. Now I am a man who can't be trusted. And what about Adeeb? Could I really leave him twisting in the wind?

He wasn't sure he could talk Rick Allen into a truce, and even if he did, if she'd accept the terms. Then there was the problem of Avery not even knowing his father was still alive, and Cate seemingly determined to keep him in the dark.

But all of that would be a moot point if Cate fled the second they landed in Aruba, and if Tack was a betting man, he'd go all-in on her running just as soon as she got the opportunity. He was a man who prided himself on seeing all the angles, and when it came to Cate, she was going to flee, not fight. It was all she knew how to do. If only he could show her the benefit of taking a stand, of not letting the bad guy run her out of town. If she was going to take her power back, she'd have to do it on her own terms. He knew it would be a long road to convince her that if she stood her ground, she just might be able to win. If she ran, she'd always lose.

"Can you still see him?" Cate asked as she concentrated on steering the catamaran.

"They're out of sight," Tack said, moving up beside her. "Looks like we lost them."

"For now," she murmured and frowned. "But I don't like that they were so close. That they saw us."

"You don't know they were following us. Could've been tourists."

"Maybe, but I didn't get this far not looking over my shoulder." Cate had stuffed on an old baseball cap she found in the wheelhouse, but her unruly blond hair jutted from under it, refusing to be contained, much like the woman's stubborn will, he thought. Her tanned face needed no makeup, and the determination in her green eyes made them sparkle with fire and grit. Tack wanted to take her again right now, right here in this wheelhouse, but he knew he couldn't. Avery was awake and the autopilot was off, and he was out of luck. Still, he wrapped his hands around her waist from behind, and she squirmed a little.

"You're the most gorgeous woman I've ever met," he whispered in her ear and then kissed the side of her neck. She shivered in his arms, a delectable little quiver. He wasn't the only one being affected by the close proximity. He knew he could drive her wild, like he did last night, and he knew she wasn't faking it, either. He'd been around the block enough times to know when a woman was playing him.

No matter how much Cate might want to run away, he also knew that he had her number. Her body responded to his touch as if she were made for him. It was just one more way they were perfect for one another. If only she'd just believe it.

She giggled anxiously. "You must not have met many women."

If he didn't know her better, he would've assume she was just being coy. How could a woman so completely perfect think she was anything but? Yet he knew the insecurity was real. The self-deprecation was no joke.

"Unfortunately, I have met *many* women," he countered. "All the wrong ones. Until you."

She leaned back into him, and the feel of her back flat against his chest felt so perfect, so right, he wondered why she didn't just give in to the sensation.

She giggled again. "How *many* women are we talking about?"

Tack scoffed. If he were honest with himself, he probably lost count. There was a long, long line of romances in his life, none of them serious. A man who looked like him didn't get turned down very often. Throw in the fact that he was in active service in his prime, and he didn't need more of a come-on line than *I'm on active duty.* Getting laid was one of the unspoken perks of serving Uncle Sam. God bless America.

"A few," he answered noncommittally. None of them mattered. Except for the fact that he knew Ms. Right when he found her.

"But none of them matter," he said honestly. "Now that I've found you."

"And how many women have you said that to?" Cate wondered aloud.

"None," he said, truthfully, and squeezed her tightly.

Cate threw her head back and laughed. "You're good, Tack Reeves."

"You mean I'm honest," he said, and this caused her to laugh more. God, how he loved to hear this woman laugh. He wanted to spend the rest of his life making her laugh. And making her come. It would be his dual life mission from here on out. That was, if he could keep her out of jail. And not in hiding.

The shores of Aruba came into view in the distance, and Tack felt a stinging disappointment. He'd wanted to stay at sea with her for longer. Land on the horizon was the visual embodiment of reality crashing in.

"I wish we could just sail on past that shore-line," he said.

"Maybe we can," Cate said, turning. He glanced down at her and saw she was dead serious. "What if we just keep on going?"

"You mean run?"

"Why not?" A light fired up in Cate's eyes, and he saw the flicker of seriousness in them. "Come with us, Tack. You, me and Avery. We could make this work."

For a second, Tack was sorely tempted.

He could run with Cate. They could be a family. He'd have the woman he loved, and did it really matter if they might have to look over their shoulders?

Then he thought of Adeeb, the man's stoic smile, the way he calmly went about his business in the middle of a war zone. The passion inside the man that had driven him to risk it all to save his country. The promise Tack made. He knew he couldn't abandon his friend, either. Getting Allen to give him a visa might be a long shot. But he had to at least try.

He couldn't let the one last hope for Adeeb slip out of his fingers. He'd have to figure out something. He just needed more time.

"I love you," he said, ignoring the fact that his words were met with a stiff silence. He didn't care if she wasn't ready to tell him she felt the same way. He didn't even care if she was never ready. He felt what he did, and he wasn't going to hide it. Not if it could make a difference. "It doesn't matter how you feel about me. I love you. And *because* I love you, I'm not going to let you and your son spend the rest of your lives on the run. It's not fair to Avery, and it sure as hell isn't fair to you."

Disappointment hit Cate. He could tell, as her shoulders stiffened and a wall seemed to come up between them. How could he make her see that he was on *her* side, that fighting was the only way she'd ever be free?

"It's a fight I can't win."

"You don't know that."

"I do." She turned on him fiercely, green eyes blazing with hurt and anger and a little tinge of fear. The invitation, the little bit of hope that had been there just seconds ago, had vanished. He wondered if he'd ever see it again.

"I know you've been through a lot."

"You don't know the first thing about me." Her words hit him sharply, like a slap across the cheek. He did know her. He'd been tracking her for a year. He'd interviewed *nearly everybody who'd ever known her.* Her father. Her college roommate. Everyone.

He realized with a start that he'd been slowly falling in love with this woman *for a year.* Meeting her just sealed the deal. He'd been telling himself he doubted her, that she was a bad person, but everything he'd ever found about her told him the opposite. He was just too stubborn to let it all in. Until he met her, and he realized that everything everyone had ever said about her was right.

"I do know you, Cate. I've spent the last year studying *everything* I could about you. I've talked to *everybody* I could find that ever knew you. Your college roommate, Kimmy. Remember her? Raved about you. Said you were a fantastic friend."

"Kimmy? You talked to her?" She looked taken aback, and her hands nearly slid off the wheel of the boat. "But I haven't talked to her in…"

"Years. She told me to tell you, if I found you, to call her. She misses you. And I talked to your prom date."

"You…what?" Now, Cate's cheeks turned from pink to crimson. "You talked to…Pete Benson?"

Now Tack was starting to enjoy himself.

"Sure did. I think he's still in love with you,

by the way. The way he talked about you… Also, he owns the Big Bar, down at Cado. In case you want to drop in. He said drinks are on him."

Cate dropped her head onto the window of the wheelhouse and groaned. "Oh, boy."

"And…I talked to your father."

Cate's jaw dropped and her face was now bright purple. "You had no right to do that."

"I was looking for you. He didn't know where you were, but he told me you had a heart of gold, and no matter what anybody said, you could never harm a hair on a fly's head. He told me the story about how, as a little girl, you'd never hook the worms for the bait, because you felt too bad for them and kept trying to set them all free. He said you damn near ran his bait shop out of business trying to let all those critters go."

At the time he heard the story, he thought maybe Cate had just been a nice kid who'd gotten corrupted somewhere along the way. Now he realized she was still that nice kid. Trying to set the worms free. It was why she was so determined to keep on running right now. Why she hated the idea of standing and fighting.

"How…is Dad?"

"Having beer for breakfast," Tack said honestly. "The man put away four while I talked to him."

"Same old Dad." Cate shook her head. "When I married Rick, I tried to send Dad to rehab. Paid for the best program. But he quit on day two and told me he was too old to dry out, so he was going to keep on drinking and just pickle himself up. He said his grandfather drank moonshine every day for all of his life and lived to be eighty-nine."

Tack couldn't help but laugh a little. "At least he's living his life on his own terms."

"Who else did you track down?"

"Your aunts. And uncle. And at least two cousins."

"Which ones?"

"Christina and Maureen."

Cate looked visibly relieved. "Good. They're great. I think one of my other cousins might be in jail."

"Never found him. But Christina and Maureen were very nice. They also had no idea where you were."

"How did you find me?" Cate's eyes were sharp, assessing. "I was very careful."

"You were very careful. So was Mark, who got you the papers. I knew you'd gone to the Caribbean because of the last bank transfer, from that bank account you kept under your maiden name."

"Nobody knew about that account," she protested. "Not even Rick."

"No, he didn't, but I found it. There wasn't much in it," he remarked, and watched her face contort into shock.

"There was ten thousand dollars in that account!" she exclaimed.

"It's not a lot when you're talking about millions," he clarified with a shrug. "Why get it?"

"It was my money. I'd earned it, back before I'd married Rick. It was my money, and I wasn't going to leave it, and besides, I needed every penny I could get." Across the horizon, the shore grew closer. Small buildings on the island came into view. They probably had ten minutes, maybe more, before they landed.

"I figured it was something like that," Tack said. "But the point is, I *do* know you, Cate. I've been living and breathing you for a year. I know the kind of person you are, and that's why I love you."

"I don't know what to say to that." Cate just stared at him, varied emotions running across her face. He wanted to pull her into his arms, convince her to see reason. But she hadn't spent a year researching him, and what she knew of him was betrayal. He understood that on a very basic level. It would take her a while to come around. *If* she ever came around.

"You don't have to say anything." He didn't want to put pressure on her. Already, she was a skittish colt about to bolt. He didn't want to give her a reason. The only thing he could hope for now was just more time to convince her. Tack wanted to know that she wouldn't run the second the boat was tied off.

"We're almost to shore," he remarked, and she stayed silent, keeping her eyes on the water. "Will you let me talk to him? Will you let me try?"

Cate hesitated, her green eyes turning a hard-to-read slate. She studied him, and he could see the calculations running in her head. *Lie or tell the truth?*

"Cate."

"I need you to go secure that sail." She nodded outward, away from her.

"Not before you give me an answer."

Cate shifted uncomfortably from foot to foot. "Okay. I'll give you three hours. You can try to talk to him, but after that…"

Three hours was short. What if he didn't even connect with Allen in that time? Still, three hours was probably more time than she was comfortable giving, especially with Derek on the loose looking for them. He shouldn't press his luck by asking for more time.

"I'll do what I can with that," he said.

"Good. Now, go secure that sail. We're coming into port." Her tone left no room for argument. He only hoped that she'd deliver on her promise and give him three hours before disappearing to wherever else she planned to hide.

Now came the impossible task of trying to figure out how to convince an egomaniac billionaire narcissist not to arrest his ex-wife on kidnapping charges.

The boat grew closer to the shore, and as they glided into the dock, Tack noticed a uniformed police officer standing near the edge. Two more were back near the street, and he saw three police cars stationed in the parking lot.

A split second later, Cate noticed them, too.

"Did you tip them off?" she cried, angry.

"No! Of course I didn't." Tack didn't call the cops. He had no reason to do that. But Cate jumped to the quick conclusion that he had. It showed just how far she really was from trusting him.

"We're not docking here," she declared, and threw the catamaran's small engine in Reverse, but by that time, a police boat had looped back around them, cutting off their only path of escape.

"We're trapped," she stated, panic clearly on her face.

A police officer on the boat spoke over a loudspeaker. "Pull into the dock slowly," the officer said. "And no one will get hurt."

"Looks like it's too late for you to try to talk to him," Cate said. "If that's ever what you wanted to do."

"Cate, I didn't do this." In the seconds before they'd be close enough to tie off the boat, Tack grabbed Cate by the shoulders. "Whatever you do, don't say anything. I can still help us. I *will* help us. Do you understand me?"

Cate frowned at him. "Why should I believe you?"

"What do I have to gain by lying to you now?" Tack asked, a fair question he thought, given that they were surrounded by cops. "I promise that I will protect you and Avery, and I plan to keep that promise. We're probably going to be arrested, and they will probably take Avery, but if you run, then things can get violent. We don't want that."

Cate nodded.

"Then do everything they say and trust that I will figure out a way to get us out of this."

The catamaran slid into its spot on the dock,

and several officers hopped aboard, handcuffs at the ready.

Now, just *how* he was going to get them out of this was another story.

...the road.

She had now begun trying to get them out of...was a much later story.

CHAPTER NINETEEN

"WHERE'S MY SON?" Cate asked for the fifth time, as she leaned through the bars of her holding cell in the tiny Aruba jail where the officers had brought her to be processed. They'd taken a mug shot and her fingerprints, and had left her in a single cell with two metal cots, a cracked floor and a single, stainless-steel seatless toilet.

Cate didn't know if anyone could hear her. She pressed her face to the bars but could only see the jail cell opposite and what looked like part of a wall. She knew a hallway lay beyond, because she'd walked down it after she'd been led through the main door, a large steel thing with a small Plexiglas window. On the other side of that was the desk where a female officer had wordlessly taken her fingerprints.

Cate squeezed her eyes shut, and a single tear slipped down her cheek. Had she been wrong to keep her son from his father? *Even if that father is a monster?* She only wanted to do what was right by Avery. Because if she'd stayed in Rick's mansion, she would've ended up dead. She knew that for a fact. Eventually, he would've gone too far and killed her.

Suddenly, she remembered Tack's vow: *I will protect you and Avery.* Did he mean that? Or was it just one more lie? And if this was his idea of protecting them, then they sure didn't need this kind of protection. Cate glanced around her concrete walls with the blue paint peeling off in huge chunks. Still, part of her hoped against hope that he *had* meant his promise. Who else would help her now? Mark? He was an island away, and he probably didn't even know she'd been arrested. Even if he did, he'd told her more than once that if she was ever caught it would be hellish to nightmare trying to get her out of jail, that she'd likely be extradited to the United States as quickly as the Caribbean police forces could get her there. She knew Mark didn't have a backup plan, because he'd said more than once if plan A didn't work, there wasn't a plan B, so they sure as hell should hope plan A worked. But it hadn't.

Because of Tack Reeves.

But did she truly believe that? Cate wasn't even sure anymore. She had been so certain he'd betrayed her on the boat, and yet part of her realized the look of shock that crossed his face when he saw the police was real. They'd led him away in a different police car, and she had no idea where they took him. A different police station? Somewhere to be interrogated? Was he getting Adeeb's visa right now? And even if he was, could she blame him?

Still, something told her he hadn't called the cops. She hoped it wasn't because she was starting to have feelings for the man. *You'll believe anything a man says if you start thinking with your heart instead of your brain.* Wasn't that what happened with Rick? Hadn't she turned a blind eye to all his faults because she'd been in love? Hadn't that led her to the worst decision she'd ever made by marrying him?

She pressed her head against the cold concrete of the cell wall. It was the only thing in the cell that was cold. A big ceiling fan circulated humid air through the jail, but the place didn't have air-conditioning. A big, brown roach skittered across the cracked concrete floor, and Cate tried not to shudder. How long would she be here? Could she even get a lawyer in Aruba? She had no idea whether she'd even see a judge before she was sent back to the United States. None of the Aruba police were saying a word, after the initial charge.

She wished she'd gotten a chance to hug Avery. That's what she thought of now as she closed her eyes and cried more hot tears, sitting on the steel bench in her cell, hugging her knees. She hadn't gotten a chance to hug her boy goodbye, not before the cuffs were put on. She hated that he'd seen her like that, being led away to a police car. What would *he* think? He must be so confused and scared. She wished she'd told him the truth. She realized her mistake. Now some stranger, probably a police officer, was going to have to tell him his father was alive, and that she'd lied to him about it. The thought felt like a flaming arrow through her heart. She should've been the one to tell him that. She could've explained. Now she wouldn't get that chance.

Tack had been right. It had been wrong to try to keep this from her son. She should've told him the truth, and she should've—to the best of her ability—explained why she'd made the choices she'd made. Then he would've at least understood she'd done it for him. Now he might never know. He might grow up poisoned against her. The thought made her feel nauseous.

There was so much about her life that she'd do differently if she had the chance for a do-over. What she wouldn't give to have five minutes with her son to try to explain.

But there was nothing she could do. Nothing to do but wait.

She swiped at the tears on her face, not caring if she smeared the little mascara she still wore. Sweat dripped down her back, and she wished there was a window in her cell, anything that might let in a breeze, but she was surrounded by crumbling cinder blocks.

Cate found herself wishing that Tack Reeves would walk through the door, and then instantly wondered why that desire popped into her head. Wouldn't he go to save Adeeb? Try to do what he could to convince Rick he held up his end of the bargain? Why wouldn't he be bargaining for a visa right now?

Because he loves you.

Maybe, it's that simple. Maybe he was a man who said what he meant. Just because everything out of Rick Allen's mouth was a lie, didn't mean Tack was a liar, too.

Hope fluttered in her chest. Did she want to believe Tack loved her, or was she just clinging to the ridiculous hope that he'd come save her? Did it matter at this point?

Her life as she knew it was likely over. Her son would grow up hating her. Rick would see to it that she never saw daylight again or felt the rain on her face. Would it matter if she knew if Tack really loved her or not?

Amazingly, it did. She realized, sitting in that cell, that she wanted to know. Did he? He'd told her he did, but was he telling the truth?

If Tack came for her, he loved her. If she never saw him again, it was because he chose Adeeb. Could she really blame him, though? Could she?

Cate hugged her knees a little tighter.

NOT LONG AFTER Cate had been taken to the police station, Tack and Avery were shuttled into an unmarked police sedan, where some-one had handed Tack an Aruba police shirt, taking them away from the docks in the opposite direction the police had taken Cate. The short drive down the shoreline left little time for Tack to plan, and the driver, a plainclothes detective with a square jaw and a mean look about him, was not amenable to answering any of his questions.

"Where are we going?" Tack asked the man, only to get nothing but steely silence.

Tack stared at the back of the man's head, and then glared at the rearview mirror, but the man never once looked up. He might as well have been deaf.

"We have a right to know where we're going," Tack said once more. "And if it's not the US

Consulate, then I damn sure want to know where else you plan to drop us." The detective sent him a quick look in the mirror, but again said nothing. "Where did they take Cate? Is she going to be processed?"

"Where's my mommy?" Avery asked, eyes wide as he glanced at Tack. He hadn't meant to make the boy worry, but of course he'd know they were talking about his mother. "Do you know where my mommy is?"

"I don't know, Avery."

"Does he know?" Avery asked once more, pointing at the back of the driver's head. He didn't turn and didn't even move. The man clearly could not care less. He'd have to have a heart made of granite not to be affected by the boy's plea.

"Hey, man, her son wants to know where she's being held, that's all," Tack said, softening his approach. "Can you do us a favor and let us know?"

The detective simply leaned forward and turned up the stereo a little louder, the sounds of Bob Marley blaring through the interior of the car. Jerk. Granite was probably too soft a rock for his heart.

"I want my mommy," the boy whined.

"I know, and I'm going to do my best to find her. I promise. It'll be okay," Tack said, trying to comfort the boy and hoping he wasn't telling a lie. Would it be okay? And where was the square-jawed detective taking them? Eventually, they'd get to their destination, and Tack would have a long, long talk with the detective's supervisor.

Tack saw as they turned onto a narrow costal highway, and thought about how much Aruba reminded him of St. Anthony's Island. He wondered if they were going to the US Consulate. That's where he'd go if he planned to repatriate the boy. They didn't have his passport, so they'd need to secure some ID there. The good news was that he had an inside man there, John Benoit, who might be able to help them. Or, at minimum, figure out what was going on.

Avery reached out then and grabbed Tack's hand, saying nothing as he did so, a small instinctual need for comfort. Tack squeezed the little boy's hand, amazed at how small it was in his own, and felt suddenly extremely protective of the boy. He'd promised Cate he'd look after them both, and he meant it. The boy was scared, and Tack just wanted to ease his worry.

"Hey, you know that your mom loves you more than *anything*, right? That she'd do anything for you?"

Avery nodded.

"Well, she won't be separated from you for

long *if she can help it*. She told me you were the sun in her sky."

Avery giggled a little. "She did?"

"And no matter what anybody ever tells you, I want you to remember that your mom loves you very much."

The little boy made a face as if to say, *Of course*.

Not long after that, the car pulled into the elegant roundabout of a luxury hotel.

"Woah!" Avery cried as he saw the blue-green ocean behind the hotel, and the blue-and-white-striped covered recliners lining the private beach.

"Are we stopping here?" Tack said, suddenly confused. This resort wasn't the consulate, clearly. Tack had a bad feeling about this.

The square-jawed detective stepped out of the front seat of the car and opened the back door, letting Avery out, but slamming the door shut in Tack's face before he could get out. A flip of the key-chain remote, and the car doors locked, trapping Tack in the back seat.

"Wait. Where are you taking him?"

Tack grabbed the door handle, but it didn't budge. "Avery!"

The boy glanced back, looking uneasy. "Tack?" he asked, fearful.

Tack nearly broke off the interior handle trying to get the door loose. Then Derek stepped out of the lobby, a huge shit-eating grin on his face.

"Nice to see you, Reeves," he said through the tiny opening of the window. Tack hurled his elbow at the window, but it didn't even make a crack.

"You better not harm a hair on that boy's head or I swear to God…"

"You can swear all you want, but you don't need to worry. I'm not going to harm him. He's my golden ticket." Derek wrapped his arm around the boy's shoulders, tugging him closer to his side. Avery reluctantly went, his worried eyes focused on Tack. "I'm taking him straight to Allen and getting my reward."

"No. You can't take him off the island. Not without the FBI involved. If it's kidnapping charges, they'd be the ones—"

"You don't even get it, do you?" Derek tilted back his head and laughed. "You really have lost a step since Kabul, buddy."

"Why don't you let me out of this car, and we'll see who lost a step." Tack planned to take the man apart. Slowly.

Derek just laughed. "No, thanks."

"I see you're still a coward." Tack had thought Derek Hollie was a sniveling coward the moment they'd met.

"You better watch your mouth."

"Or what? You'll call the MP to save you—again?"

Derek's face flushed red with anger.

"I should've killed you when I had the chance," Derek growled. "Should've slit your throat while you slept."

"Believe me, the feeling is mutual."

Derek grabbed Avery's shoulder, and the boy flinched, his lower lip trembling in fear. Tack hated that man. Hated what he did to Adeeb and hated that he was making Avery scared. All he wanted to do was make the man bleed.

Then he glanced at the Aruban detective. He was Tack's only hope at this point. "You've got to let me out," he said. "We've got to stop this man. He's got no legal grounds to take that boy. I demand we go to the US Consulate…"

"I don't think we'll be going to the consulate," Derek said. That's when he reached into his pocket and pulled out a wad of Aruban florins, brightly colored rainbow bills, and handed them to the square-jawed officer standing nearby. The detective tucked the money into his jacket pocket and grinned. That's when it became clear that maybe the real authorities, the FBI, might not be involved in this case at all. Maybe this was just Allen's way of using money once more to get what he wanted. It all clicked then for Tack—it was why he hired so many private eyes and didn't let the FBI take over the investigation. He wanted complete control of it. The good news was this meant that Cate might not face jail time, after all. The bad news was that she might never get out of jail, depending on how much money Allen used to bribe the local authorities.

"We've got a plane to catch. So sorry we can't stick around," Derek said, grinning as he led the boy to a waiting limo. He glanced at the square-jawed detective. "Take him for a drive. A loooong drive."

Silently, the detective turned and climbed back into the car. Tack didn't like the sound of that. He had a sinking feeling he didn't want to find out what awaited him at the end of that long drive.

As the detective turned the car out of the hotel parking lot, he saw Derek take Avery inside the hotel. He glanced at the bulletproof partition separating him from the driver, and wondered how the hell he was going to get out of this.

CHAPTER TWENTY

TACK SAT IN the back of the unmarked police car trying to figure out what the hell he ought to do. He wasn't handcuffed, that was the good news, but his hands weren't going to do anything against the bulletproof plastic separating him from the driver, or the automatic door locks. Tack had tried to break the back windows, but they were shatterproof, too, and without a sharp tool he wouldn't get anywhere. He glanced at the small holes in the middle plastic partition and wish he could somehow fit his hands through so he could throttle the crooked detective who sat in the front seat. Meanwhile, the detective reached over and turned on the stereo. The sound of reggae filled the car as they sped away, down a road lined with bright, tropical flowers. He thought he'd been in trouble when the police had surrounded the dock. *Out of the frying pan, into the fire.*

Then an idea hit him. *Fire.* The matches that he'd picked up on the deck of Cate's boat! He jammed his hand into his pocket and found the old matchbook, along with the safety pins that had toppled onto the ground when she'd made that abrupt turn. His idea was insane, but it just might work. He lit a match from the matchbook and carefully held it up against the back of the front seat. After a little coaxing, the fire caught, and suddenly the driver's seat began to smoke.

Tack tapped on the glass. "Hey, buddy," he called. "Your seat's on fire."

The detective turned, alarm on his face as the smoke reached his nose. It would've been comical except for the fact that he nearly careened into oncoming traffic. Clearly, he was not a man who acted well under pressure, Tack thought as he shifted to the passenger side and tried to brace himself against the car's violent turns. *You're not going to put the fire out weaving, Einstein.*

"I'd suggest pulling over, man," Tack offered, hoping that he could do that without hitting a tree. Or the bus in the next lane.

Glancing in the rearview mirror, eyes wide, the detective slammed on the brakes and skidded to the side of the road where he leaped out, and then, filled with a panic that left him careless, he clicked his key chain and threw open the back door. Tack was ready for him.

One swift kick sent the man sprawling backward. Tack rushed out of the car and tackled him, the way he'd done with dozens of offensive linemen when he'd played high school football. Piece of cake. One hard shot to the face, and the detective was down, groaning. Tack grabbed the keys.

He rushed to the front of the car, grabbed a half-consumed soda can from the cup holder, went to the back and doused the smoking seat with it. Then he slammed the door shut, returned to the driver's seat and drove off, leaving the groggy, square-jawed detective yelling at him in his rearview mirror.

He had only one thing on his mind: save Avery. He sped off in the direction of the airport, his heart pounding. He knew it was a long shot to catch them. Allen would be flying Derek back to Chicago on a private jet, no doubt. They could easily already be wheels up by this stage. Tack had spent a few weeks on Aruba just last month, and he knew his way around the small island. It took him only a few minutes to reach the airport. He careened down the narrow highway to the airport, but in his bones, he already knew he was probably too late. Private jets didn't have the same kind of security that commercial ones did. In the back of the airport, he screeched to a stop, just as a he saw a small jet roll off down the runway. Allen Enterprises was written along the side. No doubt the boy and Derek were already aboard.

Now for plan B, he thought, jumping back in his car and making his way to the US Consulate. He was going to get Cate out of jail.

CATE WASN'T SURE how long it had been since her arrest. Her cell had no windows and no visible clock, just the garish overheard fluorescent lights occasionally flickering overhead. It felt like days. She'd drifted in and out of sleep at one point, but the lights, the hard metal cot and the eerie emptiness of the rest of the jail made it impossible to get any real rest.

The female officer who'd fingerprinted her had at one point brought in water, a package of pretzels and a fish sandwich that smelled so strong she hadn't thought it a good idea to eat it. She had enough problems without adding food poisoning to the menu. Her stomach growled and ached from being empty. If that was anything to go by, she'd been here at least a full day and a night. Maybe longer. She was thirsty, tired and hungry, and feeling more and more like she'd been abandoned forever.

In the time she'd been in jail, she'd managed to catalog every single mistake she'd ever made in her life, and imagined exactly what she'd do differently. Maybe she never should've run with Avery, after all. Maybe she should've insisted on trying to find a police officer somewhere who *would* listen to her. Or she could've set up cameras throughout the house to get irrefutable proof that he'd been laying his hands on her. Everything seemed so simple and easy *now*.

Of course, she knew she hadn't been thinking rationally when she'd been married to Rick. How could she outthink him when she was always just trying to read his mood, predict the erupting of his temper and hope she could avoid the tornado that would inevitably follow. Plus, Rick made no secret of feeling paranoid that others were out to get him—his competitors, his rivals, even ex-girlfriends. If he'd found cameras *she'd* planted, then he would've killed her. Not to mention, the ever-watchful eye of the servants—the butler, the housekeeper, the cook—always seemingly everywhere at once. She was never alone enough of the time to set up surveillance equipment. They would've seen. They would've told Rick.

That had been part of the worst of it—surrounded by people, none of them ever willing to help her. Their silence bought like so many others.

Her thoughts looped endlessly around what she could've done differently, should've done differently. Should she have run the second she'd even had a suspicion about Tack? Hadn't she known something was off the second he'd climbed into her hotel minibus? A big, strapping vet who'd flirted with her had to have an ulterior motive.

He said he loved me. He said he'd look after me.

She glanced at the empty cell across the hall and couldn't help but feel abandoned. Then she heard voices from down the hallway. Loud ones. A man's voice, arguing. She stood and pressed her face against the bars. She couldn't see anything, but she heard a steel door creak open. Then came footsteps.

She closed her eyes and prayed they'd belong to Tack.

"You can't hold her here. It's been *thirty hours*, and have you even given her anything to eat? *One* meal is inhumane, Officer. And it's clearly against the law. I don't think your chief will want to hear about this. *Any* of this."

Cate craned her neck to see. The voice didn't sound like Tack's. She tried to stifle the heavy disappointment that threatened to rest on her shoulders.

The female officer lumbered into view, and

beside her stood a man she'd never seen before, wearing a smart dark suit and tie. He was striking with dark hair and hazel-colored eyes and had the kind of determined walk that said he was used to getting what he wanted. She couldn't help but feel sorely disappointed. Who was this man?

"Cate Dalton? I'm John Benoit. US Consulate. Here to see that you're safely bonded out of this facility."

"Do I know you?" Cate asked, perplexed, as the guard opened her cell and she came out.

"No, but I know you. And all your questions will be answered in due time. Now, come along. I've got someone who's very eager to see you." Cate's heart leaped. Was it somehow Avery? She glanced at the man who'd gotten her out of jail, and as they turned down a narrow passage to the steel door with the small Plexiglas window, she wondered if Mark had sent him. Had Mark somehow heard she'd been arrested?

In the front area of the jail, where the coffeemaker and two desks sat side by side, the female guard handed her a bag containing her personal effects: her watch and jewelry and phone.

She thought about the boat, and her suitcase and purse.

"What about my suitcase…and the boat?" she asked.

"I'll take care of it," John promised. "We'll get it back."

Cate simply couldn't believe it, as she walked by the desks, past the unhappy-looking guard, that she was actually leaving. She glanced backward once, and the man in the dark suit gently clasped her elbow.

"Keep moving," John urged. "Just keep moving."

She followed him out of the jail and into the blinding morning sunlight. She blinked back the light, and then, once in the parking lot, saw a tall, broad figure leaning up against a gray sedan.

"Tack?" she murmured, almost unable to believe her eyes. He *had* come for her, just like he said he would. He uncrossed his arms and jogged to her. In seconds, she was in his arms and he'd lifted her straight off the ground. She'd never been so glad to be swept off her feet. He kissed her almost instantly, running his hands through her hair like he'd been waiting years, and not just a day, to have her in his arms again.

"You came for me," she said, still not quite sure she believed her own eyes. "But what about the visa?"

"We might still be able to get it. But I wasn't going to leave you behind. Never." His full lips quirked into a crooked grin, and Cate felt her insides melt just a little bit. The man's smile still had the same effect on her.

"While this little reunion is heartwarming, I think we'd better go, Tack, before they realize you're the guy who set a police car on fire and *then* stole it," John said drily as he slipped out of his suit jacket and opened the front door.

"Stole a police car? Set it on *fire*? Sounds like I missed quite a lot," Cate said.

"You have no idea." Tack wrapped his arm around her shoulders, and they both ducked into the back of the sedan. John took the driver's seat.

"What would I do without you?" Tack said as he reached the driver's seat and clapped his friend on the shoulder.

"Rot in jail probably," John quipped and Tack chuckled, as his friend keyed the ignition and drove the car out of the police parking lot.

"I've known this guy since boot camp," Tack said. "He was the one who fainted in the mess hall."

"I had *heat stroke*," John said, quick to clarify. "So, the proper term is *passed out*. Not fainted."

"Whatever you say, London." Tack grinned at Cate, grabbing her hand and squeezing it.

"London?" Cate questioned.

"London Bridge is falling down," Tack explained, and Cate could see John roll his eyes in the rearview mirror.

"That's some way to thank the man who just sprung your girlfriend out of jail."

"They weren't even holding her on any real charges," Tack said, squeezing her hand.

Cate didn't understand. "What about the kidnapping? What about the theft? They said that I'd be on trial soon. That I'd be in jail for a long time."

"Allen bribed them, we think," Tack said. "As it turned out, he didn't want to go through proper channels, because he didn't want to have to wait. He wanted to make sure he maintained control, and the only way to do that was *not* to involve the US government."

"Where's Avery? Are we going to see him?" Cate felt hope rise in her chest. If the US authorities weren't involved, maybe that meant there was a better chance she'd get to see her boy. Then she saw Tack meet John's glance in the rearview mirror.

"We think Derek took him to see Allen. I saw them leave on a private jet."

"What?" Cate felt her heart race. Her boy was on his way to see her ex *right now*.

"The good news is we can travel. And London, here, has access to a private jet."

"I didn't say you could use it," he deadpanned, but when Cate met his gaze in the mirror he winked. "*She* can go anywhere she'd like, especially if it's with me. But I don't think I promised *you* anything."

"I told you she's *off-limits*, London."

"That's for the girl to decide, isn't it?" John was clearly flirting, but Cate didn't mind. It was good-natured, and she could tell he was mostly doing it to get under Tack's skin. The fact that it was working made Cate feel a little thrill. Tack *cared*.

"I'm not going to let you go alone with London. He has a bad rap with women."

"Women love me!" he exclaimed.

"Exactly *why* you have a bad rap," Tack said, and his friend laughed at that.

"Okay, I'm going to have you to the airport in about ten minutes."

"You're flying with us?" Cate asked, even as Tack wrapped a protective arm around her shoulders.

"Wish I could, but no. It's just you two outbound. The jet has to fly to pick up the diplomat's kid from boarding school, so it might as well take you to Chicago on the way. I've got all the papers you need. It's wheels up in an hour."

INSIDE THE PRIVATE JET, Cate glanced at the tasteful tan leather interior and the two facing armchair seats on one side of the plane, and the long couch on the other. On the far end hung a wide, flat-screen TV, plus a small table with a magazine and newspaper on it. For a second, she felt like she was back on one of Rick's jets, but then remembered this one did not belong to him and felt a bit of relief.

"Hey, folks," the captain said as he poked his head out of the cockpit. "Welcome aboard. We'll be taking off soon. It's a seven-hour flight, and it's just you two, me and the copilot up here. Keep your seat belt on for take-off, but after that you can serve yourself drinks or grab something from the mini fridge. If you need anything, knock. Otherwise, we'll probably see you on the other side." The pilot slid the privacy door closed, and it was suddenly just Tack and Cate, alone, as the engines of the plane came to life, and the plane moved away from the hangar.

"This is nice," Tack said as he slid into one of the overstuffed armchairs. "I'm used to flying coach—or cargo plane. This is something else."

Cate nodded and slipped into the armchair across from him, suddenly reminded of all the dozens of flights she'd taken in a private jet.

She'd been lucky, she knew, yet she'd paid for that wealth every single day she'd been married to Rick. "Sure, it's nice."

Tack glanced up. "But not as nice as you're used to."

"I didn't say that."

"You didn't have to." Tack studied her a minute, leaning forward and touching her knees. His big hands felt warm and protective there as he squeezed them ever so slightly. She suddenly felt a little shiver down her spine. She didn't want him to stop touching her. "Do you miss it? The wealth?"

Cate glanced out of the small, oval window. "Sometimes," she admitted honestly. "It's not easy to worry about money. I worried about money my whole life growing up, and then after Rick...everything was much harder."

Tack's hands slipped from her knees. She reached out and touched his arm. "But I wouldn't want it back. Not if Rick came with it. I know now that being poor and happy is far better than being rich and miserable."

The plane shuddered beneath them as it turned at the end of the runway. Then, the engines revved and the plane throttled forward, eventually taking flight. Tack looked out the window as the small plane took off, the airport and the island growing smaller and smaller beneath them, until it was a small dark shape in a sea of blue-green.

"It really is beautiful down there," Cate said. "I'm going to miss the Caribbean."

"Maybe you can come back," Tack said.

"Maybe."

"I don't think Mark is going to sell the resort," he said.

"He might not have a choice." It was funny, the worry of the resort had been all-encompassing just days ago, but now it seemed almost inconsequential. Not that she didn't care, but she simply couldn't focus on anything other than Avery. And getting him back.

The plane soon leveled off as they began the journey to Chicago. Cate wondered how she was going endure the entire flight when she just wanted to *get there already*. Why hadn't teleporting been invented yet?

Tack glanced at the small mini fridge near the couch. "Want a drink?" he asked her. "We've got seven hours. Might as well get comfortable."

Cate wasn't sure she *could* get comfortable. All she could think about was her little boy, and whether he was getting fed foods he'd eat, whether Derek was taking care of him, whether he was sad or scared or worried. She hated the not knowing more than anything. Being a mother had been the most fulfilling role of her life, and yet it was also the most demanding, even when Avery wasn't in her sight. Maybe *more* demanding when he wasn't. The worry ate away at her stomach.

She popped up from her seat and began to pace in the small cabin.

"Hungry? Can I get you something to eat?"

"Starved."

"I see crackers and cheese here, and wine… but you probably want water."

"Wine is good. Or anything stronger."

He glanced over his shoulder and saw the expression on her face. "You okay?"

"I'm just worried. Do you think…do you think Avery is okay?"

Tack put down the bottle and returned to her. "I think he's fine, I do." He put his arms gently on her shoulders. Cate turned and faced him, biting her lip.

"But he's all alone."

"Derek will treat him well because Allen won't pay him if he doesn't, and Derek just cares about getting paid."

"Are you sure? What if he doesn't feed him, or makes sure he uses the bathroom, or…"

"He'll be fine, Cate. Try not to worry." He looked so confident, so sure, and Cate wanted to believe him. She wanted to feel confident that everything would work out, but she just couldn't quite shut her brain off. It rattled and hummed, as if it were filled with a million bees, all of them angry and anxious. She sank onto the couch.

"How can I not worry? Even if he is fine, what if I never see him again? What if Rick uses his money and his influence and…and… what about when he finds out I lied to him, that his father was alive all this time, what if… what if he *doesn't* want to see me again? What if he hates me?" This haunted her and made her feel sick to her stomach. Cate knew she'd done her boy wrong by keeping the truth from him. And even though he was still so little, he knew what a lie was.

She put her face in her hands. "Rick is going to tell Avery what a bad mom I am, and what if he's right? What if I am a terrible mother?" Cate was losing it. She didn't know if she had the strength to face the horrible what-ifs, and her throat constricted with tears.

Tack sat next to her, wrapping his strong arm around her shoulders.

"You're not a terrible mother. You're a loving mother who did what she thought she had to do to protect her son," Tack said, gently squeezing her to his side.

"But Avery is so little. He'll believe anything Rick tells him." And Rick was so very persuasive.

"Avery loves you, and he'll always love you. Rick Allen's money and his influence and anything else won't change that."

Cate leaned into Tack, drawing comfort from him and strength. "How can you be so sure?"

"Because I saw how much you love him, and how much he loves you, and a bond like that can't be severed with money. Remember, your ex is a virtual stranger to him. Do you really think he'll immediately believe his word over yours?"

"He'll be so confused, though. And hurt. And upset." Cate felt the tears well up. The last thing on earth she ever wanted to do was hurt Avery.

She laid her face against his broad chest. "Hey, you did what you thought was right at that time. You can't beat yourself up over this. What was the alternative? You stay with Avery's father and let him beat you to death? *Then* where would Avery be? Without his mother."

Cate nodded; Tack was right.

"You did what you thought you had to do," he continued, stroking her arm. "You might have had other choices, but at the time, what could you have really done differently? You were isolated and alone, and yet you still found a way to break free of all that, and take Avery with you. A weaker person would've stayed. A weaker person would still be there."

Cate hugged Tack, holding on to him, the comfort in his body and his words. "You think so?"

"I know so. You're one of the bravest and strongest women I've ever met."

"Avery might not think so. He'll be hurt." She bit her lip. She hated imagining him angry or hurt because of something she did.

"Avery is young. And kids his age are very forgiving. Not to mention that you'll be with him soon. To explain why you did what you did. You'll have a lifetime to make it up to him." Tack nuzzled the top of her head, and she leaned into the touch. He felt so big and safe, so strong. She wanted to believe him.

"Rick could keep him from me."

"He won't. I'll make sure he won't. We *will* work something out so that you can see your son. I won't let Rick steal him away from you."

"Why are you fighting so hard for this? For Avery? For me?" She still couldn't quite wrap her head around the fact that she had an ally, someone who would fight for her.

"Because we're a team now, whether you like it or not. And I'll fight by your side for as long as it takes to make sure Avery gets to see his mother."

"Tack... If you really do this, Rick could destroy you." Cate still thought Tack didn't understand the enemy he was facing. He didn't get that Rick just got what he wanted, whenever he wanted, that he was a man who never took no for an answer, who never had to. "I've seen him make people's lives miserable. He has so much power, and so much money, he can have whatever he wants. He'll dig up your secrets, and if you don't have any, he'll make them up."

Tack stiffened a little, but then hugged her tighter. "I don't care what he throws at me. I've told you all my secrets. And, besides, I talked to my friend at the consulate. He gave me some good advice. I think I'll be able to persuade him."

"Don't underestimate him."

"I won't," Tack promised. "Just as long as you don't underestimate me."

Cate couldn't help but love his confidence, the way he stared this massive problem in the face and didn't back down.

"I wish we were there already," she said. "I don't know how I can survive seven hours on this plane."

Tack gently ran a hand down her arm and squeezed.

"By letting me distract you." Suddenly, the gentle caress made all her worries fade. All she could think about at that moment was his touch, and the heat of his body next to her. God, the man was so broad, so *solid*. She did love the feel of him against her. She felt safe, if only for a few seconds. *He came back for you.* Hadn't that been the litmus test? Wasn't that what she was waiting for to prove his love? Yet insecurities rattled around in her chest, like loose change.

"Why did you come back for me?" she murmured in his chest. She needed to hear it from him.

"Because I love you," he said softly. "Because I can't imagine my life without you in it."

The words seemed so bold. So sure. "But you thought I was a thief...worse..." He had been planning to deliver her straight into the arms of the man who'd hurt her and who would not rest until she was behind bars or dead.

He pulled away then, fixing her with his dark gaze filled with regret. "I am so sorry for that. I was wrong. I was so very wrong about you." He tucked his finger beneath her chin and raised her face. "I'm sorry for hurting you.

If you give me another chance, I promise I'll never hurt you again."

His dark eyes pleaded with her.

"I want to give you that chance. I do." Her whole body screamed for her to do just that. It would be the easiest thing in the world to kiss him right now, to believe everything he'd just said, and to start over with him. She wanted to believe that after so much had happened in her life that this could really, truly be love. *Real* love. But she thought about Rick once more, and how sure she'd been of him at the start, about how he'd changed so radically after she'd moved in.

Then, the realization that she still had doubts about Tack, even after he'd come to save her, made her worry that she might *never* heal. Maybe, she realized, the worst and most lasting wound was being unable to trust in love.

"But I'm not sure, Tack. I just…" So much was happening all at once. Her boy was missing, she'd spent the night in jail, her ex was still out there, angry and probably hell-bent on revenge. She had nothing left to give at this moment, and her head was a swirl of emotions. She couldn't think straight. Plus, the exhaustion of the last forty-eight hours weighed on her suddenly. Cate barely slept the night before, and she realized she'd been mostly running on adrenaline for the last two days. She felt shaky and exhausted.

Tack pulled her back to his chest and hugged her tightly. "I'm on your timeline," he told her. "I'm a patient man."

"I'm going to test that patience," she said, smiling into his chest. It rumbled with laughter. She snuggled into him, though, too tired to do much else.

"You already are," he murmured softly and kissed the top of her head.

CHAPTER TWENTY-ONE

CATE FELL ASLEEP against Tack, her body worn out from the mind-boggling events of the last few days. She woke as the plane touched down, jerking awake only to realize that she was still safely encased in Tack's arms on the couch in the private plane.

She felt warm and safe, until she remembered where she was and why. Rick found her, and probably right at this moment had her boy, and there was a chance that she might never see Avery again. She loved that Tack wanted to fight for her, for them, but she also knew the reality of going up against a titan like Rick Allen. She knew what the man was capable of, and Tack didn't. She'd meant it when she said that Rick played dirty, that he would find secrets or make them up. He didn't care which.

"Did I sleep that whole time?" Cate asked, yawning as she untangled herself from Tack's embrace and sat up.

"Soundly. You even snored."

"I did?" Cate felt her face grow pink. "I snore?"

"Like a congested grizzly bear," Tack said, and leaned over and kissed her on the nose. "It's adorable."

"Doesn't sound adorable." She blinked and rubbed her eyes as she watched Tack lean back and raise the window shade near the couch. Sunlight streamed in, and she could see the airport whiz by as the plane slowed on the runway. "I can't believe I slept the whole flight away."

"I can. You were exhausted. I'm glad you got some rest." Tack dipped down and kissed her lightly. Cate returned the kiss before it even occurred to her that she probably had a horrendous case of morning breath. Tack didn't seem to mind, however, as he smiled at her, which made her stomach feel warm and a little gooey. He draped his arm across her shoulders and she leaned into him once more, loving how she fit perfectly in the crook of his arm.

"What do we do now?" she asked as the plane taxied to the private hangar.

"First, you let me go talk to your ex."

Cate felt her stomach tighten with worry. "What if he doesn't want to talk?"

"Then he'll be the one doing the listening."

Tack's jaw flexed, and she saw the determination in his face. She hoped he knew what he was doing, and she sent up a silent prayer that Rick wouldn't hurt him.

"Be careful, Tack. Rick Allen is dangerous."

He hugged her tightly. "I'm always careful. You don't have to worry about me."

"And you can't go see him in that..." She nodded toward the Aruba Police shirt he wore.

"I'll ask the captain if he has a shirt I can borrow," Tack said. "In the meantime, just relax. We'll be okay."

Cate hoped he was right. But she decided she'd check with Mark. Maybe he'd have some ideas on how to deal with Rick.

AFTER BREEZING THROUGH customs thanks to the IDs John Benoit provided, Tack and Cate rode in a taxi down Lakeshore Drive, past the sailboats bobbing in Lake Michigan. The massive lake looked almost like the Caribbean, except it was a deep blue, not blue-green, and the bare trees lining the highway reminded Tack that it wasn't the balmy eighty degrees of most days on St. Anthony's Island. The chilly February air whistled into the cab through the partially open back window. He glanced at Cate, who was hugging her arms, and he reached over and rolled the window up. Then he shrugged out of his borrowed button-down plaid shirt, offering it to her for warmth. Beneath, he wore a simple white undershirt. She took it and sent him a grateful smile, which lit him up from inside, made him feel even more protective of her. He just wanted her comfortable and safe, and he was going to do everything in his power to make sure she was.

"I'm not used to seasons anymore," Cate said. "Just summer."

She pulled on his shirt, the sleeves hanging impossibly long past her fingers. She looked like a child wearing her father's shirt. It made her look even more adorable, and Tack's heart sped up a little. He didn't want to lose her. He was going to do everything in his power to make sure that didn't happen. Her phone dinged and she pulled it out, frowning as she read a new message.

"Who's texting you?" Tack asked, glancing at her phone face.

"Mark," she said. "I asked him about legal stuff. He's a retired lawyer, and he has friends who do family law. I just want to cover my bases."

"I also know a lawyer," Tack said, wrapping his arm around her shoulders and pulling her to him. "You know, one way or another, this will be okay."

Cate studied her phone, scrolling through the long message. "I hope so."

Soon enough, they pulled into the massive hospital complex in downtown, where some of the finest surgeons in the country practiced, a beacon of cutting edge research and new techniques, and Rick Allen's last resort. Tack had discovered the man had flown all over the world looking for treatments or a different diagnosis for his failing lungs. Switzerland, the Netherlands, Japan. None of them had cures for him, and so he came back home, to Chicago, where he'd found one last team of surgeons willing to try to revive his body. Tack knew the prognosis was bad. He'd heard it from Allen himself, months ago.

Cate grasped his hand and squeezed. "You're sure this is the only way?" She glanced at him, worry pinching her features. All he wanted to do was make those worry lines go away. To see her smile again.

"I am going to go talk to him. You don't have to even see him. I don't want to put you through that." Cate's shoulders relaxed a little, and Tack felt a small bit of relief. "You don't ever have to see him again, if I can help it."

Cate slipped her hands around his waist and squeezed. "Thank you," she murmured against his chest, and he could feel the sincerity of her gratitude.

"I will take care of him."

"But what about Adeeb?"

Tack frowned as the cab pulled up in the circular drive, where visitors wandered into the hospital through oversize automatic glass doors. "I want you to wait for me. Can you do that? You can even wait here, in the cab."

"No," Cate said. "I'll wait inside."

"Are you sure?"

She nodded. Once more, Tack admired her bravery. He paid the cabbie and took her by the hand. Together, they walked into the hospital and took the elevator up to ICU.

A small, furnished waiting room sat near a nurses' station. The windows would have overlooked the lake, but most of them were covered in blinds, half closed.

"You can wait here," Tack suggested, nodding toward the empty seats. Cate squeezed his arm.

She nodded, a little bit in a daze, as she sank onto a cushioned love seat.

"You okay?" he asked her.

"Yes. Just… I miss Avery. I hope this works."

"It will," Tack said with more confidence than he felt.

Tack already knew Allen was in room 1209. He pulled Cate into his arms and hugged her tightly. Then he laid a gentle kiss on her lips.

"Good luck," she whispered.

He knew he was going to need it.

What was he going to do to get a man like Rick Allen to see reason?

The hallway was mostly empty, except for a nurse filling out paperwork at the main desk. She didn't look up as he glided past, straight to 1209.

Inside, Cate's ex-husband lay still on the hospital bed, dozens of wires and tubes running from his arms to the adjacent monitors. They quietly beeped around him as colored numbers denoting blood pressure and heart rate continued to change. The once-powerful man looked pale and shrunken. Anyone could see the man was not long for this world.

He also realized that as frail as the man was, he still shouldn't count him out. Cate had said he was dangerous, and Tack needed to keep on his toes. *Never underestimate your enemy.*

Allen cracked one eye open, his breathing labored, and the oxygen tube in his nose not doing much. "You failed," he said. "If you're

looking for your visa, you can keep on looking. Derek brought my boy back. And I had to
pay extra to make sure they put that no good
woman away. It wasn't cheap to make sure
she rots there."

Tack felt anger prick his skin, and he clenched
one fist. He'd let his temper get the best of him
before with Derek. That got him court-martialed. This time, he had to keep a level head.
For Cate. For Avery. For Adeeb.

"I found her," Tack said calmly, realizing
that one of his advantages was that Allen had
no idea Cate was free. He could use that. "You
owe me."

"I don't owe you anything." Allen took a
shaky breath. His body looked so frail, his
useless legs stretched out before him, even
smaller than Tack remembered. What muscles the man used to have in his shoulders and
arms had now also atrophied, and he looked
immeasurably older and frailer. Still, a fire
burned in his eyes. The man wouldn't let go
of revenge, even now, on his deathbed. "You
were too busy looking at my wife's ass to do
your job. I heard Derek's report. He'd been
watching you two."

"*Ex*-wife. And besides, I was just doing
what I could to get close to her," Tack lied.

"Give me the visa you promised. Derek would never have found her on his own. You and I both know that."

"Maybe." Allen struggled and then clicked the button next to him, and more painkillers dripped into his IV. Tack hoped he could use that to his advantage. "But I think you planned to betray me."

"I had them both on the boat. I was going to deliver." The lies came out easily. "You have the boy at your house right as we speak, don't you?"

"No." Allen wheezed. "But I give you credit for trying to find out. I know you've fallen for Cate. You're working for her now. You can't fool me."

Tack realized it was no use in pretending, and besides, he wanted to tell the man exactly what he thought of him. "You're right. I love her. I plan to marry her."

Allen let out a hoarse laugh. "I don't want her anymore. You're welcome to her. And, just so you know, I've instructed my attorneys to draw up papers to declare her an unfit mother, so no matter what happens to me, she'll never see Avery again."

"You won't get away with that." Tack felt his blood pressure rise. "I'm here to talk about how you're going to make sure that she sees her boy. How you're going to apologize to her for everything you've done, and how you're going to make sure there's a fair custody hearing."

Allen laughed, but dry coughs cut off his bitter mirth as he struggled to get his breathing under control. "You don't have anything I want, therefore, you can't negotiate with me. I'm going to tell *you* how this is going to go. *I'm* going to file charges against Cate for parenting kidnapping, and then I'm going to make sure the judge knows just how *unstable* she is, how she is *delusional* and how she's been seeing a therapist for years for her disorders."

Tack felt off balance as he let Allen's words sink in. Cate hadn't said anything about a therapist. And she wasn't crazy, so that meant… "Cate never saw a therapist. She doesn't have any issues."

Allen smirked. "I've *paid* a therapist, so she's seen one."

"You're going to bribe a therapist to give a *false testimony* in a custody hearing." Tack shook his head. "Just like you paid the local police to look the other way when you beat your wife."

Allen closed his eyes, and for a minute Tack thought the man might drift off.

"I didn't have to pay them," Allen murmured, the extra painkillers beginning to take effect.

"No? Is that what you call the extra campaign contributions to the mayor and the local alderman? Then, low and behold, everyone gets a little boost to their pension plans." Tack had done his research. Now that he'd known where to look, the money trail seemed obvious. Not that he could prove it in court, but still.

Allen chuckled. "It's not a bribe if it's part of our political process. Money talks. I just happen to have a lot of money." He laughed a little, sounding almost drunk on morphine.

"That you used to make sure nobody believed Cate. What about the scar on her chin? How are you going to explain that? That makes for some powerful proof that you laid your hands on her."

"That would've never have happened if she'd stayed where she belonged." Allen clicked the main medication one more time.

Tack would've felt sorry for the shriveled shell of a man before him if he weren't still trying so hard to hurt the woman Tack loved.

"You're dying. This is your last shot to make

amends, and instead, you want to hurt the mother of your child."

"She hurt me first," the man said simply, his voice growing weaker as the meds took effect. Now he had trouble keeping his eyes open.

Tack took a seat near his bedside.

"You're not going to hurt Cate anymore. Do you understand me?"

Allen gave a low chuckle. "What are you going to do? Threaten to kill me? I'm already dying. You can't do anything more to me than that.

"And, just so you know, she doesn't get a dime of my money. I divorced her. I wrote her out of the will. My will gives it all to charity. I'll go down in history as the world's biggest benefactor. With some set aside for Avery, of course."

"Which we both know is a lie." Cate stood in the door, still wearing Tack's plaid shirt, with the sleeves pushed up.

"Cate…" Tack cried, surprised.

She glanced at him, but then turned her attention back to her ex-husband.

"You…" Allen growled, his heart rate increasing on the monitors before them. "What are you doing here?"

Cate smirked and shook her head slowly.

She walked right up to his IV, which was plugged into the morphine machine, and she unplugged it with one sharp jerk, cutting him off from all painkillers. Then she unplugged the nurse's call button, too. Now he was cut off from help.

"I'm here to get my son. You're going to sit there, and you're going to listen to me."

CHAPTER TWENTY-TWO

CATE HAD THOUGHT seeing Rick again would be the worst moment of her life, but right then, she felt more empowered than she'd felt in years. Rick wasn't the strong, overbearing man she remembered—he was weak, a shell of his former self, hardly someone she could imagine being scared of.

She took in his sickly appearance, his pale skin and slightly blue lips, and was glad she'd gotten up from that waiting room couch and stepped into the room. She decided she couldn't let Tack do this alone. This was her fight as much as it was his, and it was long past time for her to join in.

She took in Rick's withered body, amazed at how much he'd changed since the last time she'd seen him. He had wasted away. Literally. His blue eyes glared at her, pure hatred and menace. She could feel how badly he wanted to hurt her, even lying there on the hospital bed.

"Plug me back in."

He looked down at his morphine drip and nodded to the wall. For a second, his rumbling voice put her right back into walking-on-eggshells mode. The old Cate would've apologized and scurried to plug the morphine back in. She was surprised by how strong the urge was to cave, to do his bidding. It was almost like a Pavlovian response. He shouted, "Jump," and her body wanted to ask, "How high?" But those days were gone. She was a different person now, a stronger person. She'd been on her own a long time, taking care of herself, and she wasn't about to stop now.

She glanced at Tack, who watched her carefully, as if waiting for his cue to pounce on Rick. She didn't need that. Not yet. She was okay. She could *do* this.

"I *said*, put my line back in."

Now, she thought, he sounded just like a petulant child. And she wasn't going to give in. Not this time. Cate had no intention of making him comfortable.

"This is how this will go," she said, ignoring his request as if he were a toddler throwing a fit. "You're going to tell me where Avery is. You're going to let me see him, *and* you're going to give me custody. Then you're going to make the call you need to make so that Tack gets that visa his friend needs."

Rick laughed weakly. "You're delusional. You think not giving me morphine will make me do that? I'm calling the police." He struggled to raise his arm for the phone.

"Go ahead," Cate said. "Tell them how you bribed police officers, how you lied about the abuse. I bet you even lied to the FBI. I'd bet money you didn't *want* kidnapping charges filed. You wanted to find me yourself. You didn't want them to find me first."

"Lies," Rick croaked, but his voice was weak.

"Tell them how you wanted me dead so that *you* wouldn't have to pay me half your estate, which, by the way, you still owe me. I've confirmed it with *my* lawyer. It doesn't matter that a judge granted you a divorce decree in my absence, because that decree grants me *50 percent* of everything you have, if I am ever found. I've already filed a motion to freeze your assets."

Now Cate started to see real fear on his face. She'd hit him where it hurt: his wallet. "No." He shook his head.

"Documents don't lie, and I have a copy of the decree right here." She held up her phone to show him the email Mark had sent her. She was entitled to 50 percent of everything he had, will or not.

"I'll fight you. I'll sue. I'll contest *every-thing*. You're not getting my money."

"I don't want your money." That stunned Rick into silence. "What I want is for you to give Tack the visa he needs."

Tack whipped his head around and glared at her in shock. "You don't have to do that."

"I do," Cate said, resolute. She had never felt so sure of anything. Tack's friend needed that visa. He'd served a country not even his own well, and it wasn't right to abandon him.

"The visa isn't worth five hundred million dollars," Rick growled. "You'd sign away your part of my fortune?"

"You give Tack the visa. You agree to let Avery live with me, though I will bring him to visit you every day in the hospital as long as you live."

"How can I trust you won't just run again?" Rick struggled in bed. "You'll run."

"You promise not to pursue *any* charges against me. We get it in writing, all past offenses forgiven, on the condition that I bring Avery to see you as much as possible in your last days." Cate took a step forward, feeling more and more confident that she was doing the right thing, that Rick would never be able to hurt her again. She was finally standing up for herself. This was different from running. This was making a stand.

"And...you do not pay out the reward money you offered to Derek Hollie."

"That's a long list of things. Why should I agree?"

"You're going to do what I ask," Cate said, her voice sounding suddenly powerful in her own ears, "because you have no choice. Because I will fight you with *your own* money. Because you know as well as I do that you can't get custody. You're too sick, and you won't survive a legal battle that will take months, if not years. You will do this now because it's *the right thing to do*, and for once in your life, before you die, you're going to do the right thing." She took a breath, her hands shaking with emotion. "You tried to kill me. To take away my will to live, but I am going to survive you. And I am not just going to survive. I promise you, I'm going to thrive."

And then, just when Cate thought Rick would start yelling, throwing a fit, threatening to kill her, he simply started to cry.

The man she'd been so afraid of was *crying.* The man who'd kept her under his thumb for years sobbed like a baby. Tears slid down the man's cheeks, and for a second, all Cate could do was stare. What was this? A trick? The painkillers in his system?

"I'm dying, Cate. You don't care that I'm *dying*." She heard the hopelessness in his voice, the sorrow. Cate just stared at the man as he sniffed. "Don't you love me at all? Don't you *care*?"

Cate glanced at Tack. Had he heard this? Was this *actually happening*? She expected something far different. For him to be furious, for him to want revenge. The angry Rick was the one she was expecting. Not this sad, blubbering mess.

"You lost the right to have her empathy the moment you laid a hand on her," Tack growled.

"You stay out of this," Rick snapped. "Cate, can we talk…alone?" He glared at Tack, but Tack simply glanced at Cate, unsure.

"It's okay," she said. "Let me talk to him."

Reluctantly, Tack left. "I'll be right outside. You need anything, just yell."

Rick blinked at Cate, looking tired and worn out.

"Sit down," he commanded. When she didn't budge, he added, "Please."

Cate took a seat, but kept herself out of reach.

"I loved you, Cate. I *still* love you even though *you* did this to me." He sniffled. "I just wanted to see you again before I died."

"Is this some kind of trick?" Cate couldn't help but ask. "Because…"

"It's no trick. I love you. I thought you loved me. We have a *child* together. But you don't even seem to care about that. You've treated me so badly, Cate. And all I wanted to do was love you."

Cate snorted. "You *hit* me."

"Cate. You know you drove me crazy sometimes, I loved you that much. Don't you love me at all? You're so cold, Cate. Don't you care, even a little? It seems to me that you don't care about me at all."

Cate had a flash of memory then. About how he would be *just like this* after one of his episodes. About how he'd be apologetic with a splash of passive aggressiveness. This was part of the cycle. Anger, then guilt—it was exactly how he'd controlled her so well. He'd take away her ability to be mad, because he'd make her feel guilty for not being *good enough* or not *loving him enough*. All she'd had to do to prove it was forgive him, take him back, let the cycle start all over again.

"You never listened to me, Cate. If only you'd *listened*, you would've known how not to make me mad. I told you so often what you needed to do, but you wouldn't *listen*."

There it was—the blame. This was all her

fault. Cate had heard it before. So many times. It had worked, too. That's the part she was ashamed of.

"It's not my fault that you hit me." She wasn't budging from that.

"I'm not saying that. I'm saying I loved you, and you didn't love me enough or you would've been obedient."

"Obey you? That's all you really wanted. You never cared about love. You only cared about making me do what you wanted. You have a messed up sense of love."

And that was it, in a nutshell. He was twisted and broken and unable to be anything else but selfish, thinking only of himself, unable to understand or care about anybody else's needs.

"Cate, why don't you love me? Why?" Rick looked so sad then, so forlorn.

"It's too late for us," Cate said. "It was too late the first time you hit me."

"Can't you forgive me? I don't want to die knowing you don't love me. How can you be so cruel?"

Cate thought she'd feel anger and indignation welling up in her chest, but instead, all she felt was pity and…indifference.

Rick only cried harder. "I'm *dying*. How can you talk to me like that?"

"Because it's the truth."

"All I want is to see my son before I die. And I don't want you to tell him you hate me. That I'm a bad person. I know…I didn't handle everything as well as I could."

She felt strangely detached. She almost… pitied him. She thought about her son, about how she didn't want him to know his father was an evil man. How that would affect *him*. She didn't want him to feel badly about his father, or himself. "I won't talk badly about you when you're gone."

"You really don't love me, do you? Did you ever?" Rick sniffled.

"At one time, I did love you. If you wanted to keep me, you should've treated me better." She said that without anger and without emotion. It was a fact, plain and simple.

"I know." Rick blinked fast. "I can see that."

"I'd like to see my son today."

Rick nodded. "Okay."

Cate felt her heart lift.

"And the visa for Tack's friend?"

Rick frowned. "Why do you care so much about that man?"

Because he's amazing in all the ways you're not. Because he loves me in a way you never could.

"The visa is the right thing to do, Rick. I know you're not a religious man, but do you really want your last act on earth to be one that condemns a man and his family to die?"

Rick thought about that a moment.

"I'll do it," he said. "But I'll do it for you."

"MOMMY!" AVERY RAN from the elevator at the hospital and straight into his mother's arms. Cate hugged him so tightly Tack thought the poor boy might burst.

Derek was right behind him. Tack felt his whole body tense.

Derek smirked as Avery jumped into his mother's arms.

"I missed you, Mommy!" he cried.

"I missed you, too, sweetheart." Cate wiped tears from her eyes. "Are you okay? Did everyone treat you okay?"

"I rode on a plane with a *huge* TV!" he exclaimed, a little excited. "I watched cartoons."

Tack thought the boy would be just fine.

At one end of the waiting room stood vending machines, and Avery caught sight of them. "Can I have a snack?" he asked, bright-eyed.

"Sure, let me take you to the vending machine."

Cate sent Tack a worried look, but he ignored it. He was going to deal with Derek, once and for all.

"You should know that Adeeb will be coming to the States," Tack said. "So, your sick and twisted revenge didn't work."

"You're pathetic, First Lieutenant," Derek said. "All these years and you've still got your panties in a bunch about a *translator*? Who cares? They all knew what they were getting into when they helped us. It was their choice." Derek slouched against the wall near the elevators, looking bored. Tack wanted to punch him right there, but managed to contain his rage.

Don't hit the man.

"We promised them asylum, and you broke that promise. But it's done. *You're* done."

"No, I'm rich."

"Really? Because Allen won't be paying you the reward money." Tack grinned, watching all the blood drain from Derek's face. The SOB deserved it. God, but he loved delivering bad news to this man.

"That can't be." Derek scurried to Rick Allen's room, and Tack couldn't help but laugh a little. He got what he deserved, the weasel.

Cate came back, with a happy Avery munching on cheese-flavored crackers.

"You okay?" Tack asked. Cate nodded, sniffing, but beaming with happiness.

"More than okay," she said. Avery sat in a nearby chair.

"I'm proud of you, you know that?" he said. "What you did wasn't easy."

Cate smiled through her happy tears. "Looks like you got your visa, and I got Avery. A happy ending."

He reached out and grabbed her hand. "Cate, you shouldn't give up a fortune for me. For Adeeb. We can work on finding another way, maybe."

"I want to do this. I want to bring Adeeb home."

Tack pulled Cate into his arms. "I love you."

"I love you, too," she said, and Tack felt a rush of emotion—surprise, shock and then delight.

He felt a huge grin spread across his face. "You do?"

"I really do."

Tack dipped his head and kissed her hard, leaving her breathless. There was no place else he'd rather be.

CATE KEPT HER PROMISE. She took Avery every day to visit his father. None of those visits were easy, and Cate battled her own little flame of guilt, knowing that Avery's only memories of his father would be as a sick, dying man. Rick Allen died three months later, and Cate, Tack and Avery attended the funeral. Cate kept her promise not to fight for Rick's money, but in the end, he surprised her by setting up a trust for Avery worth millions. She sent some of that money to Mark on St. Anthony's, ensuring the resort would be up and running for a long time to come because Avery had so many memories there as a young boy, and in some ways that would always be Avery's home.

Cate and Avery settled into an apartment in Chicago in Tack's own building, and the three spent much of their time together. They also planned to spend every winter on St. Anthony's Island.

Now, Cate, Avery and Tack stood together in the baggage claim of Chicago's O'Hare International Airport, waiting for their guests to arrive.

"What's the girl's name again?" Avery asked, excited.

"Medeeha," Tack said. He craned his neck to search the crowd as people filed in from Customs. A slim man, his young wife and three-year-old daughter walked out then. Cate watched Tack as he ran to his friend and gave him a bear hug worthy of a brother.

"How the hell are you?" he cried, clapping him on the back.

"We're glad to be here," Adeeb said, grinning. Cate took Avery by the hand and they began introductions all around. Medeeha shyly waved at Avery, and the two became fast friends, as Avery showed her his little Matchbox car.

Cate could see the joy on Tack's face, and on Adeeb's, and she felt her heart swell with emotion. She was so proud of Tack for not giving up on his friend, and she knew then that the man's stout loyalty knew no bounds. She knew he'd never give up on her, either.

She'd spent so much of her time feeling like she was a lost cause. Tack helped her see that she still had her whole life ahead of her, and she planned to live it with him.

He put his arm around her, and for the first time, she felt truly loved, and 100 percent safe. She'd finally found the shelter from the storm she'd been looking for all these years. She leaned into him, and for the first time, truly let herself feel happy.

* * * * *

If you enjoyed this story by Superromance author Cara Lockwood, you'll also love her most recent books:
THE BIG BREAK
HER HAWAIIAN HOMECOMING
Watch for her next book, coming in February 2018.
...ilable at Harlequin.com.

Get 2 Free Books,
Plus 2 Free Gifts—
just for trying the Reader Service!

Get 2 Free Books, <u>Plus</u> 2 Free Gifts—

HARLEQUIN *Presents*

just for trying the *Reader Service!*

Get 2 Free Books,
Plus 2 Free Gifts—
just for trying the
Reader Service!

HARLEQUIN
HEARTWARMING™

Get 2 Free Books,
Plus 2 Free Gifts—
just for trying the Reader Service!

◈ HARLEQUIN

INTRIGUE

YES! Please send me 2 FREE Harlequin® Intrigue novels and my 2 FREE gifts (gifts are worth about $10 retail). After receiving them, if I don't wish to receive any more books, I can return the shipping statement marked "cancel." If I don't cancel, I will receive 6 brand-new novels every month and be billed just $4.99 each for the regular-print edition or $5.74 each for the larger-print edition in the U.S., or $5.74 each for the regular-print edition or $6.49 each for the larger-print edition in Canada. That's a savings of at least 12% off the cover price! It's quite a bargain! Shipping and handling is just 50¢ per book in the U.S. and 75¢ per book in Canada.* I understand that accepting the 2 free books and gifts places me under no obligation to buy anything. I can always return a shipment and cancel at any time. Even if I never buy another book, the two free books and gifts are mine to keep forever.

Please check one: ☐ Harlequin® Intrigue Regular-Print   ☐ Harlequin® Intrigue Larger-Print
                    (182/382 HDN GLP2)   (199/399 HDN GLP3)

Name _____ (PLEASE PRINT) _____

Address _____ Apt. # _____

City _____ State/Prov. _____ Zip/Postal Code _____

Signature (if under 18, a parent or guardian must sign)

Mail to the **Reader Service:**
IN U.S.A.: P.O. Box 1867, Buffalo, NY 14240-1867
IN CANADA: P.O. Box 611, Fort Erie, Ontario L2A 9Z9

*Terms and prices subject to change without notice. Prices do not include applicable taxes. Sales tax applicable in N.Y. Canadian residents will be charged applicable taxes. Offer not valid in Quebec. This offer is limited to one order per household. Books received may not be as shown. Not valid for current subscribers to Harlequin Intrigue books. All orders subject to credit approval. Credit or debit balances in a customer's account(s) may be offset by any other outstanding balance owed by or to the customer. Please allow 4 to 6 weeks for delivery. Offer available while quantities last.

Your Privacy—The Reader Service is committed to protecting your privacy. Our Privacy Policy is available online at www.ReaderService.com or upon request from the Reader Service.

We make a portion of our mailing list available to reputable third parties that offer products we believe may interest you. If you prefer that we not exchange your name with third parties, or if you wish to clarify or modify your communication preferences, please visit us at www.ReaderService.com/consumerschoice or write to us at Reader Service Preference Service, P.O. Box 9062, Buffalo, NY 14240-9062. Include your complete name and address.